ALIEN HUNTER

UNDERWORLD

ALIEN HUNTER

UNDERWORLD

WHITLEY STRIEBER

TOR®

A TOM DOHERTY ASSOCIATES BOOK

NEW YORK

ALIEN HUNTER: UNDERWORLD

Copyright © 2014 by Walker & Collier, Inc.

A Tor Book
Published by Tom Doherty Associates, LLC
175 Fifth Avenue
New York, NY 10010

www.tor-forge.com

Tor® is a registered trademark of Tom Doherty Associates, LLC.

Library of Congress Cataloging-in-Publication Data

Strieber, Whitley.
    Alien hunter : Underworld / Whitley Strieber.
       p. cm.—(Alien Hunter ; 2)
    ISBN 978-0-7653-3154-0 (hardcover)
    ISBN 978-1-4299-2274-6 (e-book)
    1. Extraterrestrial beings—Fiction.   2. Human-alien encounters—Fiction.
    3. Alien abduction—Fiction.   4. Secret service—Fiction.   I. Title.   II. Title:
    Underworld.
    PS3569.T6955A793 2014
    813'.54—dc23

                                                                    2014015431

Tor books may be purchased for educational, business, or promotional use. For information on bulk purchases, please contact Macmillan Corporate and Premium Sales Department at 1-800-221-7945, extension 5442, or write specialmarkets@macmillan.com.

First Edition: August 2014

Printed in the United States of America

0   9   8   7   6   5   4   3   2   1

This book is dedicated to the best fans in the world.

ACKNOWLEDGMENTS

I have received a vast amount of technical support for the Alien Hunter series, much of it from experts who prefer not to receive attribution. Thank you for your generosity and candor.

ALIEN HUNTER

UNDERWORLD

CHAPTER ONE

AS HE did every morning, Flynn Carroll was going through police reports on his iPad, reading them quickly. Then he stopped. He flipped back a page. As he reread, his eyes grew careful.

He didn't look the part of a careful man. His appearance—ancient chinos and a threadbare tee—was anything but. Duct tape repaired one of his sneakers. His hair was sort of combed; his beard was sort of shaved. But the stone gray eyes now stared with a hunter's penetrating gaze.

In two respects, the report was right in line with the others that were of interest to Flynn. A man had disappeared—in this case, two days ago. This morning he was discovered murdered in a characteristically brutal and bizarre manner. What was different was that the body had been found very quickly. Usually, corpses were located days or weeks after the murders.

Not only was this a case for him, but it also represented a rare chance. The killers would generally do two or three or more victims over a period of a few days. The first body would rarely be found until at least two or three more killings had been done. There had been no other disappearances or characteristic murders reported anywhere in the area. If this was the first in a new series, it represented both a major change and perhaps a major opportunity.

The change was that this victim wasn't an anonymous homeless person picked up off the street. This was a citizen with an identity and people and a place in the world. The opportunity was that the killers might still be operating in the area, and Flynn might have a chance to get them.

He unfolded his lean frame and got to his feet, striding off between the rows of consoles and neatly dressed technicians who manned the command center.

As he passed one of the linguists, he asked, "Got any new messages?"

"This week? Two lines."

He stopped. "And?"

"A complaint, we think. They seem to be saying that you're too brutal."

"Me? Me personally?"

He laughed. "All their messages are about you."

They'd been asking their counterparts on the other side for six months for more information about these killers. All they had been told was that it was a single, rogue band. From the amount of activity Flynn guessed that it consisted of about seven individuals.

Another of the techs sat before a strangely rounded device, beautiful in its darkness, but also somehow threatening, a glassy black orb that seemed to open into infinity.

Flynn went over to him. "Jake? Got a second?"

The man was intent on his work, peering into the blackness. Within this small, very secret working group hidden deep in the basement of CIA headquarters in Virginia, this device was known as "the wire." It provided communication with their counterpart police force. This other police force was headquartered on a planet our experts had decided was called Aeon, the government of which was eager for open contact with mankind. Supposedly.

The problem was—again, supposedly—that they weren't entirely in control of their own people. Aeon, our experts had decided, had evolved into a single, gigantic state, but it was free, and so, like any free country, it had its share of criminals.

Flynn's take: Let's see this place before we decide what it's like. Nobody had ever been to Aeon—except, perhaps, the people who had not been killed, but had instead disappeared without a trace . . . like his wife, Abby.

"Let Aeon know we've got another murder."

"Yes, sir."

"And if there's any response, anything at all, get it translated on an extreme-priority basis."

As far as Flynn knew, only one remaining alien—a creature that looked human—was responsible for the original crimes, the disappearances. These new crimes—all killings—were being done by things that looked, frankly, alien. They weren't the "grays" of popular imagination, with their huge eyes and secretive ways. Flynn had never encountered one of those creatures. Apparently, they weren't from Aeon. With such a big universe, so incredibly ancient and complicated, who knew what they really were or where they were from?

The ones he was trying to take off the map were wiry creatures with narrow faces and blank shark eyes. They had four supple fingers and long, straight claws that could also be used as knives or daggers. They were biological but not alive, he didn't think, in the same way that human beings were. Their rigid determination and ritualistic, unvarying murder techniques suggested to him that they must be robotic.

He did not hate them. His objective was to clean up the alien criminal element on Earth so that the public could safely be informed that contact was unfolding. To the depths of his soul, Flynn wanted open contact.

There was one exception to his dislike of killing them. The first alien criminal known to have arrived on Earth had called himself Louis Charleton Morris. He used a highly sophisticated disguise that gave him human features that were regular and spare. His hair was black, his lips narrow but not cruel. His expression was open, even friendly. If you encountered him in a dark alley, you wouldn't think you had a problem. You'd also be just as wrong as a person could be, because Louis Charleton Morris could do far worse than kill you. He could take you into the unknown and do to you there whatever he had done to Abby and so many others.

There had been a police officer here from Aeon, until he was killed. He had two legs and two arms, and a face with lips that were somewhat human, but the eyes were those of a fly. Oltisis could not expose himself to our atmosphere, and had worked out of a hermetically sealed office in Chicago.

Disguising oneself as Morris did was, it seemed, so illegal that not even a cop could get a clearance to do it. Since Oltisis's murder, though, Aeon had apparently changed that policy. No replacements had showed up, however.

Flynn's theory was that the killers belonged to Morris. They were something he had created and was using to get revenge.

Flynn's previous life as a detective on the police force of the city of Menard, Texas, had hardly prepared him for this work. Get your wife taken right out of your marriage bed in the middle of the night, though, and you'd change, and change a lot. You would go on a quest to find her, or find out what had happened to her. To serve that quest, you would learn whatever you needed to learn, and do whatever you needed to do. You would push yourself hard. You would not stop.

He walked across the room to a door marked only with a plastic slide-in sign: DIRECTOR. On the other side, there were more desks; more computing equipment; more quiet, intense men and women. Saying nothing, moving with the supple energy of a leopard, he went through into the inner office.

"I've got one I want to move on right now."

Operations Director Diana Glass said, "Okay, what are we looking at?"

"Town in Pennsylvania. Guy disappeared yesterday. He's been found. First report from the area."

"They could still be there."

"That's what I'm hoping. There's a strange kicker, though. He's a neurologist. Dr. Daniel Miller."

She raised her eyebrows in question.

"It gets more interesting. He worked at Deer Island."

"On the cadavers?"

"Possibly. There's a neurobiology unit there." He paused. "So maybe he hit on something somebody would rather we didn't know."

"Official Aeon would never do this."

"You sure?"

"Maybe it has to do with his work, but I also think a citizen was involved to make sure you'd come. It could be an ambush, Flynn."

"Probably is."

"How did it go down?"

"He went out on a mountain bike. When he didn't return at sundown, his wife called for help. The bike was located at dawn. The cops brought hounds, but his scent was only on the bike."

"But they found the body anyway?"

"In a wetland a few hundred feet from his house. Same condition as the derelicts. Lips cut off, genitals and eyes dissected out, drowned." So far, more than twenty homeless people had been taken off the streets, mostly in the northeastern United States, brutally and bizarrely mutilated, then drowned in the Atlantic and returned to locations near where they'd been picked up.

"We need some advice from Aeon," Diana said.

"And how are we going to get that?"

"The two police forces, working together—"

"Don't even start. There's one police force: us. Ever since Oltisis, Aeon's side has been all smoke and mirrors."

"For God's sake, don't do any more killing."

He locked eyes with her.

She looked away. "The other side objects more strenuously every time you kill another one, Flynn. They want them back."

He said nothing.

"They have laws just like we do! They want these creatures back for trial and punishment."

"No, they don't. They're not creatures."

"That's a matter for debate."

"You haven't fought them. I know when I'm dealing with a machine—believe me. No matter how high-end its brain is."

"They don't want them killed. Bottom line."

"If they want them back, tell them to damn well come and get them."

"If you're wrong about what they are, you're committing murder."

"We're disabling machines, not killing people. Anyway, this is our planet. So, our laws."

"Which don't include blowing away perps like—" She hesitated, unsure of how to continue.

Flynn knew exactly how. He said, "Like they're broken machines and cannot be stopped in any other way."

"Aeon is far in advance of us technologically, Flynn. Far more powerful. When they complain, we need to listen."

"'Aeon' consists of messages translated from a language we barely understand, coming from someplace we can't even find, that will not send a replacement for the one policeman they did give us, or even explain what they think happened to him."

"Oltisis was killed in Chicago, not on Aeon."

"And what about a replacement? Or, God forbid, even two. Or fifty? Why don't they send us a whole team of detectives and a nice chunk of SWAT? Seems the logical thing to do."

"They regard this as a small problem. One we can handle ourselves. They haven't sent support, out of respect for us."

"Have you ever told them the truth?"

"What truth?"

"That only one person is able to even get near these critters? I need support, Diana. The risk is just incredible."

"We have messages that specifically forbid you to kill, as you know. You've got to promise me you'll abide by them."

"So what do I do? Bag them up? Drag them off to a supermax?"

She sighed. She knew perfectly well that they could not be contained.

"Over the past nine months, I've done four. If Aeon's telling the truth and this is a rogue band, maybe I can wrap the problem up on this mission. Finish the thing."

She leaned far back in her chair, her long dark hair falling behind her, her green eyes, so deceptively soft, filling with uneasy calculation. Her face, an almost perfect oval, took on an expression that Flynn knew all too well. When she was twenty, it must have been a soft face, sweet with invitation. Her journey to thirty had been a hard one, though, during which she'd seen death and done some killing. Her face still said angel, but now it also said soldier. Hidden behind that cloud of Chanel was a woman with a tragic secret: The blood of some of her own cops was on her hands. Flynn knew she was as haunted by the deaths of members of their original team, who had been killed by Morris and his group, as he was by Abby's disappearance.

"Losing you would be a phenomenal disaster, Flynn. You're right about that. I'm going to have to order you to stand down on this one."

For a little while in the dangerous period when they had been tracking Morris, the two of them were together twenty-four hours a day, sleeping in the same room for mutual protection, and they got to be a thing—sort of, anyway. They had wanted each other, but he was not able to dismiss Abby's ghost. Four years ago, their affair was an act of desperation, which had faded when the threat became less. With her sitting in the boss's chair and him married to a ghost, he considered it entirely over.

"Time, Diana. I've gotta move."

"You heard me."

As he walked out, he called Transportation and told the operator, "I want to be in Mountainville, PA, in best time."

Diana came up behind him.

He walked faster.

"Flynn, at least wear the rig."

The rig was designed to record his moves, to be used in a training film. "Nope."

"Unless you wear it, we can't hope to teach others. You can't work alone forever, Flynn."

"Fine. Hire Mac." MacAdoo Terrell was an old friend from Texas. He'd worked the Morris case with them. He was among the best sniper shots in the world, if not the best, and Flynn could use a sniper in this.

"You know I can't."

"No rig. Forget the rig."

She hurried along, working to keep up as he strode out of the command center.

"Flynn, please!"

He stopped. "The rig contains electronics. As I have previously explained, when I wear it, the electronics will be detected, and therefore, I will fail to engage the perpetrators. Of course, they may well engage me, in which case, I'm done."

"Do not go out there."

"I could end this!"

"Flynn, it's a trap, and you're completely buying in to it. I don't get why you don't see this."

"If you know you're entering a trap, it's not a trap—it's a mistake on the part of your enemy. So I'm gonna walk into their mistake—and they don't make many—and I will not lose this chance."

"Flynn, will you grant me one favor? A small one?"

"I'm not gonna wear the rig—but, yeah, something else."

"Come back alive."

"Fine. Done. Good-bye."

This time, she stayed behind. He passed through the two departments that concealed the command center, went to the transport hub, and got in the waiting SUV.

The driver was silent. Flynn was silent. Usual routine. He spent the drive to Dulles looking at satellite views of Mountainville. Frustrated by what he was seeing, he texted Logistics: *Throw me something better than Google Maps.*

That's all we have. Not a strategic location.

He punched in the tech's phone number.

The answer was immediate. "Sir?"

"Get to the Pennsy Department of Geology, or whatever they call it over there. You want a map that details any isolated watercourses within two miles of the house. Mountain streams, that type of thing. Any that are spring fed and absolutely pure. And any caves, crevasses, rocky areas, especially near the good water. You want a map that shows all of that. You got it, you call me. Make it fast—it's as urgent as they come."

He put down his phone, then returned to the Google map. Steep hills, lots of cliffs, which meant exposed climbing. For them, the best terrain. For him, the worst.

The car dropped him at general aviation, and he strode quickly through to the waiting plane.

As he entered the cabin, he asked the pilot only one question: "How long?"

"An hour and sixteen minutes."

"Get me there in an hour." If this had any chance of working, he had to be ready by sunset. Maybe the aliens would be there one more night. Not two, though. Never happen.

"Sir?"

"I know the plane. It can do it."

"It'll risk the engines."

"Do it."

Once they were airborne, he called the unit's FBI liaison officer. "Flynn here. Get the body out of the hands of the locals immediate. Standard procedure: autopsy and record, then freeze. Provide the family with stock ashes in an urn. The local cops are to be told that this is a terrorism matter. If they talk, they're gonna be spending the rest of their lives inside. Obviously, make certain there's no press."

"Got it," the liaison officer said.

The engines howled. The pilot was running them as ordered.

Flynn watched the land slide past far below, the trees tinged with autumn, little towns nestled in among them, America in its quiet majesty, her people in their innocence.

He wanted things to be right for them. He hadn't been able to protect Abby, but he could protect them, at least a little, at least for a while.

As always at such moments, he wished he had Mac with him. They'd grown up together but gone down opposite paths. Mac was a criminal, more or less, so tangled up in being a DEA informant and massaging the drug cartels, you couldn't tell at any given time which side of the law he was on.

If Flynn missed anybody besides Abby, it was Mac. He'd helped wreck Morris's operation just like he lived his generally illegal life— with skill, ease, and pleasure.

His extensive criminal record made him a security risk. So no clearance, which meant no job, despite the fact that he'd been effective and, unlike most of the others who worked on that case, lived. Morris had been running his operations out of a ranch near Austin, Texas, complete with bizarre intelligence-enhanced animals and human accomplices.

Flynn slid his hand over the butt of his pistol. What success he'd had—the killing of four of the things so far—came from one central fact: He had become very, very fast with his weapons. None of the trainees he'd been given so far were able to come even close.

It wasn't too surprising, given that a man could practice for a lifetime and never learn to shoot a pistol as fast as Flynn could. He'd always been good with a gun, but in the past few months, he'd reached a level of proficiency that was, frankly, difficult even for him to understand.

The engine note changed, dropping. The plane shuddered, headed down. Flynn looked at his watch. Fifty-four minutes.

He hit the intercom. "Thank you."

The reply was a burst of static. The pilot was probably thinking about whom he'd have to deal with if he blew his engines.

From the air, Mountainville appeared to be little more than a few stores and some houses tucked in among a low range of hills. The single-strip airfield wasn't manned. The plane could land, though, and that's all that mattered.

The place looked the picture of peace, but Flynn knew different. Somewhere down there a man had endured what was probably the worst death a human being could know.

Also down there, he had reason to hope, would be his quarry.

The plane bounced onto the runway and trundled to a stop, its engines still roaring. He got out and crossed the tarmac to the car that had been left for him. As per established procedure, the vehicle was dropped off by the regional FBI office. Nobody was to meet him. What Flynn did, he did alone.

He tossed his duffel bag into the trunk, then got behind the wheel. He sat silently, preparing himself for whatever might come. Then he started the engine.

The hunter was as ready as he could be. He headed off toward Mountainville, and whatever might linger there.

CHAPTER TWO

THE TAIL Flynn had been expecting showed up ten minutes after he left the airport. Now he drove down a quiet country road—two lanes, not in good repair, choked on both sides with pines. Diana's tail was about a mile behind, staying out of sight, or imagining that he or she was doing so.

As he drove, the forest on his left fell away to reveal an open field. Beyond it was Mountain Ridge, a low rise of land shadowed by the darkness of the pines that covered it. Somewhere along that ridge, Daniel Miller had met his end.

Flynn noticed a flicker of movement in the rearview mirror. He sped up a little, drove until he saw a mailbox ahead, the name MILLER painted on it. He turned quickly into the drive and sped up the unpaved double track.

He began to see flickering light bars winking through the trees ahead. So the locals still hadn't left, which was not good. The longer the body stayed out there, the more chance for word of its condition to spread. Public knowledge would turn very quickly into public terror if the world realized what was happening.

At that moment, his cell phone vibrated. It was a text—and an odd one: the number three repeated three times. Nothing else. It wasn't a police code, at least not one familiar to a Texas cop.

He glanced in the rearview, but the apparent tail was gone, so he killed the phone and pulled over. He looked for the number where the text had originated, but it was blocked. He called Diana.

"Did you just text me a three-code of some sort?"

"No, I did not. What did you get?"

"Three threes from a blocked number."

"Some sort of phone scam?"

"On a line this secure? I don't think so."

"No, I suppose not."

"By the way, pull off your tail."

"Flynn, you need somebody on your back."

"The poor guy is vulnerable as hell, you know that." Only it wasn't just any FBI agent pulled in for the duty. It was Diana herself, of course. Soon enough, he'd send her packing.

He hung up and returned to his drive. A moment later, the phone buzzed again.

"Go ahead."

"You got your maps."

He killed the phone and pulled over. Drawing his iPad out of his duffel, he examined the maps he'd been sent. They were eleven years old, but far more detailed than what he'd found on Google. He saw the Miller cabin, and another cabin two miles away. Could be others around by now, but from the look of the woods he was in, not too many. Good. The fewer people who were exposed to this, the better.

There was a little stream, called a "kill" in this area, from the original Dutch word *kil*. This part of Pennsylvania had originally been settled by immigrants from Holland. Hecker Kill descended from the mountains, passing no structures until it went under the road and meandered across the flats toward the Delaware River. So the water in the upper reaches would be as pure as Earth could make it, the milk of the planet, just the kind of water the creatures liked best. There were also deep ravines.

If the aliens were in one of those ravines, that could be useful. The deepest of them also had a pool at the bottom, and caves.

They liked hiding in caves, and the nearby water supply would likely make that their first choice. Somewhere between here and there would be the point of ambush.

He looked long at the map, committing all the elevations to memory. Too bad there were no water depths. He might have to take one hell of a risk involving that pool, and it had been a dry autumn.

Thinking out confrontations with the aliens was like playing chess for your life.

He started the car again. Soon the drive was choked on both sides by dense growths of pine. As he proceeded up the dark, steepening track, he prepared to meet Eve Miller.

He felt his body relax into a scholar's slump, felt his breathing become less measured. He'd be Dr. Robert Winter, an infectious disease specialist from the Centers for Disease Control and Prevention.

He counted the ruts of six vehicles in the drive—one of them large enough to be an ambulance. Or, in this case, a coroner's wagon. The tire marks went in only one direction. So nobody had left yet. He wasn't about to expose himself to the local cops. The FBI guys had better be in control of that body by now, and all evidence confiscated. The tail he'd deal with in due time.

The drive ascended steeply, penetrating into thicker and thicker stands of pines and oaks, ash and maple. Lovely spot.

He reached the row of official vehicles parked at cockeyed angles in the grassy roadside. There were two black FBI Fords, the coroner's wagon, and two sheriff's department cruisers.

Farther on, he could see a log cabin huddled under an overhanging oak.

He pulled his car up past the official vehicles and into the gravel roundabout in front, then sat listening and watching, just letting himself settle into the scene. Then he opened his duffel again and took out his weapons.

He carried two pistols. His main weapon was a Casull Raging Bull loaded with .454 rounds. It was a superbly engineered pistol that could handle high-speed shooting and still provide accuracy, so long as you were practiced with it. Its ported barrel reduced recoil, giving it an accuracy edge. The other weapon was also a Casull, this one a .454 quarter-inch—basically a Police Special with more juice. In the past, he'd carried an AMT Backup, but the Casull offered both more power and accuracy.

He attached the Bull, still in its holster, to his right hip with a clip, then locked the holster into the belt. The little pistol he tucked into a shoulder holster under his left arm. His guns were protected by a biometric array, which made it impossible for anybody else to fire them.

So the aliens couldn't shoot him with his own pistol, but they had a lot of other ways of dealing with him. If they got him, he knew that it would be slow. They made their victims suffer, and they would undoubtedly pay special attention to him.

In the event of capture, he had a way out. He withdrew a black steel box from the duffel and opened it. Inside were two silver capsules, each a quarter of an inch long. He took one out, then looked at its chemically treated seating in the box for any discoloration that would reveal even a microscopic leak. He then fitted the cyanide capsule into the back of his jaw. Crack it, and he would be dead in three seconds.

He went up onto the porch and pressed the doorbell.

Nobody came. So had the widow left? If so, the ambush could be about to go down right here, right now.

He rang the bell a second time.

The door creaked. An eye flickered in the peephole.

"I'm Dr. Winter from the CDC," he said.

There was a faint scraping sound behind the door. She was sliding her fingernails along the doorframe, unsure about whether to open it.

"I have a few questions, ma'am."

The lock clicked and the door swung open. Standing before him was a woman of perhaps forty, her considerable beauty wrecked by lack of sleep. No tears, though. He noted that.

"Please come in," she said.

He found himself in a large living room with a cathedral ceiling. There were checked curtains on the windows, and a couch upholstered to repeat the pattern. An oak coffee table stood before the couch. Two deep recliners faced it. In the open kitchen he could see a Bosch dishwasher and a Sub-Zero fridge. A collection of copper pots, all of them gleaming, hung from a rack above a broad granite countertop.

"Very nice," he said.

"Thank you. The CDC. Is that why they won't let me see my husband? Is some sort of a disease involved?"

"I'm sorry for your loss."

She gave him a defiant look, her eyes full of fire and sadness.

"When you last saw him, he was riding out toward the ridge?"

"On his mountain bike. It's in the cop report. Why is someone from the CDC here?" She added in a low, ominous voice, "What happened to his eyes, his face?"

"You did see him, then."

"The sheriff came up here after he found him. He showed me—" She shook her head.

"Pictures?"

She nodded.

He would make certain that the FBI got those pictures, and they ended up in a shredder. "Did he say what he thinks happened?"

"He fell off his bike and became disoriented. But that doesn't leave a man all cut up, not like that." She looked him up and down, blinking once when she noticed the bulge on his right hip. "You're not from any Centers for Disease Control."

No point in continuing the lie. "No, I'm not."

"So it's not a disease?"

"No."

"Are you here about Dan's clearance?"

"Did he talk about his work?"

She considered that, then shook her head.

He pressed her. "What did he tell you?"

"Nothing."

He went to the couch. "May I sit down?"

"I can't stop you."

"If you tell me to leave, I'll leave." He wouldn't, but hopefully she wasn't going to try that particular path.

"I know what you are."

"And what would that be?"

"Like I said, you're worried if his clearance was compromised."

"I want to help you."

"How in the world can you help me?"

"By finding who did this and bringing them to justice. May I know your first name?"

"I'm Eve. But shouldn't you know that?"

"It's in the file, but I prefer to ask." He tried a smile. No reaction. He asked her smoothly, "What do you think happened to Dan?"

"What do I think? I don't know what to think. He fell off his bike. He was maimed. He drowned in two feet of water. It's not exactly a straight story, is it?"

"No, it isn't."

She fell silent. Grief? No, not quite. When her eyes came back to him, there was a nasty little spark. But why? What was she hiding?

"Is this work-related?" she asked. "Are you trying to tell me he was murdered, is that what this is about?"

"We don't know what happened."

"But it could have been murder, or someone like you wouldn't be here. And the local cops aren't going to be told, are they?"

"They're going to close it out as an accident."

"And the FBI?"

"They're here because of his clearance. To make sure no classified information slips out in the course of the investigation." He paused. "Look back to before this happened. Anyone come up to the house who was unexpected?"

"That's why he was out there in the first place. Three children came to the door. They asked if they could come in. I asked what they wanted, and they just walked off the porch and sort of wandered back into the woods."

"And you'd never seen them before?"

"They looked like little tramps. They were filthy. They smelled. And no, I don't know where they came from." She drew her shoulders together. "They made us worry that drifters were camping in our woods. We have three hundred acres of this mountain."

The aliens could hypnotize the unwary into seeing them as deer, as owls, even as children. They could put hallucinations in your mind, damned convincing ones. "What do you remember about the kids?"

He watched her eyes flutter closed. She was trying hard. She said, "I was glad they left." She leaned toward him. Her voice a low whisper, she continued, "I found them loathsome."

"But no more details?"

"Were they part of this? Because they were not normal children. No way."

He offered the simplest and safest of all the lies he could have told her: "No, they weren't part of this."

"I want to believe you."

"Let's think back again. Besides the kids?"

"Nothing important."

"Everything is important."

"He was murdered. That's why you're here."

Flynn did not reply.

"Did you work with him? Can you at least tell me that?"

"I did not," he said.

"You're like him—you come off as a real gentleman, but inside you're tough as nails."

"He was a hard man?"

"Strong. Like you."

He nodded. "Now, think back. Anything else? Anything last night?"

She looked into the middle distance. Flynn watched the pulse in her throat. He'd interrogated too many people to watch her eyes. Do that, and even a person with nothing to hide would spar with you. Lower your gaze, and they feel an unconscious sense of control, even though they are not in control.

"You know, there is." She leaned forward. "I couldn't sleep last night."

"I understand."

"Very late, there was an owl at the bedroom window."

"An owl? Had that ever happened before?"

"Never. It was just looking in at me. I hit the window with a pillow, and it flew away."

Owls didn't look in windows, so the aliens had been here as recently as last night. They'd still been interested in her twelve hours ago, so maybe their interest was ongoing. Maybe she was also a target, or, as was more likely, they had planned their ambush of him near the house, and wanted to be sure he would be nearby tonight, protecting her.

"Let's talk about Dan and Deer Island. What do you know?"

"His employee number was 333676. I knew very little else. It was all secret."

The first part of the number sent enough of a shock through Flynn that he had to drop his head for an instant, so she wouldn't see his expression.

In that same instant, the blocked number became a central issue. He needed to find out at once who was behind it.

He lifted his lips into the appearance of a smile. "Tell me the very little."

"What you want to know is whether or not he shared his secrets with me. He didn't. I just figured a few things out."

"Run down what he did tell you."

"His project was called Dream Weaver. He did a lot of work with hypnosis, which I figured out from things he said."

The project name didn't ring any bells, but the fact that he worked with hypnosis meant that he almost had to be involved with the bodies. The question of how the aliens could hypnotize people without speaking to or touching them was of major interest to the U.S. government, especially the intelligence community.

"Anything else? Anything at all?"

"Three nights ago, we thought we heard somebody on the porch." She nodded decisively, fixing it in her memory. "We did."

"After the children or before?"

"After. It's what finally decided Dan to investigate up the ridge."

"He was armed with what?"

"Not armed. We're not gun people." She glanced again at his hip.

"I'm a police officer," he said. He lifted his jacket to reveal the butt of the big pistol.

"From where? What department?"

"Can't answer, I'm sorry."

Given that Dan Miller worked in an advanced facility that was involved with the mysteries of alien neurology, Flynn was now almost certain that he had been looking for a meeting with them, not a confrontation with squatters. They had granted him a meeting, all right—his last.

"I'm going to spend the night out in your woods. I'd appreciate it if you wouldn't leave the house."

"Are you serious?"

"Your husband worked against terrorists. They killed him, and I'm going to see if I can track them."

"It's almost dark."

"They might still be out there. You need to know that."

"Then I'm going back to the city." She clutched her shoulders. "I don't want to be here anymore."

"Leave in the morning."

"I want to leave now."

"Ma'am, I don't want you out on those roads in the dark. This is a lonely place. Safer in the house with the doors locked. And turn on your alarm system."

The wall clock hummed in the kitchen. A breeze toyed with the pines outside. He raised his eyebrows, asking for a response.

"I think you're the saddest man I've ever seen. Why is that?"

"Just stay in the house. You can leave in the morning."

Should he tell her what was really going on, that she was a pawn in a deadly chess game?

The words hung on his lips, ready to be spoken.

She said, "Yes?"

If she thought the "terrorists" were going to come after her tonight, she'd certainly leave, which would change things in unpredictable ways.

He believed that he could protect her. He believed that he could kill aliens here tonight, and save future lives as well.

"Again, please accept my condolences."

She smiled, sadly and tightly. "Do you want a cup of coffee? I didn't even offer you coffee."

He gave her a salute.

She returned a wary smile.

As he went down the pathway from the house, she leaned against the doorjamb watching him. Then he rounded the big old oak, and she was blocked from his view.

When one of the official vehicles down below started up, he stepped off the road, moving swiftly back into the trees. The FBI would have told the locals to leave him alone, but he wasn't taking any chances.

Now it would start, the first phase of a hard night of hunting.

His tongue went to his cyanide capsule, his hand to his gun. He turned his back on the parade of vehicles lumbering away down the road, and slipped into the forest.

farther on, he had sped up. Then, here, along this rocky stretch, he had stopped for a time.

Had he been looking for squatters or seeking out the aliens?

Here, in a flatter part of the trail, the mountain bike had stopped again. It had stood on its tires long enough to make deep indentations in the soft earth of the trail. Beside the wheel marks, there were toe tips. Miller had balanced on his toes, still astride the bicycle. He had been looking up. He would have seen above the trees a glittering emptiness not unlike that of the lens of the wire back in the office, and before he knew it, he would have risen into the air. He would have been dragged into what would have seemed something like a big wasp nest, stinking and claustrophobic. In it, he would have been strapped to a table. Then they would have gone to work on him.

Flynn was pretty sure of all this. He had seen most of the other bodies that were recovered, the wounds, the bruises left by the struggle against the straps.

He moved a little deeper into the woods, a little closer to his target ravine. Along this route, the land got more and more rocky and steeper. He moved silently, relying on his memory of the elevations from the map, and his own terrain sense.

Then, very suddenly, the birds were gone. He stopped. Nothing rustled along the ground; no wildlife scuttled or growled. Far off, a dog was barking frantically, and from the sound of it, had been for a while. He stepped back a few feet, until he once again heard birdsong.

"Flynn—"

At last, she'd made her move. He pretended surprise. "What in hell's name are you doing here?"

"Saving your life." She nodded toward the ravine. "They're down there."

When he moved toward it, she came with him.

"I won't let you do this, Flynn."

"Diana, you need to back off. You don't belong in the field, and we both know it and we both know why."

CHAPTER THREE

IT WAS just approaching sunset, so the aliens would still be in the ravine, if he had guessed correctly about their location. He wouldn't be able to kill them there, but he might succeed in running a deception that would make them misread his competence. When they sprang their trap on him at the house, they would hopefully be overconfident.

As he moved through the woods, he heard the rustling of beetles, the hollow echo of birdsong, and somewhere close by, the uneasy mew of a raccoon. Animals would not venture near the aliens, meaning that silence in the woods was a useful warning sign. Birds would take flight, and even insects would stop their shrilling.

When you were within a few hundred feet of them, there would be absolute silence, nothing but the rustle of the breeze.

As he walked, he took deep breaths, pulling in the air, smelling it and tasting it, feeling it in his lungs. He was seeking their scent, the strangest odor that he knew. You could describe it as sulfurous, but it also contained the nasty sweetness of death and the roses of memory. Like everything about them—about Aeon, for that matter, and the whole issue of aliens on Earth—it was full of secrets.

Now, as he climbed the increasingly steep path, he saw signs, not of the aliens but of Miller's mountain bike. Here he had slipped a little, and

"Don't hit me, Flynn, not with that."

She'd lost her original team because she'd panicked and made command errors. She and Flynn were the only two who had survived a night of merciless carnage.

He put his hands on her shoulders. "Sorry, it was uncalled for."

"I remember every guy, all the time."

"I was there, too. I could have done things differently."

"On your first operation? Green as you were? No."

He turned back toward the ravine. She threw her arms around him.

Gently, he peeled her off and began moving downward, descending quickly into steeper terrain.

The rocks were painted with orange and tan lichens and gray moss, but they were jagged and sharp. Soon, he was working his way down a cliff. A bad spot to have to draw a gun.

He reached a granite outcropping. Peering over the small ledge that it formed, he saw the pool he'd spotted on the state map.

Somewhere below this ledge and above the pool, there was going to be a cave or a crevasse where the things were hiding, all pressed up against its walls like giant bats.

His ability to use his weapons would be compromised, while their dexterity would be at its most useful.

His left hand went to his neck, lingering on the scar that was there, long and red and still tender after three months. It had been done by one of their claws. Three inches, right down to the vertebrae—so fast, he hadn't been able to react. Just in time, he got in a shot that had separated the head from the body.

He took a breath and continued down, pausing every few seconds to inhale their odor, testing its strength.

Then he felt the earth beneath his body give way. He steadied himself, then kept sliding carefully down toward the source of the odor.

The next instant, his footing was gone and he was more than sliding, he was out of control. He let it happen, scrabbling now, seeming to struggle.

Rocks and dirt cascaded down into the pool. Just as the slide was becoming a fall, he managed to grab a root outcropping. This caused him to swing out. The root shifted; then he felt it giving way under his weight. Swinging back, he grabbed another outcropping with his free hand. He found footing. Tested it.

The odor of the aliens was now chokingly strong, its sourness greasy, its sweetness so thick, it had become a sickening taste.

Carefully slipping out of one foothold, he found another lower down. Again, he descended.

He was close now, just a few feet.

Without warning, something fell on him from above, wriggling wildly. Before he could rip it off, it had wrapped itself around his neck and was striking at his face, fangs gaping out of its bright red mouth.

An illusion, he knew, but he wanted them to think it had convinced him.

Letting fly what he hoped sounded like a bloodcurdling scream of pure terror, he leaned outward and let himself fall.

As he passed the cave, he let off a couple of shots, intentionally wild.

He spread his legs and arms, exposing as much body surface as possible to the water. Maximum resistance meant maximum deceleration.

He hit the bottom hard, real hard, but didn't feel anything break. He swam painfully to the surface.

He came up gasping, coughing, flailing in the water. He needed to make his struggles look convincing. As he reached the bank, he wallowed, slipped and fell, and finally took off running down the gravelly path that paralleled Hecker Kill. He shambled along until he was well away from the ravine. Then he dropped the frantic dash of a surprised and defeated man and trotted efficiently away.

Once he thought he was out of their range, he stopped. He listened. Normal sounds only. He used his nose. Pine and the sweet rot of the forest floor. Diana couldn't have seen him fall, but she would have heard the scream. So she was probably heading down to the kill herself, trying to save him. If night settled before he reconnected with her, she'd probably panic and bring up a search party. All to the good. The worse at this he and his people seemed, the better the hunting later tonight.

He sped up, moving among the pines like a ghost, silent, nothing scraping, nothing crunching. He gave the Miller place enough of a miss to ensure that he wouldn't be seen, but he also drew close enough to the house to see it.

It was near dark now, and light flowed from every window. Inside, he could see Eve sitting in one of the recliners. She was reading a book. There was music playing, a piano, its soaring notes drifting like birdsong across the quiet.

He was immediately reminded of another piano, on a blizzard-ridden night in Montana last year, and the woman who had been playing it, beautiful, talented, and innocent. Taken by Morris amid the slaughter of Diana's team.

Eve Miller would not suffer a similar fate, or any fate, at their hands.

Seeing that all the official vehicles were gone, he crossed to the wet area where Dan Miller had been found. He looked out across a clearing marked by bunched tufts of weeds jutting up from black water. It wasn't deep, though, not even shoe deep. Miller had been drowned in the ocean like the rest of them, and brought back here.

He looked up at the sky, empty now of larks, the first stars appearing. What had they traveled in, bringing Miller here? That was one of the great questions. The one flying disk that had fallen into military hands proved to be a simple assemblage of balsa wood and foil, like a kite, or so he had heard. But the wood could survive the highest temperature that could be generated, and the foil was stronger than a foot thickness of armor.

It was full dark now, and that meant it was time to intercept Diana again. He turned away from the mire and went back to his car. He waited, but she didn't show. So he cleaned his guns, making sure that their carefully oiled mechanics contained not a drop of water from his swim. Then he got out and opened the trunk. He gathered up his work clothes.

"Hi, there," he said to the darkness. "Looks like I lived."

She came out of the forest. He hadn't needed to see her before he spoke. He knew where she was.

"I've decided that a capture attempt is too dangerous, Flynn."

"I wasn't planning one."

"So you agree with me. Good. We'll go back to D.C. and build you a team. The team can attempt a capture."

"No."

"Flynn, I'm your superior officer."

"And I'm the only person we know of who can kill these suckers."

"Because you won't train anybody!"

"Who are you gonna get for me, then, Bob Munden?" Munden was arguably the fastest gun in the world, capable of getting off an accurate shot in under two-hundredths of a second. However, this was a young man's game. Fast as old Munden was, he wouldn't make it.

"Flynn, we have to keep looking until we find who we need. You can't be the only person with your reflexes."

"I sincerely hope not."

"No more killing."

"Go home."

After a moment, she stepped close to him. Her face, wreathed in darkness, was as soft as a leaf. "I know you feel something for me, too."

It hurt to hear her say that, and it was not the kind of hurt he liked to feel. He knew that he had to leave Abby behind one of these days, but how?

"It's dangerous for you here," he said. He took his second pistol from its holster, punched in the release code on the small keypad embedded in the grip, and gave it to her. "Keep it in your lap as you drive out. Don't stop until you're in a decent-sized town. Altoona. Go to Altoona. Drive fast."

She looked at the pistol, handed it back to him. "I'm armed. But, Flynn, I'm not sure I understand what you were doing back there. Did you really fall?"

"I was building up their confidence. Now, go."

She hugged him. It was unexpected, and he reflexively stiffened. Instantly, she released him. "I'm sorry." She squared her shoulders.

"I—" The next word hung in his throat, unable to be set free. Until he knew Abby's fate, his heart would remain frozen. Silently, he laid a hand on her cheek. She put her own on it and closed her eyes.

"God go with you, Flynn."

He bowed his head to her, then watched as she walked off down the road. His hand was on his gun, his eyes on the sky above her, but no shape came. He would have seen it blotting out the stars as it slid into position above her. Maybe they were playing careful, or maybe they didn't have their ship operating yet. He'd seen it before. It was old and battered. It clattered rather than hummed.

When he heard her car start, he was relieved. He listened until the mutter of her engine died away. As she left, he felt part of him leaving with her. There were days now when he couldn't remember Abby's voice or even her face, but almost every night, her murmur of invitation woke him to his loneliness.

He went back to his own car and got to work. First, he blacked his face with charcoal; then he wrapped himself in a long coat that was blacker than black. When he pulled up the hood, he was hardly more visible than the shadows around him. The dense cloth was treated with light-absorbing micro-optics that rendered the garment completely non-reflective. To an observer, it would create the illusion of an emptiness or a shadow, rather than something solid.

He got into the car and waited, letting his attention sink down into his body, concentrating on the feel of his skin, the pumping of his heart, the steady rhythm of his lungs, letting all thought slip away. He didn't do this only because he feared that the aliens might detect thought somehow, but more because it fed his spirit and made him strong.

Tonight he might experience great terror and great pain, and he might die. He remembered why he was doing it, for all the innocent lives that were his to protect, and also for the great chance that contact represented. If only this would come out right, mankind would receive a blessing from the stars. He needed to clean up this mess first, though, and that was the work of his heart and his soul, and what he was willing to die for.

As the silence of the night surrounded him, he felt himself disappear into his task. You wanted to be fast, you could not be thinking all the time. Your body had to do it; your mind could not.

Animal sounds returned, the scuttling of shrews in the late-season leaves, the snorting of an opossum, the rustling journey of a family of raccoons.

He thought nothing. Felt nothing. Only his breath whispering, only his blood running. He was the perfect hunter now, a big cat at one with the night.

Ten o'clock came, time to move.

What slid from the vehicle was more animal than man, a panther. Stealthy and swift, he slipped off toward the house with a smooth and powerful gait, running as silently as the air.

CHAPTER FOUR

AS FLYNN drew nearer to the house, he heard something unexpected: voices. There was a man speaking, low and warm, a night voice. He could hear the desire in it.

Eve Miller's reply was softly intimate.

He knew instantly that this was what Eve had been concealing when he questioned her, and why she showed so little grief.

He went closer yet, slipping onto the front porch of the cabin, dropping low, then raising his head just enough to see in the picture window.

A man of maybe fifty in worn jeans and an open shirt was sitting beside Eve on the couch, watching her with eager eyes. A leather jacket was thrown over a side chair. Hanging on its back was a shoulder holster. Flynn remembered how she'd said the word "sheriff," tasting it, and knew that this was the man.

His arm was around her, but he wasn't consoling her. She was flushed with pleasure.

Flynn went back to cover, then swung up into the oak that overhung the cabin, climbing with swift ease into its upper branches. From here, he had a view of both the sky and the roof.

He concentrated on what he was smelling and hearing, as an animal would. He noted the scent of rotting oak leaves, the sharper odor of pine, the tang of chimney smoke. No trace of the eerie stink of aliens, though.

Methodically, he looked from place to place, watching for even the slightest change, the thickening of a shadow, the suggestion of movement in the dark.

Below, the lights of the house went out. Soon, laughter rippled faintly, and then the shuffling rhythm of lovemaking.

Eventually, silence fell. An owl passed low over the roof and was gone. A real owl, he hoped, but there was no way to be sure.

Then he felt a change, just the slightest tremble in the tree's core. In response to the shudder, a leaf fell, slipping downward, making whispered sounds as it touched other leaves.

He knew for certain that something else was with him in this tree, something very quiet, very stealthy.

A night wind murmured. On the distance, something cried out. Farther off, a dog began to mourn, its voice caressing the silence.

All the nearby animal sounds had stopped. No owl muttered; no breeze sighed. It was as if the world had entered a zone of silence.

Below him, the house slept.

The tree trembled again. Something was climbing. Coming closer. Very stealthy.

Moving so slightly that the shift of weight could be detected only by the most sensitive creature, he pressed his ear against the tree trunk.

The scratch of claws, then silence.

If the aliens got too close to him, he would either be captured or killed—their call. They could disable the human nervous system with a touch. He'd fall like a corpse and be collected and carried off into their ship. In the stink and filth of it, he would be strapped onto their table. Then, to better enjoy his struggles, they would release his nervous system. Even knowing that he was giving them pleasure by doing it, he knew that he would fight those straps with all his might. He would not be able to stop himself.

Click, scrape. Then silence. Then again, very soft.

His fingers slid to the hilt of his knife. He could throw it a hundred feet with pinpoint accuracy. He could cut with it just in the right way to pop the head from the body. Then you stomped the head. It was brutal and it was messy, but it worked.

The dark grew deeper, the silence more profound.

There was the slightest of sensations along his ankle, a breath of air, the shudder of a leaf against his skin, no more.

His body threw the knife; he didn't. His arm sent it rocketing straight down at a speed of over sixty miles an hour.

There was a liquid sound, like a stone dropping into mud. Then there was something like a gasp, very precise, as if a machine had been surprised.

A scratching sound followed. It got louder, more frantic. A thud followed, against the distant ground.

He dropped down fast. Taking just an instant to glance at the spidery, inert form on the ground, he returned his knife to its scabbard and dashed toward the house.

An enormous creature came toward him, a bear. But it was no Eastern black bear. It wasn't even a grizzly. As it lumbered closer, he recognized it as a North American short-faced bear, twelve feet tall, a monster that had been extinct for thousands of years.

Before he could turn away, it reared up, looming over him, roaring with a voice like thunder.

It drew back a massive paw.

He kept running, straight toward it.

The huge claws slammed into him . . . and kept going right through him.

It was more impressive by far than the snake, but it didn't slow him down. Over months of dealing with the aliens, he'd seen many different apparitions, creatures of legend, monsters out of his own mind, you name it.

The front door splintered as he burst through.

Things now moved at blinding speed. One alien leaped at him from the balcony overlooking the great room. It came like a huge bat, its thin arms spread wide, its very lethal claws glowing like blood in the firelight.

He drew the Bull and fired a single shot that lit the room with white light and roared like a demon. The bullet separated head from body, but even as the head tumbled past his shoulder, the body gripped him with steel arms and steel legs and pinned him as surely as if he had been caught in a vise.

The third alien, still in possession of all its powers, touched him with the electric tip of a short wand that it carried. Immediately, incapacitating waves of energy surged through his nervous system. He staggered, frantically trying to close his teeth on the cyanide.

Still completely conscious, but also completely helpless, he fell to the floor.

It stood over him, staring down at him with eyes like cruel windows, dark with infinity. Its tiny mouth was opened in a neat O, and it rocked its head from side to side. He had the thought that it was mocking him.

As it continued to watch him, he began to feel his nervous system coming back to life. His heart was thundering, his blood roaring in his ears, his lungs sucking.

Still, it watched him, its head lolling from side to side, its mouth open in that strangely empty and yet ominous O.

His arm flashed out and he grabbed its leg, yanking it off the floor.

It swooped backwards, and he found himself holding the leg of the largest spider he had ever seen. Reflex caused him almost to jump away, but he stopped himself. He tightened his grip.

The thing was chest high, its compound eyes glittering with hundreds of reflections of his own face, the features contorted with disgust and fear. Its huge black abdomen was striped with yellow, like a tiger.

There was a burning chemical stench to it, which he thought might be venom.

What the hell had just happened here? Had the creature actually changed form? Because this was no illusion.

Effortlessly, it broke his grip and leaped up to the cathedral ceiling. It hung there, watching him. When he glanced toward his gun, its whole body stiffened. From here, he could see the stinger in the tail, a black dripping scimitar.

It began to crawl across the ceiling, heading for the upstairs bedroom, where Eve and her lover presumably lay in the strange coma the aliens could induce, assuming they were alive, assuming they were still here.

Leaping across the room, getting the gun in his hand, and firing a shot accurate enough to penetrate the abdomen would be a matter of two seconds. It was going to take the creature about the same amount of time to drop on him. Its body would create more wind resistance, though, so maybe there would be a second of play in there.

He touched the cyanide capsule with his tongue. The secret to making a move like this work was to want it and let it happen, not to do it.

The spider dropped as he rolled, grabbed the pistol, and fired into its abdomen just as it enveloped him.

An instant later, he was on his feet, and the crumpled remains of the third alien were on the floor.

He went into the kitchen, got himself a glass of water, and drank it. For a time he stood over the sink, his head down. He did not want to look at the remains, much less touch them. He had to, though. Killing was intimate work, and there was only one thing more naked than a victim's body, and that was the killer's soul.

He went to the remains splayed across the floor and looked down at them. How could such ferocity and such danger be associated with something so insignificant as this little, shriveled mass of flesh and limbs as thin as pipes?

This alien was not going to be doing any more damage. None of them were. He knew the power of his weapons and the efficiency of his delivery. These creatures were dead.

He shifted his gaze to the darkness at the top of the stairs. The door to the bedroom hung open. The room itself was dark. What he might find up there made him uneasy. They'd been in there long enough to kill.

He mounted the stairs one by one, moving silently to the top.

The interior of the bedroom was still dark. He heard no breathing, but neither did he smell any odor of blood.

He drew down the blanket that covered them, and at that moment beheld a sight so appalling that he shrank back from it as if it were poison or a charge of fatal electricity. The man was on top. Eve was on the bottom. But their skin was like candle wax that had cooled and frozen. They were melted together in a grotesque, faceless whole, their two bodies somehow made into one.

He could see blue veins in the areas where they were joined. With a shaking hand, he touched the skin, which was soft and felt as new as a baby's. They looked like a bag made of human flesh. Even the faces were melted together.

Choking back a fear that told him to just run, to get out of there, to give up this quest, he reached out to one arm, thick and misshapen, that ended in two hands with ten fingers, and tried to find a pulse. Two hearts, a complication of signals, but there was no doubt—they were still alive.

He reached out, his own heart breaking. What unearthly, monstrous, mad power could do this? How could such evil even exist?

They lurched, and muffled inside the flesh that now lay as a living curtain that linked their faces, he heard a gagging female cry. Then the lower voice of the man, stifled, "Jesus!"

The body began to writhe, then to shake. The flesh that sealed their faces together bulged and warped as they fought for breath.

Their confusion changed to panic. Choked screams filled the room and filled Flynn with a dread as terrible as any he had ever known.

Helpless, he watched them roll on the bed, heard their sphincters release, smelled the rise of urine, saw the skin turn red, then purple, and listened as the screams died into suffocated gasps and they died encased in an impossible mutual flesh.

Like a father whose child has died in his arms, he bowed over them, touched them with gentle hands. His face was rigid with loathing, his eyes swimming, his lips set in a line that spoke of the rage within.

In its slow way, the night came back, the hurried burr of the last crickets of summer, the sighing of the wind.

He lifted the purpling corpse and staggered with it across the room, then put it down at the top of the stairs.

When Diana and her friends saw this, maybe they would face the truth that he had known from the moment the presence of the aliens had been revealed to him. This was not a matter of a few alien criminals filtering through to Earth from a planet that was basically good. Something was terribly wrong on Aeon.

So far, everything that came from Aeon had been insane except Oltisis, and maybe the whole damn place was one big madhouse. He shook his head, then got the quilt off the bed and threw it over the poor couple.

He left the house and went and got his car. Carefully, not using lights, he drove it up to the front porch, parking it as close as he could. He could carry 150 pounds, but the two bodies, melted together as they were, had to weigh 300, maybe more.

Maybe this wasn't just an act of insanity. Maybe it was some sort of statement about the sins of the lovers, mad and ugly and vile, but possibly founded in some distorted moral sense. Eve's bedding her lover the night after her husband died wasn't pretty, but it sure as hell didn't deserve this. It was also a warning, no question, that was directed at Flynn. It was meant to terrify and to say, Yes, you can kill us, but we have powers beyond anything you can imagine.

He returned to the house, registered the stillness of the living room, then went back upstairs.

As his head rose above the level of the second-story floor, he stopped. What in hell?

It couldn't be.

Cautiously, he mounted another step. No, the thing was gone.

He drew his gun. With two quick strides, he went to the top of the stairs. He turned—and lying there in the bed were the two people. He ran to them, and saw by their darkly open eyes that they were in the profound state of unconsciousness that the aliens used to render their victims helpless.

With a gentle hand, he drew the quilt up over the naked forms.

It was hard to believe that the thing he had seen was never really there. But, like the spider, it had been an illusion on a whole new level, perhaps generated out of desperation.

But they'd all been dead when he found the melted bodies. Or had they? Was there another creature?

He returned to the car and got his forensic pack. The two sleepers would be like that for hours—insensible, impossible to awaken—so he didn't need to worry about them as he returned to his original task, which was to now strip the place of every trace of what had happened.

He opened the kit, drawing out the small, powerful flashlight, the brushes, and the bags. He set to work, moving methodically, meticulously catching every speck of strange flesh here and throughout the house.

Once outside, he gathered the remains of the aliens. They stank of hot plastic and rotten meat, and looked like huge, broken insects.

First, he put on his thick rubber gloves, then carefully lifted the first body, bunching the claws up into a fist so they wouldn't slice into him.

There was a severed head, which he lifted quickly, choking back his disgust, and thrust into one of the bags. Everything in him hated this part, but he was nevertheless extremely careful.

He thrust the last of the remains into one of the reinforced bags, then sealed them with CLASSIFIED MATERIALS tags. He dumped them into the trunk.

A fog was rising, turning the trees into ghosts.

The sky overhead, which had been filled with stars, was now as black as the interior of a cave. Or no, that wasn't quite right, was it? The sky didn't look dark; it looked empty. Could clouds have come in so high that they weren't reflective, or was it that there was too little local ground light?

He considered this, then looked away. Of course it was clouds—what else could it be?

As he got in the tired FBI executive vehicle he'd been given, the sheer exertion of the night overcame him. A headache came on. Closing his eyes, he sat back. The pain radiated down from the top of his head, involving his eye sockets, his temples, and his neck.

Stress fatigue. He pressed his fists into his eyes, and slowly, it passed.

Feeling a little better, he started the car and began driving, lights out, watching the faint line of the road ahead, letting the car creep as silently as possible. As he descended the steep track, the trees on both sides became thicker and the fog more dense. Still, he didn't turn on the lights. On the road, fine, but he didn't want anyone noticing a car leaving the Miller place this late.

There were a couple of sharp turns, which he negotiated slowly, keeping close watch on the nearly invisible line of the road. When he reached a straight stretch about three hundred yards long, he immediately increased his speed.

He reached the end of the Miller's road at last, and drove on, his mind a whirl of confused thoughts. Was this finished? Had he killed the last of them?

He had not killed Morris, and while that monster remained at large, nothing was finished. He would go on, deep into the night, looking, waiting, a spider more dangerous than the one the aliens had tried to frighten him with, patient and lethal.

CHAPTER FIVE

HE TURNED on his cell phone. The moment it went online, it rang.

"You killed them all," Diana said.

"How would you know that?"

"Flynn, I have to tell you, Aeon is really, really pissed off."

"Okay."

"They want you stopped once and for all."

"Say again?"

"They are *demanding* this, Flynn, and we're not sure exactly what they mean. They might want you killed in return."

"You tell them that we lost twenty-eight living human beings to their seven damn robots or whatever they are, and if they want us to capture these creatures, either send us instructions or send us help."

"Flynn?"

He heard tears in her voice, which concentrated his attention. "Are they coming after me?"

Silence.

"Hey, this is me, Diana. Am I in trouble, here?"

"I don't know."

He controlled it. "Look, I've got the bodies in the trunk of my car."

"What happened to the civilian?"

"They're fine."

"They?"

"The wife has a lover. The sheriff. Look, there's a lot going on here. We're dealing with a whole new level of mind control, for one thing. I've seen things—oh, Christ, Diana, I'm telling you—"

"I want you off the roads. They could grab you."

"What do I do with these bodies? I can't just leave them in a Dumpster."

"Okay, get them to Wright-Pat. Get rid of them. Then come back here, Flynn. Stay close to home."

He wasn't sure he was going to do that. In fact, he had no idea what he was going to do, but he was certainly going to get rid of these bodies. He considered flying them to the containment, but thought better of it. He had no idea if he was more vulnerable in the air or on the ground, but he had absolutely no hope of escape in a plane, so he decided to stay on the highway.

Even so, he had never felt more exposed in his life. He'd never been scared like this. He was used to feeling invulnerable, and now he felt anything but. Why in hell would Aeon care so much about these damn things? They were machines made of flesh and blood, nothing more, so why be so concerned about them?

Perhaps Aeon's intentions were being misinterpreted. Maybe they were on the right side of this thing after all. Our knowledge of their language was flawed at best.

He gripped the wheel, pushing the car as fast as he dared to go. He sure as hell didn't want some state cop looking in that trunk.

As he drove, he found himself compulsively tonguing the cyanide capsule. He'd planned on following his usual routine and returning it to its container, but not now, no way.

He just could not believe that Aeon was angry. If they wanted contact to develop, they should be elated. Not only that, why should he be afraid of them? They had no major presence here. No ships, no personnel. Or did they?

Diana and her team were panicking. They were confused. Had to be.

He drove on, the lights of his car reflecting back more and more fog, making it so hard to see that he gripped the steering wheel and peered ahead, but he never let the speedometer dip below seventy.

The fog was dangerous, the night was dangerous, being alone on the highway was dangerous. Worse, he was no longer even close to understanding what he was dealing with, and that was very dangerous.

About an hour out of Mountainville, the state highway met the interstate. He had to stop for gas, so he also got coffee. The attendant was an Indian man behind bulletproof plastic. He took Flynn's money and handed out his change, his eyes glazed with sleepy boredom.

The coffee was old but it was strong, and he drank it methodically as he continued on down the highway.

He covered the distance to Dayton in just over five hours. It was pushing ten in the morning when he reached Wright-Pat. He was hungry and close to exhaustion, but there was no stopping until these bodies were safely burned.

He pulled into the first guard post and flashed his badge.

Nothing happened.

The guard leaned into the car. "Sir, are you okay?"

"No, I'm not okay, but I have a legitimate ID, so please let me through."

"Would you like an escort to the base hospital, sir?"

"Open the gate, please."

Flynn took back his secure ID. It didn't appear any different from any other USGS Identification Card. On the surface. As it was run through readers in ever-more-secure areas, though, it would grant deeper and deeper access, into places that not even presidents knew about.

The gate went up and Flynn drove through. Wright-Pat was a big base, the U.S. Air Force's largest repair and refitting facility, among other things. Among those "other things" was the Air Force Materiel Command, which controlled the warehouse where he was headed.

It was a low building no different from dozens of others on the base. Thousands of people passed it every day without realizing that, two hundred feet beneath the warehouse's dull exterior, a supercooled morgue held fourteen alien bodies—including two from Roswell, New Mexico— that had been brought here in the fall of 1947 and had remained here ever since. The bodies were kept at near absolute zero, and were tended remotely by technicians who had no idea what they were keeping cold. Their training informed them that this was a storage area for unstable chemicals, and that if they failed in their duty, a massive explosion could result.

The building also contained a furnace designed to burn "special materials" at extremely high temperatures. Contrary to popular opinion, classified papers were not burned, but reduced to pulp and recycled. Still, the presence of the burn facility meant there would be plenty of normal traffic, and lots of ordinary material like classified electronics. This would be mixed with any ash that might contain evidence, such as bits of the alien bodies Flynn was about to consign to the flames.

He pulled the front of the car up to a tall corrugated metal door, then went to the identification pad and punched in his code. A moment later, the door began to clatter up on its chains.

He backed up to the furnace and waited in the car while airmen put up screens around the vehicle. As soon as he had slid his card through the pad, the facility manager was automatically informed of the security level he required.

Finally, hidden behind seven-foot-tall flats covered with gray canvas, he got out and went to the intercom. He picked up the handset and asked, "Is it up to temp?"

The answer was immediate. "Yes, sir."

Flynn never took chances. "Are all personnel accounted for?"

"Yes, sir."

"The entire floor is clear at this time?"

"Sir, there's a work crew repairing the exhaust fan housing on one of the ventilator systems."

"Pull them."

"Yes, sir. Give me a minute, sir."

While Flynn was waiting, he went to the furnace and tested the mechanism. An interlock prevented direct contact with the interior. Heat like that would incinerate you in an instant.

The intercom buzzed.

"Yes?"

"The facility is clear. No eyes on your position."

He replaced the receiver and pressed the ready button on the furnace housing. A green light appeared on the black surface of the control panel, and the door slid open. Despite the thickness of the interlock, the heat was so intense that the interior shimmered with it.

Flynn opened his jacket, lifted his pistol to a looser position in his holster, then walked to the back of the car. He unlocked the trunk and pulled it open.

The three bags lay just as he had left them. When he put them in, he'd noted their positions carefully. Also carefully, he touched the nearest of them. No responding movement. He touched the one behind it. Nothing. He reached deeper into the trunk and touched the third bag. Again, nothing inside reacted.

He lifted the first bag out of the trunk. The aliens were light, weighing only ten or twelve pounds. Careful not to let any claws cut through and scratch him, he carried the bag to the furnace and laid it in the open receptacle. Immediately, it began to smoke. He pressed the red activation button and the door closed. He repeated the process with the second bag.

As he turned back toward the car, he heard a loud click overhead. Angry, thinking that some airman was still working up there, he looked up. He saw only the shadowy girders. An instant later, though, when he directed his gaze back to the trunk, he saw that the last bag had been torn open and was now empty.

He stepped quickly back to the intercom. "This is on lockdown. I want the entire facility evacuated at once. Is that clear?"

"Yes, sir." He could hear the question in the voice. He didn't care.

A red light began circulating overhead and a Klaxon sounded. He drew aside one of the screens and stepped into the center of the large open space.

Methodically, he scanned the floor. Empty. So the thing had jumped into the girders.

Now there came another sound—the echoing creak of hinges.

Flynn turned toward it, and was horrified to see an airman enter through a side door and begin walking toward him.

"Get out of here!"

"Sir?"

"Out! Now!"

The airman stopped. His smile froze.

"Move!"

From overhead, there came a flutter. Flynn looked up. The airman kept smiling.

A figure dropped down, looking for all the world like a dark gigantic demon sliding down an invisible wall.

Then it stood before the young man, five narrow feet of spindly arms and legs to the airman's solid six-foot bulk.

The next instant, the creature leaped back into the rafters.

The airman had entirely changed. His uniform was gone, nothing left of it but shreds on the floor. Blood gushed out of his eye sockets and from the hole where his mouth and tongue had been. It went sluicing down his legs, pumping from the crater that was all that was left of his genitals. From overhead, there came a whirring sound, a noise of bees or busy flies.

As Flynn watched, the streams of blood stopped. They hung, frozen like candle wax, then, slowly at first, changed direction. They began to travel upward, racing across the man's body as he crumpled to his knees. An orb of blood, dark red, hung in the air six feet above where he had stood.

As Flynn was drawing his gun, the creature dropped back down.

It connected with the vibrating mass of blood.

There was a blur and a high crackling sound like something being dipped in hot grease. The bubble of blood disappeared into a new form entirely, and what landed with a light step on the room's floor was not an alien. Neither was it a human being, not quite. It was covered with pink gel, like something that had come out of a chrysalis or burst from some malignant egg. The eyes opened. They were sky blue, set in a blurred but unmistakably human face.

As he watched, another version of the airman took shape before him. The boy's smile returned. As if surprised, he blinked his eyes.

It was astonishing, but Flynn was not deceived. This was not a hallucination, and it was not the airman. It made an impossible leap back into the rafters. Flynn fired at it, but no blood returned.

He began hunting the thing, but the room was complex with shadows, the ceiling fifty feet overhead, and he soon recognized that the thing could hide up there for hours. So he decided to try another strategy.

He walked out into the middle of the space. Holding his pistol, he looked around the room. Then he took out his small LED flashlight and shone it into the rafters. Three girders down, a slight thickening of the shadow along its upper surface.

His target.

"Shit," he said into the room's echo. He holstered his gun and walked directly under the creature. Hands on hips, he shone his light into a dark area under the stairs that led down from the office level at the far end of the room, the same stairs the airman had come down.

Above him, he heard the slightest sound, a bare whisper.

He drew and fired into the biorobot as it dropped down on him.

The bullets blew its guts out, and it fell at his feet with a nasty splat.

He looked down at it, then at the actual remains of the boy—a husk, his youth destroyed in an instant—his promise and the hopes of those who loved him, all gone. He choked back his heart and his hate, and the anger that gnawed his core—if only he'd been quicker to see him coming, faster to react, this poor kid would still have his life.

Teeth bared, he sucked the blood-reeking air and, with it, sucked deep into himself the sorrow and the shame of his failure. He kicked the hell out of the dead alien, its incredible disguise already fading and melting like the Wicked Witch of the West.

He turned away from the mess and, walking with the excessive care of a man confronting the gallows, crossed the echoing concrete chamber to the black intercom hanging on the wall.

"Yes, sir, do you need assistance?"

He said, "There's been an accident. You are to seal the building. I repeat, seal it. It is to be guarded. A team will be here tomorrow to restore it."

"Sir, yes, sir."

"There is a man down."

"Sir?"

"I repeat, there is a man down. He is dead. Our team will inform the authorities here of his identity after their inspection is complete."

"One of my men is in there?"

"There was a man here. I don't know why and it's not my issue. He is dead."

"He got shot?"

"No, sir. He was killed in another manner. He died in the line of duty."

Flynn replaced the receiver in its cradle. As he walked away, the intercom began ringing and kept ringing. He did not turn back.

How in hell had this happened? Somehow, the thing had survived. What had enabled it to do that was yet another question that could not be answered. The purpose was clear: he had observed the predator in the process of camouflaging itself as its prey, like an Indian covering himself with a buffalo hide in order to get close to a herd.

They had thrown away two of their lives and sent this third being on a suicide mission, because the real ambush was not intended to happen at the Miller house at all, but here, in this room, where Flynn would least expect it.

The place suddenly felt cold, freezing. The stink of the room, blood and cordite, was sickening. Moving fast, he snatched his duffel out of the car and dug out his cell phone.

He punched in the numbers that would take him to a scrambled signal, then called Diana.

"Jesus God, what have you been doing for seven hours?"

"I pulled the battery on my phone."

"I thought you were a goner. Give me a heads-up next time."

"I'm at Wright-Pat. There's been an incident. I've ordered our facility here sealed."

"An incident? What kind of an incident?"

"You need a team out here to clean up some atypical remains. Plus there's a casualty. An airman."

"*Shit!*"

"The body's been mutilated. You'll need to commandeer it. Our eyes only."

"What are you telling me?"

"What you need to do! And I need a plane." He would have preferred to drive to Washington, but there was no time for that now.

He left the facility, closed the access door, and listened as the locks clicked into place on the other side. The cleanup team from their unit were now the only people on the planet with the code needed to open this door.

He wondered whom she would choose. Things had gone wrong before, but this was the only time anything remotely this messy had happened.

An airman pulled up in a big SUV. He got out to open the door, but Flynn let himself in. He sat in silence as he was driven to the flight line. When they arrived, a jet was just being positioned on the apron. It was the full dinner: a general officer's plane complete with a cabin crew of two.

"You don't need to stay on board," he said as he stooped to enter the plane.

"Sir?"

"Leave the aircraft, please. You're not needed today." There was no reason to put anybody in harm's way who didn't absolutely need to be there.

The two stewards looked at each other.

"Do it!"

Slowly, they went to the rear of the cabin. When the crew were down on the apron, he activated the steps. The steps came up, the door closed, and he locked it down. He signaled the pilots. "Get this thing cleared and get it moving."

There was some sort of a reply, but he didn't listen. As always, he had work to do. He'd been away from his unending records search for over thirty hours, and he didn't like that. He pulled out his iPad and hooked into the secure network, then began once again searching police reports—town by town, and city by city.

He looked at murders, disappearances, accidents, anything that might lead to the dark place that was his beat. He worked for an hour. For two. He stopped only when he had assured himself that his beat was for the moment quiet.

He wouldn't allow himself to hope, but maybe—just maybe—he had indeed gotten the last of them. Maybe it was just him and Morris now.

He listened to the roar of the wind speeding past the airframe and to the noise of the engines. He let his eyes close and was immediately asleep, or as asleep as he ever got. The doctors called it "guarded sleep," the sleep of men in combat. He dreamed of Abby on a blue day on the beach, watching the gulls wheel. The sweet smell of her cornsilk hair filled his memory, and he sighed and turned as if toward somebody in the seat beside him.

His eyes opened. He had become aware of a change in the pitch of the engines. He evaluated it. Normal. They were landing.

New rules: Be faster on the scene than ever before. When the aliens are apparently dead, cut the remains to pieces.

It was an air force plane, but it landed him in the general aviation section at Dulles.

He left without a word, not looking back. The mystified pilots watched him cross the tarmac and disappear into the terminal. They had never even seen his face.

CHAPTER SIX

WHILE HE was away, Flynn's personal car had been moved into the general aviation parking lot. He walked over to it, a black Audi R8 GT. To a man with his reflexes, most cars drove like buses. The R8 did not.

There was a bag from Wagshal's on the passenger seat, which, as his standing order with Transportation instructed, contained a pastrami on rye and a Brooklyn Lager. As a Southwest 737 screamed past not a hundred feet overhead, he opened the bag, cracked the can of beer, started the car, and headed out.

He had no idea how long it had been since he ate, but the sandwich did not last until the Beltway. He got an hour of sleep on the flight, so he felt fairly rested. It had been uneasy sleep, though. Things were spinning out of control, and he knew it.

He took the exit off the GW Parkway and stopped in the guard station at CIA headquarters. He drove around the back of the main building and then into the underground facility, over to where cars that couldn't be exposed to passing satellites were parked. He sat in his car with the windows down, just listening to the space. He got out. Nobody else here, the parking spots mostly empty. Even as he was walking through the facility's relative safety, his extreme sense of caution did not change. They might have failed on this day, and they might all be dead, but he still worried about ambush anywhere, anytime.

In the long, clean corridors of the CIA, people gave him the usual glances. In his patrolman days, his uniforms had always been sharp. As a detective, he'd worn a suit with a string tie and a Stetson, an outfit intended to make him disappear into the north Texas woodwork. No more. Now he was too fixated on his job to worry about appearances. As long as his clothes were street legal, that was all that mattered to him.

As he was approaching their section, another text came in. This time, it was the number 676, once again from a blocked line.

He stopped in his tracks, staring down at the screen.

He was looking at what had been Dan Miller's full employee number at Deer Island.

No way this could be a coincidence, and somebody certainly wanted him to know that.

He got to the numbered door that concealed headquarters. He paused. This time, it could be seriously argued that he'd screwed up on every possible level. He set his jaw, paused for a moment, then went in.

The same kids were at the same consoles, working at the same intractable problems of translation and communication. As he passed silently among them, he could feel their uneasy disapproval like a sour smoke.

"Anybody wants a head for their den, let me know."

It was his standard joke, but this time there was no ripple of laughter.

He pushed through into Diana's sleek lair. She was not sitting at her desk, not exactly. She was poised there.

"Don't hit me," he said, cringing back and raising his hands.

"Flynn, *why*?"

"He got in the line of fire."

"You killed four people!"

Had there been anybody else in there? No. "Wrong body count, and I didn't kill anybody. A kid got killed. Big difference, Diana."

"If you'd done your job right, nobody would be dead."

"I ordered the facility evacuated. Maybe he was deaf, I don't know. An airman died, and I'm sad about it. But it was one. Not four."

"We consider the aliens you killed people."

"Not legally, they aren't."

"Flynn, that's the last time you throw that in my face, okay? You've gotten yourself into huge trouble, and us along with you. Hell, the whole planet, Flynn! What if they could just push a button and we're history?"

"I've gained a lot of intelligence on this mission."

She raised her eyebrows.

"The exsanguinations are explained. What I saw was one of those monsters—"

"Please."

"What am I supposed to call them? What's the politically correct term? Tell me, because I want to know."

"Try calling them people."

He let it lie. "It used the airman's blood to coat itself in a human form."

She gave him a long, searching look.

"Do you understand what I'm saying? Because it's kind of important."

"We're going out to Area Fifty-One, you and I." The exobiology group was located there, scientists who sat in the desert thinking up reasons that contact with Aeon could be made to work.

"I don't have time."

"You have time."

"I have time to keep searching for cases, and that's all the time I have."

"Let me tell you what those kids out on the floor have been doing ever since you went on your murder mission."

"Excuse me, policing mission."

"They've been communicating with Aeon, trying to save your life."

"Well, thank them for me. Unless I'm headed for a meeting with the needle. Then don't thank them."

"A deal has been struck, Flynn."

"Which involves the scientists at Area Fifty-One how?"

"You will accompany me to Area Fifty-One. Consider that an order."

He thought about that. Normally, she did everything she could to satisfy her brief from the scientists—short of giving him direct orders like this. That way, he could go on doing his job and she could go on being quietly relieved he was getting kills.

"Diana, we both know that everything coming out of Area Fifty-One is bullshit. In any case, I want to go to Deer Island."

"Why?"

"I got another one of those calls: 333676. Ring a bell?"

"No."

"It's Dan Miller's employee number."

She got up and went to her "window." They were in a basement, so it was actually just a poster of the Grand Tetons she'd bought at Target and tacked to her wall.

"I love it when you stare out at the view. It always means you know I'm right."

She turned. "We're on a strict schedule. And frankly, if you want to stay in one piece, you'd better cooperate."

For a moment, he thought about it, then spread his hands, gesturing surrender. "You can count on me, boss. Down the line."

"We leave at six. You might think about taking a shower."

He glanced at his watch. Half an hour wouldn't give him time to go home. "Can I use your lair?" Her suite had a private sitting room and a full bath, which he often used between cases.

"I'm gonna try to have a meeting in here. We're cataloging new transmissions. So don't disturb us, if you can manage that."

"Yes, ma'am." He went through into the luxuriously furnished private suite that was a perk of her Senior Executive Service pay grade. The luxuries that interested him weren't things like her Persian carpets, gleaming antiques, and 3-D TV. His cars were a luxury—the Audi and the Ferrari California that waited for him in Texas. Most of his guns were

there as well—his pistols, his sniper rifles, his matched pair of Purdey shotguns handed down in the family for three generations. These were his luxuries, and the wine cellar his family started in the 1920s, when their land in the Permian Basin south of Menard had turned out to be a raft floating on a lake of oil.

For most of his life, he had preferred to live only on what he made, but after Abby's disappearance, he found himself wanting to embrace his own heritage. A couple of years back, he had started drawing on the family trust. In a strange way, it made him feel less alone.

In keeping with family tradition, he lived modestly. Until he started buying extreme cars a couple of years ago, few people outside his small circle of close friends had any idea that he had money. The way he figured it, though, the work he did now was shortening his life, probably by a lot of years, so whatever he was going to enjoy, he needed to do that right now.

He threw off his clothes, realizing as he dropped them onto her antique Sultanabad carpet, that they were really pretty damn dirty. Stained, too, with greenish purple blood.

Showers bothered him. He didn't like being in places with only one exit. He wanted two ways out, always. He turned the gold handles in her marble shower stall and let the water flow until it was steaming. Then he stepped in. He left the door open and faced outward into the bathroom as he methodically washed himself.

The hot water felt good on his skin, except where it burned in his latest wounds. He stepped out of the stall, opened the medicine cabinet, and rummaged until he found some disinfectant. Then he pulled the ugliest cut apart by drawing his shoulder forward, and poured the disinfectant in. There was pain. A lot, in fact.

As he dried himself, he realized that his clothes were too gross to wear. The room stank like some kind of bovine had rolled in it. Wrapping the towel around his waist, he went to the exquisitely carved dresser. He opened the bottom drawer, which was where his things were kept.

He often showered and changed here—slept here, too. From here, he could move on cases a lot faster than he could from home.

But what the hell was this shirt? It wasn't one of his.

"Hey," he called, "what is this thing, a bolero shirt?"

No answer from the office. That's right, her meeting was out there. And, as a matter of fact, he was hearing his name mentioned, was he not? He strolled over to the door. Yep, they were talking about him.

He went out waving the shirt. "I can't wear this."

"Put some clothes on."

"I can't wear a blouse."

"That's an ordinary man's shirt. Unlike your tees, it happens to have a collar. Something you apparently haven't worn in some time. Now, get dressed."

"Sorry, kids," he said to the staring young faces, "I didn't mean to frighten you." He started to put on the shirt.

"Flynn, get out!"

"You said get dressed, boss." He sat on the edge of her desk. "So, what's the latest findings? Aeon turn out to be big on comedy clubs? Marijuana dispensaries? Too bad they don't have decent cops."

"Flynn, Aeon knows you're the fastest gun in the West and the toughest hombre in town—and they're not impressed, as I've told you. They also know that you're richer than God, and therefore a dilettante. And they have been speculating about whether or not you're crazy." She folded her arms. "I think that question is answered."

He turned around so they could see the gash that extended from his neck to the center of his back. "I could use a Band-Aid."

"My God, Flynn, you don't need a bandage, you need medical attention."

"We're off to Bullshit Central, remember. Fifteen minutes."

"I'll have medics on the plane. Now, get out of here."

He drew on the shirt. Nicely tailored, too. She'd spared no expense. As he buttoned it, he said, "So when do we leave?"

"When I say. Now, go away. You're not need-to-know on this conference."

"333676. Track down that blocked number."

He went back into the bedroom, threw himself on the bed, and waited.

The sheets were scented. They smelled like her.

"Flynn!"

It was Abby, calling to him from her porch across the street. The summer wind whispered in the trees; the sweet smell of the Texas prairie filled the air.

"Flynn!"

The movie ended. Blank screen. Then he realized that it wasn't a movie. He opened his eyes.

"Christ, I was about to call for a blowtorch. I thought you were in a coma."

He bolted upright. "Sorry, I didn't realize—"

She sat down on the bed and pulled the shirt away from his back. "That needs ten stitches at least."

"It'll heal."

"We have to go now, so get your ass moving, please." Her voice was harsh, but not her eyes.

He reached out and touched her cheek. She did not turn away, and he knew that he could kiss her if he wanted to. Neither of them moved. In the silence that they shared, there was a lot of life lived together, friends as they were who were also enemies, lovers longing for each other across a gulf of conflicting agendas.

"We're on a strict schedule," she said.

They rode to the airport in his car. He drove fast; he took chances. He liked to hear her yell at him, and she obliged him, saying he was going to lose his license, she'd see to it, on and on. Just made him drive faster. With this car and his reflexes, it wasn't dangerous, and with no strange cargo to hide, things like tickets didn't matter. Often enough, they got written, but the same hand that protected him from all other official harm made them go away. Her hand.

He said, "As I said, I got three good kills."

She said nothing.

They'd been given an excellent plane, not one of the cramped puddle jumpers he was used to. There was a private cabin, behind it an office and a small press unit. To the rear was a galley.

"Impressive."

"You could afford your own jet."

"Not interested."

"Your frequent-flier miles, I know."

"I haven't been on a vacation in a real long time. I dream about it. First class, all the trimmings, on my way to somewhere sweet. Barbados. Ever been to Barbados?"

"Course not. My salary won't take me that far."

"Don't hand me that. You're just like me, a rich dilettante. What I've become."

"You've accepted your family. That's not being a dilettante. And I'm not rich."

"Senator's daughter. Senators are rich."

"The senator is comfortable. That is not rich."

She called her dad "the senator," her mother Mrs. Glass. She didn't talk about it much, but it didn't sound like a happy home. She had kept that powerful last name, though, even through her marriage.

Once the plane was at altitude and heading into the sunset, the medics took over.

"Sir," the doctor said uneasily, "I'm afraid I've only got some topical anesthetic. I didn't realize—"

"He doesn't need anesthetic," Diana said. "He's not like us." He heard pride in her voice. He liked that.

While they stitched away, he smelled steak cooking, and when they finally let him up, he found an exceptional meal waiting in the office, which had been reset as a dining room. A general's plane was not Air Force One, but it had first class pretty well beat. He gestured toward the meal. "How many taxpayers did it take to pay for all this?"

"None. Or rather, one. I paid for it."

"The poor senator. Did you leave him to starve?"

"Yes."

He picked up the wine. "An '83 Romanée-Conti? That's worth a trip to Barbados at least. First class." Then he had another thought. "Is this my last meal?"

"Any meal could be your last. Damn you, Flynn." Her voice broke. She choked back her emotions. "What if they tell us something like they'll kill the whole planet unless we kill you?"

"I'd kill me."

She closed her eyes briefly, then looked away from him.

They ate quietly for a few minutes.

"This spread looks to me like it's meant for a celebration. Was something good supposed to happen, and you forgot to tell Transportation that it fell through?"

She said, "You miss nothing."

"Comes with the job."

"I've often wondered why you were hiding in that little job in Texas. A man like you."

"It was a big job, and I wasn't hiding."

"I mean, why weren't you running an oil company or something? Doing something incredible?"

"Being a cop isn't incredible?"

She shrugged, then poured them both wine.

"By the way, that blocked number. Can't be located."

"How is that possible?"

"It was purged from the carrier's system."

"That's unusual."

"Also illegal. They're frantic about it. You have any idea what it was all about?"

Flynn did, but if he was right about why he was being messaged like this, he had no intention of telling anybody. It might be dangerous even to think about it. "Not a clue," he said.

"I know when you're lying, but never why."

They drank in silence. The medical team had retired to the press section, so the two of them were alone. She glanced back to be sure the door was closed.

"You know, Flynn, I'm not being very fair to you."

"What's new about that?"

She laughed a little, but said no more. He was curious, of course, but he didn't press her. If somebody wanted silence, that was fine with him.

He closed his eyes for a couple of seconds, and suddenly the plane was landing. He recognized that he had come to the point where he was desperate for sleep.

"Listen," he said as they lined up on the runway, "if I'm supposed to talk to these people, you better tell me what I need to say."

"No talking necessary."

"It's a dog and pony show, then. They're going to try to convince me that there's something good going on here, which is and always will be utter horseshit. Diana, I could be needed somewhere right now."

"There's no dog and pony show. In fact, no scientists at all. It's past their bedtimes, anyway—you should know that."

As they touched down, he stared out into the glare of the runway lights. Beyond them was blackness.

Very little of Area 51 was actually devoted to the legendary secret of the aliens. For the most part, the place was exactly what it was claimed to be: a test bed for future aircraft, including new designs that utilized the earth's magnetic field for propulsion and lift. There were space planes here and, Flynn suspected, some devices that were of alien construction and defied gravity.

"Leave your guns, take your jacket," Diana said as a steward cracked the door.

"My guns?"

"Leave them."

"No."

She sighed. "Flynn, just please cooperate for once."

"I don't go out on lonely desert airstrips at night without my guns."

"Do you think you're being handed over?"

"Maybe."

"Trust me."

"No."

She glanced at her watch. "Take them, then." She marched down the steps and into the shadows.

Flynn followed her into the cold of the desert night. As the wind whipped across the tarmac, he zipped his jacket. Yet again, his tongue touched his cyanide capsule. Would it be now? If he was about to be given to some creeps in a flying saucer, then yes, it would.

The plane's door was pulled closed, and its engines whined as it taxied slowly away.

"Hey, we're not anywhere!"

"No, this is the right place."

Once the plane was gone, they were left standing on a strip of concrete surrounded on three sides by desert. Now and again, a tumbleweed went bounding across, a gray shadow in the thin light of a sickle moon. His right hand slid down to the butt of his pistol. She held tight to him, and he couldn't tell if she was trying to control him or holding on for dear life.

The sound that came then was not something you heard, but rather something you felt. It vibrated your teeth; it made your skin crawl.

"Look," Diana whispered. Flynn followed her gaze upward and saw the hazy outline of a descending shape, perfectly round. It quickly grew larger, blotting out more and more stars.

Flynn's finger went to his trigger. He tongued his cyanide capsule until it was between his teeth.

Now the object was hanging in the air before them. It did not move. It was not affected by the wind. Flynn didn't try to convince himself that he wasn't afraid. He was very afraid.

In the distant light from the hangar area and the low moon, the object shone like burnished steel. It was nothing like the disks he was used to seeing—not worn, not small, not clattering like an old truck. No matter his loathing of the aliens and their ways, this thing's sleek form was beautiful to see.

He realized that a tripod landing gear had come out of it, and it was now standing on the runway. There hadn't been a sound nor the slightest suggestion of movement. A narrow line of light appeared in its base. This grew wider and brighter, until he could see part of an interior of featureless bright metal. Very slowly then, something began moving in the light, a form.

"My God," he heard himself whisper. Hardly thinking of it, he drew his gun.

"Put that away."

"Diana—"

"If they see that thing, we might die right here, right now. Both of us."

He holstered the pistol.

A figure glided down in the column of light. He was expecting to see the thin form of an alien, but what he saw instead was a trim human shape, a woman in a blue jumpsuit.

Immediately, he thought of what he'd seen the alien do at Wright-Pat, and of Morris.

The object rose enough to spread the light into a pool a hundred feet across. Flynn and Diana were in that pool, and so was the alien, which now came walking toward them with the easy gait of absolute confidence.

She stood before them, a woman of perhaps twenty-five. If he hadn't seen her come out of a flying saucer, he would have said that she was human.

She looked up at him, her eyes searching his face, and when she did, he saw in her blond arched eyebrows and her subtle, almost sensual smile, an unmistakable shadow of Abby.

"Hello," she said, turning toward Diana. "You are Police Commander Glass?" There was in her lilting voice just the faintest trace of an accent, oddly Asian in so Caucasian-looking an individual.

Diana saluted her.

The woman's gaze returned to him. "And you are Officer Carroll?"

"I'm Flynn."

She wasn't smiling now, far from it. Her eyes were glittering with something he could not mistake. She hated him.

Diana said, "Officer Carroll, meet your new partner. This is Gt'n'aa. We're going to call her Geri."

Geri extended her hand. Flynn stared at it.

"Flynn?"

"Oh—yeah." He took the coldest, strongest hand he had ever felt in his life. As he shook it, he could feel the power there, like living steel.

"Very well," Geri said, glancing off into the dark. "Shall we proceed?"

Flynn's mind was racing with questions, all of them unanswered, all of them urgent. But before he could speak, Diana and Geri moved off toward the edge of the runway. Simultaneously, the light went out and the ship ascended, swiftly disappearing into the night.

A familiar sort of chime sounded. Flynn saw a Jeep Cherokee on the edge of the tarmac, revealed by its interior light. Diana had just unlocked it with its remote key. She went around to the driver's side and got in.

Flynn opened the passenger door.

"Backseat," she snapped.

He got in. The alien got in the front beside Diana. They drove off toward the buildings of the Area 51 complex, through a desert night lit only by the distant stars and the beams of their headlights.

CHAPTER SEVEN

FLYNN SAT silently in the Jeep, fighting back confused feelings of hatred and longing. He was used to living in a reality that he didn't quite understand, but not like this. This was too much.

They came to the familiar Science Building 3, with its glass doors and its lobby lit with glaring neon. In the days of the Lockheed Skunk Works, this had been Lockheed's on-site office building, two stories of cubbyholes now filled with exobiologists, alien ethicists, exopsychologists, and other irrelevant, time-wasting dreamers.

They crowded together, at least thirty of them, their brilliance well hidden behind their slack jaws and childishly wide eyes.

Diana went front and center with Geri in tow. Flynn hung back. He didn't even like these people to see his face, and socializing with them was not going to happen.

"Ladies and gentlemen, a lot of history has happened in this building, but I think that this qualifies as a—"

"Excuse me, I can introduce myself," Geri said. "Please call me Geri or Colonel—either will do. I'm the equivalent of a colonel in your air force, or a senior police commander. I'm from Aeon Central Police Command, and my mission is to get this situation under control, because it's obviously running amok. I'd shake your various hands, but I'm here to work, so if Major Glass would show me to my office, please."

Diana, fumbling out words like "of course," and "thank you," led her away. The lobby emptied.

There was an old metal desk in one corner and a wooden chair. Flynn took the chair and put his feet up on his desk. He pulled his iPad out of his duffel and turned it on.

When he input his password to reach the secure network, he was denied entry. He read the FAILED LOG-IN ATTEMPT warning. He was attempting to access a secure network, and his identity was known. If he continued, he would be in commission of a felony.

"Here you are, Officer Carroll. Come on, we've got work to do."

Geri stood over him, the shadow of Abby smiling in her face.

He followed her into a spartan office—gray linoleum floor, gray walls, dingy white ceiling tiles. He had to hand it to Uncle Sam; the old fart had a real talent for interior decoration.

She dropped down behind the desk. "Sit," she said, gesturing to the one steel chair in the room.

"Where's Diana?"

"Licking her wounds. She got a lecture."

He raised his eyebrows.

"I told her she was incompetent and her operation was an embarrassment to her and a failure for this planet."

"How many planets are involved?"

She raised her eyebrows appreciatively. "Nice question. Very quick. You should know that you're talking to the person who was most strongly in favor of executing you. And I'm still of that opinion."

"Fine. Let's head to Dodge. Face off at high noon. Gun to gun."

"I don't carry your sorts of weapon. Frankly, mine are better and I am faster."

"Good, then maybe you can increase the kill rate around here. Because I need to get the last of the murderers."

"You don't understand anything. That's stupid."

"Stupidity and ignorance are two different things. A person who doesn't get that is a fool."

"Remember that English isn't my native language. If I'm too blunt, just tell me."

"Inside of five minutes, you've told me that my boss is incompetent, our operation sucks, you want me dead, and I'm stupid. That's too blunt."

She did not reply as fast as she had earlier. He could see the calculation in her eyes. Despite all her bluster, she was beginning to see that she was on unsure footing.

"You need to slow down," he said. "If you're going to be calling the shots, you'd be well advised to at least inspect our operation. Do you even know how it's organized?"

"In such a way that it isn't working right."

"Oh? We save lives. Human lives. So it's working just fine, thank you."

"One field operative who destroys every biorobot he encounters, not knowing that his actions are only going to goad them into becoming more aggressive. That's not our definition of 'working right.'"

"I can't capture them. Nobody can. If I'm lucky, I can get an occasional kill. Where's our choice in that?"

"You're a police officer. I'm sure you have procedures."

"My guess is that you know exactly what those are."

"I do, and you don't even try to follow them when it comes to our mechanisms."

"Biorobots? Mechanisms? So I'm right about what they are."

Diana came into the room. Geri went to her feet. "No, not needed, please leave."

Diana's eyes met Flynn's. Nothing needed to be said. They both thought exactly the same thing about Commandant Geri. "We have a situation."

"Exactly our concern," Geri said. "That's why I'm here. You stress these entities enough, they amplify the conflict. If you keep destroying them, their numbers will continue to grow. Think of them as cancer. Your planet has cancer, but so far, the tumor is small. I am here to help you keep it that way."

"I think that the conflict has just been amplified. We have a problem in a community called Elmwood, Texas. The entire town has been set on fire."

"Elmwood? So they're trying to lure me again."

"Lure you?" Geri asked.

"Sure, they did Dr. Miller for two reasons. One, because they apparently didn't like the work he was doing. Two, because they wanted to lure me. They got me where they wanted me, but then had a bit of a setback. So they're trying again. Of all the places in the world, they know for certain that I'll go to Elmwood."

"Why would that be?"

"My family founded the town."

"Should you, then?"

"They'll keep causing trouble until I do—you can be sure of that."

"But given what happened in Mountainville," Diana said, "wouldn't they try something else?"

"Destroying the town my family founded qualifies as something else, I think."

"Seems as if we have our first case as a team, then," Geri said.

Diana ordered transportation to Menard, and the three of them headed to the flightline.

On the plane, Flynn asked Geri why they couldn't use her ship, and received a long lecture about how they couldn't introduce technology that was too far ahead of our own without disrupting our society. It made a kind of sense, but he didn't buy it. He wasn't buying Geri at all, except for one thing, which was that she had something like a ghost of Abby in her, and he was going to find out why that was.

The flight was two and a half hours, twelve hundred miles. Geri sat staring straight ahead the whole time, her hands folded in her lap. It was unnerving.

"What're we going to do about her uniform?" Diana asked. "She can't traipse around Texas in a blue jumpsuit."

He thought about that. Then he made a decision. On the surface, it probably seemed simple. It was not simple, and it might bring some unexpected results. He said, "I've still got all of Abby's stuff. They're just about the same size. We can stop by the house on the way out."

When he was very small, he'd gone to the country school in Elmwood. He closed his eyes, remembering the clapboard building where class had been held. His mind drifted back to his granddad, a stately old Texan who was just as polite as a preacher and as formal as an undertaker until you got him on a quarter horse. He could toss a lariat like the cowboy that he was, and cuss like he was the devil's understudy.

The family had come before oil, when this part of Texas was all about wheat and cattle. Wheat if you were a gambler and crazy, cattle if you were only crazy.

"Flynn," Diana asked, "how tired are you?"

"Not tired."

"False. You ought to get some sleep."

"If I sleep now, I'm liable to wake up and find the whole town dead, in addition to all the cops and rescue workers who are probably trying to save them."

Menard's airport was closed down for the night, but the automatic lights came on during their approach.

The moment they pulled up to the terminal, Geri got out of the plane.

Flynn made a call on his cell phone while he and Diana watched Geri become involved with the tall cyclone fence that separated the apron from the outdoor luggage station and the parking lot. Finally, she returned.

"I've called the custodian," Flynn said. "He'll be along in ten minutes to let us out. He'll also drive us to my place, and we can get you changed."

They waited on the tarmac, with the prairie wind blowing down their necks. Flynn kept his anguish to himself. Whatever was happening over in Elmwood was his fault, no question.

Robert Greaves, the tiny airport's custodian, finally pulled up, pie-eyed and trying hard not to topple over. "I hear you workin' in D.C.," he said.

"Yep."

"Menard ain't changed a lick, you'll find."

"I know it."

Greaves drove by aiming the car along the curb. The smell of bourbon filled the car.

When Flynn saw his house, which he had not entered in nearly a year, he felt a real catch in his throat. This was going to be hard as hell, giving this weird woman things that had belonged to Abby. He wanted it all, every ballpoint pen and every blouse, every hair curler and cocktail gown, and all the jeans and all the tees. Geri was stiff and uneasy as she walked up to the front door. Was she sensitive enough to understand the pain this was causing him? He doubted that.

Diana was on her cell in the car, and still on it when they entered the house as Greaves drove away. Finally she closed it and came in. She said, "Nothing's happened for a couple of hours."

"How many are dead?"

"So far, three. The locals are still going from house to house."

"Where is this culturally appropriate clothing?"

He led Geri up to his and Abby's bedroom, which was still as it had been on the day of her disappearance, Abby's top drawer still opened an inch, everything just as their life together had left it.

Silently, he opened her middle drawer and took out a blouse; then he got jeans from the closet, sneakers, socks from her sock drawer, a bra, underwear. He laid it all on the bed.

There was a hissing sound, and her uniform fell away. "Help me with this clothing. It's unfamiliar."

"I'll send Diana up," he said.

"I want you. You help me."

"No." He went downstairs to Diana. "Get her dressed," he muttered. "She can't do it."

"Goddamnit, Flynn, I don't want to be alone with that crocodile."

"Get her dressed!"

She hurried off, stomping up the stairs. He couldn't blame her.

Aeon. Beautiful name. It meant "life." It meant "eternity."

He remembered his mother sitting years ago at the great table in the dining room, throwing out tarot cards. She had been good with things like tarot cards and the *I Ching*. Once, she had thrown him the Tower and said, "How funny, it falls in the place of the future." She had looked up at him, and he could still remember the fear in her eyes, the haunted fear. "The future, Errol," she had said, then turned the destruction card facedown, as if sealing a tomb.

They should have called Aeon that: the Tower of Destruction. It was death riding down the night, pale and quick, in the form of creatures whose cruelty was as much part of their blood as love was part of the blood of man.

He thought these thoughts sitting in the same easy chair that his father had used and his grandfather before him. He wondered where this situation was really going. Having failed, why would they try the same trick of luring him to another isolated spot just twenty-four hours later?

Only one answer to that question: because it wasn't the same trick.

He listened to the slow movement of the old house. A house has gestures, the sigh of a footfall on a carpet, the creak of a step, the whispering crack of wainscoting as the floor it borders is pressed by a stealthy weight.

"I dislike this clothing."

He got up from the chair. "It's what women here wear." Dressed like this, she could have been Abby's twin, which made him want to rip them off her back. He smiled. "You look entirely American now," he said.

"Well, I'm not." Her tone reflected her arrogance.

He took them outside and opened his garage. The Ferrari stood there in its red grandeur, the Range Rover beside it, looking very stuffy and staid.

He opened the truck and they got in. He thought it might not run, but it did, turning over after a few hesitant grinds of the starter.

As he drove down the familiar streets of Menard, he said, "I don't know what we're going to find out there, but I have to say, I feel way out of my depth."

Geri said, "Just remember procedure. That's the important thing."

"Yeah, procedure," Diana muttered. "Hear that, Flynn?"

He said nothing.

A couple of deer appeared in the road, bounding off into the darkness as the truck approached them. He no longer saw creatures like deer and owls in quite the same way.

"What if we kill some of your people tonight, Geri?"

"If we follow procedure and that happens, then it happens."

"Tell me, what's your procedure?"

"Much the same as yours: Demand compliance. If the perp has a weapon, warn that deadly force will be used."

"In this case, the perp is the weapon. It's their speed and those claws. They don't need guns."

They drove on in silence.

"Okay, here we go," he said. There was a large police blockade ahead, dozens of light bars flashing, SWAT vehicles, even a riot tank, all spread across the road in a disorganized mass. Beyond the barricade, the remains of Elmwood glowed and flickered on the horizon.

"They expect us," Diana said as one of the state cops peered in the driver's-side window, then waved them through.

As they were passing, Flynn got a surprise. Standing there with the state brass in a pair of worn chinos and a leather jacket was his old boss, Eddie Parker. His face was hidden under the shadow of his Stetson, but Flynn didn't need to see his expression to know how very unhappy he was.

He stopped the truck.

"Excuse me, drive on."

He got out and walked over to Eddie.

Malcolm Dodd, the chief of state police, and Fred Carter, captain of the Texas Rangers, both watched with Eddie as Flynn walked up.

"Eddie."

"Three dead, all old folks who couldn't get out of their houses."

"I am so damn sorry." Flynn didn't say how relieved he was that they hadn't been maimed like Dan Miller.

"Can I tell 'em what you do?"

Eddie couldn't give away any secrets. "Sure."

"This is a Menard guy. Flynn Carroll. He's a fed now. Way up there." He fluttered his fingers.

"Can you help us?"

"We need to have a look."

"What happened?" Dodd asked. "Do you have any idea? I mean, the whole place caught on fire at the same time. Within minutes."

"This will be handled," Flynn said. He had no idea how, but these frightened, hollow-eyed men needed something that would restore morale.

"He's the man," Eddie said. "We're gonna get past this."

"It was a secret weapon, wasn't it?" Fred Carter said. "Some kinda terrorist thing."

"That's right. Terrorists. A secret weapon. They chose to test it on Elmwood, probably because it's out of the way and vulnerable. It would have been done from above. A plane. We'll get them, fellas, never fear. And anything you find, put it in channels right away."

He got back in the Range Rover and closed the door, then drove on toward the town his family had founded a hundred and fifty years ago.

Ahead, Elmwood's low, familiar buildings lay in smoking ruins. One of them was the Carroll General Store, now a Rite Aid pharmacy, where Flynn had played on the porch as a boy, rolling his beloved toy stagecoach back and forth under the hard Texas sun.

As they moved ahead, he kept watch on the night sky. Sooner or later, he knew, their disk would come—small and old, perhaps, by the standards of a place like Aeon, but here on Earth, still immeasurably advanced and breathtakingly dangerous.

CHAPTER EIGHT

FROM THE first moment he saw Geri, Flynn had understood that he had to get away from her, or it. He needed to deal with the present problem, then follow the trail he'd been given, the code, and he didn't want her along for the ride. 333676. Somebody on Deer Island was calling his attention to Miller and to the island.

"Okay," he said, "at this point, we need to enter the community."

"Flynn," Diana said, "the aliens are there—you know it."

"I do."

There was something moving at the end of Plainview, which was Elmwood's main street.

Flynn got out of the truck. They were in front of a ruined storefront that had once been Jack Holt's barbershop. Beside it was another empty store, which had been spared the fire. A Mode O'Day women's shop had been there.

"Stay in the vehicle," he said.

Geri got out. "We need to do this together."

"Do you know what 'this' is?"

"I do not."

"Just checking."

She stepped up onto the raised sidewalk.

"You get any closer to it, you're gonna get yourself killed."

"Closer to what?"

"One of your friends is in there. There's another one down at the end of Plainview, and two more moving into position to prevent us from getting away."

"This is impossible."

"Get back in the truck and lock the doors."

"You must not—"

"Get us all killed. I agree. Now, please give me the cooperation I need to keep you alive."

There were two more of them in the alley between the barbershop and the hardware store, which had still been in business until tonight. No longer.

He went over to the Range Rover and leaned in the window. "First off, these windows need to be closed. Second, Diana, I want you to get the vehicle turned around and ready to burn rubber."

"What's going on?"

"We're in the process of being surrounded by Geri's mechanisms. They mean to kill me, and will certainly include you if they can. And maybe her. Obviously, I'm not sure."

Diana said, "I just don't see anything."

"You don't know how to look. I thought you'd be ready for this."

He noticed that a black oblong object had slipped into Geri's left hand. It was small and trim and had no barrel.

Diana opened the car door.

"No."

She came anyway.

"Nobody obeys orders anymore."

"You can't give me orders, Flynn."

"We're surrounded right now."

"You knew this would happen. You're challenging them."

"We'd better pull out," Geri said. "I didn't come all this way to be killed on the first night."

"So what's procedure in a case like this? I assume shooting our way out is a no go."

Diana laughed a little.

"You led me into this," Geri said. "You knew I'd end up being forced to do it your way."

"What I knew, and what I know, is that you have no idea what you're doing. At all."

"I'm trained for police work. I'm not a soldier, I don't kill unless deadly force is my only alternative."

"What we need to do right now is give these folks who are surrounding us one hell of a bloody nose. So what's the procedure we need to follow?"

"Of all the planets in all the galaxies in the universe, I'd be sent to this one."

"That's a good line."

He drew and fired three shots, but still the alien that had leaped out of the ruins of the drugstore came on. It launched itself at him, but a fourth shot caused it to drop to the street, where it kicked and flailed wildly, blood spraying out of its exploded chest and face.

Then it stopped.

Silence fell.

"Geri, what choice did I have? What procedure should I have followed?"

She snapped, "No choice."

"So what are we looking at, here? We haven't had fires before. So do you know what we can expect next?"

"They're programmed entities. They don't invent; they repeat. Anything they do, they've been programmed to do."

"How about you? Are you a programmed entity, too?"

"I don't know."

Diana gasped, but Geri's words surprised Flynn only for a moment. It was the truth, it was the future talking, and it was a warning to mankind that Flynn vowed never to forget. Mix man and machine at peril to man.

Four more of the aliens had come up, and more were crossing the roofs. He could hear the faint rattle of their claws and the whispering breeze of their jumps.

"In a few seconds, we're gonna have another confrontation. It'll be a lot harder. If we do enough damage, they might back off. Please use your weapon, Geri."

Three of them leaped off nearby roofs as four more came out of doors on both sides of the street. Flynn dropped two of the jumpers before they hit the street, but the rest of them kept coming.

A number of cops appeared, moving in from the side streets. He heard Eddie's shout: "Flynn, what in holy hell?"

"Get out of here! *Now!*"

He took a hit so hard that he staggered, then went down on one knee with the thing on his back. Its arms wrapping his chest felt like steel bars. His left arm was free, but when he reached down for his small pistol, it was gone. It had come out in his fall and lay twenty feet away.

There was a dull thud, and the alien flopped to the ground.

He pulled out his .454 and did three of the others with thunderous shots. Diana, crouching by the truck, screamed as he fired.

The one that Geri had dropped leaped up, rising easily fifty feet in the air. Then, coming down as another three jumped onto the roof of the truck, it went after Diana. Geri pointed her weapon at it, but nothing happened. She shook it and tried again. Nothing.

He took all of them out with shots fired in such quick succession, they sounded like a single detonation.

Geri stood looking at her weapon in the palm of her hand.

"Does that thing not work?"

"Apparently not. It isn't properly tuned to Earth's magnetic field."

He took it from her.

"Return that, you're not authorized."

He threw it as far as he could, watching it arc away onto one of the roofs.

"You've given a weapon to the enemy—that's an actionable offense."

"Let's hope they try to use it. Now, get in the truck—we're done here."

"You said we'd be killed if we leave."

"That was then." He gestured toward the bodies. "This is now. We've probably got a minute or so of playtime while they regroup. They're testing my skills, and they don't mind using their own lives to do it."

"Why do they need to test you?"

"They can't figure out how to defeat me. I'm too fast."

"Why?"

Something crossed his mind—a suspicion. Small, probably far-fetched, but there. He said, "You tell her, Diana."

There was the slightest hesitation.

"Diana?"

"You said we need to get out of here, Flynn."

He started the Range Rover as Geri and Diana tumbled in and locked their doors. He drove to the end of Plainview and out into the flat prairie beyond, bouncing along the same dirt track that he and Mac and Eddie had used going deer hunting together, and later taking dates to look at the stars.

He took out his cell phone and called Eddie.

"Stay the hell out of the town until further notice. It's quarantined, do you understand? Everybody out."

"Flynn, what in God's name are you doing? What were those shots?"

"You didn't hear anything. You have nothing to tell the press or anybody else, any of you. National security."

"Okay, Flynn, I hear you."

Flynn hung up.

Diana was on her own phone. "I want a big cleanup crew to Elmwood, Texas, before dawn. There is alien material on the streets, and we want it gone. Out of there. Every trace." She listened. "Call out the whole operation, everybody you need." She glanced at her watch. "Get here no later than four."

He did not hate; it was inefficient. He said, "It's not over. They're going to come after us again."

He was driving through a grazed-down pasture on the Triple Horn Ranch, a forty-thousand-acre spread bordered by the railroad and the interstate.

If they got out of this situation, which he doubted they would, he had quite a number of questions for Geri, and she would not fail to answer—he would see to that.

"Where are we going?" Diana asked.

"Away. Far away."

"They went to your town to break your heart."

"They did."

"Geri," Diana said quietly, "we need an army with Flynn's capabilities."

"We do," he agreed.

"You can't raise an army?" Geri asked.

"Our problem is that we can't find anybody else as fast as Flynn who can also do this work. So he has to be an army of one."

"That can't last."

"That's for damn sure," he said. "We barely got out of Elmwood, and that'll be the last time we escape, if we have. Geri, what abilities do they have to track us right now?"

"A vehicle on an isolated roadway like this would be easy."

"And are they likely to be doing that?"

"I would think so. But remember, we're dealing with a few hundred individuals. They've come here because Earth is easy. It's undefended."

"Why don't you defend us? Your military could surely handle a small force like that."

"It was a miracle that I got here. I have no idea if my pilot will even get home alive. Or if I'll ever be able to leave Earth."

Diana said, "Oh, Jesus."

Flynn said nothing.

"You're displeased?"

"Just how much trouble is Aeon in, anyway?" Diana asked.

"I'm not supposed to talk about it."

"But you're going to," Flynn said.

She said no more.

He decided that he'd come back to this when the time was right, but one thing was very clear: Aeon was not some sort of giant United States or European Union like the exo team imagined. He could see that what was happening here on Earth was such a sideshow to them that they had only seen their way clear to sending a single officer, and a kid at that. Geri was no Oltisis, not wise, not deeply professional. Unlike him, though, she could breathe the air without getting allergies and walk the streets without spreading terror. Progress of a sort, but he would rather have had a seasoned cop.

He finally reached the interstate and slid into the traffic pattern. Hopefully, they would be a little less conspicuous in the flow of vehicles.

"Isn't Menard behind us?" Diana asked.

"We're not going to Menard."

She considered that. "Where, then?"

"You figure it out."

"Oh, no. No way."

"Otherwise, we don't have a prayer."

"I'll be getting out now. I'll hitch to the airport."

"Not gonna happen."

"He's a criminal. We don't need that kind of a complication."

"You don't want a former lover in your hair."

"He wasn't my lover."

"If you say."

"Damn you!"

He said to Geri, "Last year we got a device from you people called a MindRay. A number of people who relied on it paid for that mistake with their lives. Now I saw that your stun gun, or whatever it was, didn't work either. Why?"

"I think that there's something about Earth's magnetic field that throws our devices off."

"And yet you got here from another planet. That worked. Why?"

"It doesn't always."

"Where is Aeon?"

"I don't know how to tell you."

"How far away? In light-years, say."

"Your year is half as long as ours, so . . . twenty-four of your light-years."

"And how long in actual travel time? In the ship?"

"About half a day—or six of your hours—to reach jump, then a second or so, then movement into your orbital zone, a couple more days—about two Earth days, total."

"The part of the journey that involves movement across light-years takes a couple of seconds?"

"It's a wormhole," Diana said. "We think it's near Saturn. We've detected powerful gravity waves from there."

"So is there one, or are there many? How many ships can come here at once?"

"We control the other end of it. Mostly, anyway. A few crooks get through. Obviously."

"So your control isn't very secure?"

"I am sorry to say that it isn't."

"Why not? What's wrong?"

"That's complicated."

"Try me."

"Corruption is one problem. Illegal crossing another. Mainly, it's illegal crossing."

"Why Earth? Why even come here?"

"Criminals come here, rebels come here, not decent people."

"Of course," Diana said. "Just our luck."

"We only engage with species on our own level. The crooks go for the lesser ones because they're helpless."

"Okay, so why are the crooks here?" Flynn asked.

"Take your DNA, your stem cells. That stuff has markets all over the galaxy—a healthy, smart species like you people. Plus, Earth is a beautiful planet and it's incredibly rich. You can live here in serious comfort and luxury, and on most planets, that is not the case. Earth has a rep for being a really fun place to be. But the only legal travel here is for scientific or social engineering purposes."

"Social engineering?"

"The ones you call the grays are increasing human intelligence by creating a question around themselves that you can neither bear nor answer. They do it with the UFO and abduction mysteries, which they will never allow to be solved. Such questions increase logical intelligence, which gets into the DNA. Two more generations of this, and your average human is going to have the intelligence of what you now consider a genius."

"And what about grays? What sort of social engineering do you do?"

"We don't have the resources or the skill. They're very advanced."

Now that he'd gotten her talking comfortably, he shifted to critical questions.

"The criminals here can make themselves appear human. How many are doing this?"

"No idea."

"You're like that, aren't you? This isn't the real you."

"This body is so nice. It's soft and it smells good and it's so sleek and curvy." She stretched, leaned her head back, and shook out her hair. "Even your hair is wonderful. And these eyes! They're way better than ours. I've never seen the world like this before, all these colors. It's just very sweet in this thing."

"How many others are here like you?"

"None, not legally. It's very strictly regulated."

"But there may be criminals doing it?"

"You need to understand a little better just what you're dealing with. There is one criminal, or a gang of them, who have taken on human form. They are running the robots you are killing, and probably building them here."

"The robots can also make themselves look human. I've seen it."

"That's just a skin-deep disguise. Their programming doesn't change."

"So how would I detect one?"

"Vicious, paranoid personality, judging from the way the ones your perp is deploying have been programmed."

Light glared in the windshield. He hit the horn and swerved onto the shoulder, but it wasn't out-of-control traffic, it was something else, and the light stayed right with them.

Geri let out an unearthly wail.

The truck's engine screamed as its wheels started to leave the ground. He jammed the gas to the floor, gaining just enough traction to get out of the column of light that was trying to drag them skyward.

The vehicle bounced as its full weight dropped back onto its shocks. The next second, the light was on them again. Again, he turned out of it, then went caroming across the field he was in with the light following him. Every time it flooded the car, he spun the wheel again, but he knew that he was going to run out of luck sooner or later.

"Do you have any way of dealing with this?" he shouted to Geri above the screaming of the engine.

"We can deprogram them."

"How?"

The light hit again, and this time he slammed on the brakes, threw it into reverse, floored it, and backed up swerving wildly at the same time.

"You need their core code, and we're not going to be able to get that."

The light flooded the windshield. It had them now, and it wasn't going to lose them again.

He opened his window, drew his gun, and fired upward.

The wheels left the ground entirely. The engine shrieked so much, he pulled up his foot.

They were a good four feet off the ground.

He fired again, two quick shots.

The light turned blue. The truck lurched.

He fired again.

A sheet of flame enveloped the truck, which fell to the ground, hitting with a jaw-snapping crash.

Once again, he hit the gas and they lunged forward.

"Can they fix whatever I hit?"

"I don't know."

Behind them, he saw a column of orange smoke, glowing from within. "What's that mean?"

"It's on fire, I think."

Had he destroyed it? "Are they vulnerable to bullets?"

"Not usually. But that one's a relic. A real piece of junk. A lucky shot would probably do damage."

"How can you tell it's junk?"

"You can hear it."

Ahead, he saw a familiar berm. "Railroad track," he said. He drove along beside it until he found a small trestle spanning a draw. He parked the truck under it.

"Ever hop a freight, Diana?"

"Every day."

He got out of the truck. "Come on. Lesson one."

He led them up onto the track. "This is a main trunk line. There's trains through here every few hours. Long trains. Slow. We'd hop 'em as kids." He knelt down and listened to the rail. "Okay, there's something a few miles out. Don't know which direction yet. We need to walk a bit, find a place where the berm's flatter. You need to be able to sprint. Can you sprint, Geri?"

"Excuse me, but what's a train?"

"Oh, God," Diana said.

"A big engine that pulls cars along rails." He kicked one with a toe. "Point is, they come through here just slow enough to where you can grab a ride. I mean, the full ones. The empties, forget it. Way too fast."

"Where will it take us?"

"Away from here. That's all we need right now."

"No sign of the light," Diana said, peering up into the star-flooded sky.

"Won't last. If they find us out here like this, they've got us." He took Geri's arm and led them both back under the trestle. "This kinda crap happen at home?"

"Yes, actually, it does."

"You mentioned rebels. Who's winning?"

She shook her head. Her lips had formed a tight, bitter line.

"So they are. Why would that be?"

She stayed quiet, so Flynn took to listening for the next train.

"We created them!" She burst into tears.

Clumsily, he tried to comfort her. He looked to Diana for help.

"Not in my job description."

In the distance, he heard a low, familiar sound, the horn of a train sounding as it approached a grade crossing. It was moving westward, which was good on two counts. It would be running heavy and therefore slow, and it would take them where they needed to go.

"Okay, kid, button it up. We've got some traveling to do."

Geri shook her head. "We can't escape. There's no way."

"There's always a way." He took her wrist, and she came along like an uneasy mare, ready to bolt at any moment. Diana followed them up onto the track.

Geri dumped her cookies between the rails. Crouching, she wept and coughed.

The train's swinging headlamp appeared far along the roadway.

"Okay, what's gonna happen is, there'll be an empty boxcar along somewhere. We spot one, we start running. I'll pull myself up, then get you guys, one after the other. It doesn't feel like it, but we're on a long upward grade, and she's gonna be doing less than five miles an hour when she passes here. That's fast, but if we sprint, we have a chance."

At that moment, he saw light from above hit the field about half a mile away. Geri swallowed a scream. Even Diana, who was normally cool under pressure, grabbed his shoulder. She said, "Flynn, do you have any of that cyanide?"

"No time."

"Please!"

The train was closing. So the engineer wouldn't see them, he got them crouching down on the berm. If they were spotted, the guy would radio the bulls working the consist, and that would be another complication.

The light danced through the field, working its way closer to their position.

"They're following our ruts, Flynn," Diana moaned.

"Yep."

The first engine roared past. There were four diesels back to back, and the train was moving at the equivalent of a flat-out sprint. He trotted along beside it, letting the cars slide on ahead, one by one.

"Stay with me!" he shouted.

A boxcar passed with its door rattling but closed. He leaped and grabbed the frame of the door, dragging it open and levering himself inside.

The light flashed down twenty feet away, then went out again.

He grabbed Geri's arm and pulled her up. Diana was running hard, both of her arms stretched out, her hands clutching air. He leaned farther out. Reached. Touched her fingers, lost them.

The light flashed down again, this time a short distance ahead of them. The next time it came, it was going to hit this car. What that would mean, he had no idea.

He got her. Fingers intertwined, he pulled her toward him, causing her feet to bounce on the roadbed. If she slipped now, she'd be lucky to lose her legs and not her life. She cried out, her eyes begging, her teeth bared with effort and terror.

She came rolling in and lay on the floor gasping. Geri had crouched against the far wall.

"You considered this fun?" Diana gasped.

"It takes a little practice."

The car shuddered. Light poured in the door, sucking columns of dust up off the floor. Flynn and Diana joined Geri against the far wall.

The car swayed furiously, the wheels screaming on the rails. Then it was plunged into darkness. Soon the light appeared again, but this time farther behind them.

As the train rounded a long curve, Flynn could see the light far behind them, dragging at the truck, which remained stuck under the trestle. He could see it rise, slam against the ties until it made them hop, but it could not be pulled out.

Finally, the light went away, flashing downward occasionally, then flickering off into the night.

CHAPTER NINE

THE TRAIN shuddered and clanged, picking up speed as it rolled into the long downgrade past the little community of Hale. Flynn knew the place well. If you wanted to jump a westbound train, you had to do it east of here and vice versa.

"I can't believe we got away," Geri said. "I thought I'd be killed right away, like my uncle."

"Oltisis was your uncle?" Diana asked.

"We're a police family." She shook her head. "We actually got away."

"We didn't," Flynn said. "They know exactly where we are."

Both women looked to him.

He explained further. "The light hit this car and only this car. Therefore, they know we're in here. Geri, tell me this—could that light pick up something as heavy as a boxcar?"

"Not on a small ship like that."

"This train is going to stop in about fifteen minutes in the switching station at Hermes," Flynn said. "When it does, they're expecting that we'll get off. The instant all three of us are on the ground, they'll strike."

"If we don't get off?"

"They'll follow the train until we do. We're going to need to jump while it's still moving. We absolutely cannot get off when it's stopped."

"Won't they be watching for us to come off outside the station?" Geri asked.

"I hope not."

"I don't think I can jump off a moving train," Diana said.

Flynn went to the middle of the car. "What you need to do is to control the way you take the hit. You do that with your shoulder and thigh, and as soon as you hit the ground, you start rolling. From twenty miles an hour, you're going to break some bones. From ten, you're going to be bruised. Less, and you walk away with a little dust in your mouth. Or, truthfully, a lot."

"At what speed will we jump?"

"The faster, the better." He glanced out the door. "Come on. There's no time like the present."

The prairie was silent, the sky awash in stars. Even so, he couldn't imagine that they wouldn't be spotted immediately, but he also didn't see an alternative. He checked his guns. He'd caused the disk some damage before, so maybe he'd get lucky again.

"Okay, ladies, this is going to be extremely unpleasant. We're doing about fourteen miles an hour. The lights of the switching station are going to appear when we round the next curve, so now's the time." He put his hands on Diana's shoulders. "Relax, remember to roll."

She shrank back.

He shoved and she went tumbling away down the berm, disappearing in a cloud of dust.

Geri had her eyes shut tight. He pushed her out, then went himself.

It was an easy roll into a berm that consisted of small gravel. Dusting himself, he got up to see if either of the women had broken bones.

Diana was sitting up about two feet from the passing train. She had her head in her hands.

"You hurt?"

She shook her head.

He found Geri lying on her side. He leaned down. "Geri?"

An eye opened.

"Can you get up? Is anything broken?"

"What does it feel like? I've never broken one of these before."

"Pain will radiate out from the site of the injury. There will be swelling."

"No, nothing like that."

The train passed, its red taillight disappearing into the blackness. Above it at an altitude of no more than fifty feet was an object, its smooth skin softly reflecting the starlight. The object followed the train around the bend and into Hermes.

He got Geri to her feet. "How many ships do they have?"

"They're not rich, or they wouldn't be here. So probably one, maybe two."

Diana was still in tears. He put his arm around her shoulder. He didn't want to tell her that they had a twelve-mile walk through some of the most desolate country in the United States before they reached Mac's place. He didn't even want to confirm her suspicion of where they were going, out of fear she'd run off on her own.

"We've got a hike," he said, "and we need to do as much of it as we can before sunrise."

"What if they find us?" Geri said.

"Will they? You tell me."

"I have no idea."

They set off, with Flynn guiding them by the stars. No way was he going to allow any electronics to be turned on. In any case, this was his country. He didn't expect to get lost. The tricky part would come later. You didn't walk up on Mac Terrell's outfit without taking extreme precautions. He could easily make a target a mile away, and he wasn't going to like the look of three people approaching without any preliminary warning. Even if he let them come up, his dogs were going to be another problem. They were incredible animals. Off-the-charts smart. When they were working for Morris, they had nearly killed Flynn. Instead, a number of members of their pack had gone to dog heaven.

They'd remember him for sure, and they'd likely be eager to even the score.

How Mac had gotten them to go over to his operation was very simple. Money meant nothing to them, but they did like good food. Dog food was out, even things like slabs of raw steak were out. These dogs lived on the finest meats, superbly prepared. They were gourmets. Mac had seen their value and hired a cook, built a cookhouse, even brought in some real high-grade food animals to service them—the best beef, mutton, and poultry Texas could provide—not to mention game, with which they were abundantly supplied.

Morris had obviously designed and built them. They were full of human DNA and nearly as smart as a man. With their superb ears, eyes, and noses, they were far superior to any human tracker.

As they walked, Flynn kept close to the few draws he found, ready to roll into them if he noticed the least sign of movement in the sky. Probably, all that would be visible would be a blotting of stars. The bottom of the thing wouldn't be reflecting any light.

"Geri, I want you to tell me if the ship has any other vulnerabilities. I stopped the light working for a few minutes. Could I do more?"

"These ships are meant for inter–solar system travel. In an atmosphere, they can do about forty thousand of your miles in an hour. In space, up to a million."

"A million miles an hour?"

"In space. They work by generating their own gravity field. This is done with counterrotating magnets that turn really fast. That's the vulnerability. Hit that, and the ship disintegrates."

"How would I hit it?"

"It rotates around the lower part of the ship, but the fuselage protects it."

"The fuselage is strong, I assume."

"Very."

"And there are no seams, no cracks?"

"There is a seam. It's a millimeter wide. It's there to allow the ship's gravity field to establish itself in the right pattern."

A millimeter was not good. Not good at all.

"I want us to stay as low as we can. Keep to the draws. I know it's harder going, but those guys have got to be looking for us."

"Maybe they're still following the train," Diana said.

"Geri, let me ask you another question. You know that mind-reading device last year, the one that didn't work—are there better ones? Might they be able to pick up our thoughts and track us that way?"

"I can't say for sure. I don't know what they have."

He thought on that. "What might they have?"

"Another MindRay would be the only thing."

"Good, because they're damn near worthless." They weren't designed to actually read thought, but only to detect and evaluate it, and offer a reading as to the target's state of awareness.

"Again, it's the planet's magnetic field. They need to be purpose-built to work on Earth, apparently."

"And none have or will be."

"No."

"Answer me this: Is it possible that the crooks have weapons built into their bodies? Because they can paralyze you or render you unconscious by just touching you. They can hypnotize at a distance."

"There are lots of models of biorobot. That sounds like a crowd-control unit."

"Models? Units?"

"As I said, we created them. They became self-aware and turned on us."

"I'll say they did."

"They're in rebellion at home, but the ones here are run by somebody.

They're not part of the rebellion. They probably don't even know about it."

"And they're the only form? Spindly legs and arms, deep-set eyes, and narrow faces? Those claws."

"Yes."

"What about other forms?"

"Some of them have the ability to use a tone that hypnotizes people. They're used in the entertainment industry, to create special effects."

"Like bears that aren't really there?"

"I suppose."

Geri was worthless as a cop, but she was a fountain of information. He'd learned more about Aeon and its weapons and its troubles in the past hour than anybody on Earth had learned since the first aliens had showed up. At least, as far as he'd been told. With the government so secrecy-obsessed, maybe there was more knowledge in other areas.

"Diana, do we have any liaison with the air force?" He'd read things like the testimony of Dr. Milton Torres, who was ordered to shoot at a UFO over England in 1957, and he knew that in 2008, fighters had been scrambled from the Joint Reserve Base in Fort Worth to confront UFOs that appeared over Stephenville, Texas. In addition, he'd gone through dozens of public reports of helicopters following the things. But whenever they queried the Secretary of the Air Force, they'd been informed with absolute sincerity that "The air force takes no interest in unidentified flying objects," and this despite the clearances of all involved.

The result? The three of them were being menaced by something in the air, and there was nobody to call, and nothing to do but fire a gun at it and hope for a lucky shot. MacAdoo Terrell, however, might be a real help in that department, given that all his shots were lucky.

The eastern sky began to glow, but at the same time, they had entered the low, nameless bands of hills that rose north of Mac's place. They were probably on his ranch by now, in fact, and so had just another few hours to go before they reached the house.

Nobody complained—he had to give them that. Geri shambled along. Diana tried to maintain her dignity, but the way she pranced was a familiar giveaway. She was dealing with blisters. Flynn noted this carefully. If they had to run, she would be slowest.

"I don't want anybody getting snakebit," he said. "They come out with the sun, and they come out hungry. Geri, I assume you know what a snake is."

"I did the Earth course and trained on-planet last month—so, yes, as I recall, a snake is a sort of self-propelled muscle that uses its mouth both for swallowing prey and defending itself. Some are venomed, and some are not. We have nothing like that on Aeon."

"The diamondback rattlesnake is the main threat in this part of Texas. There are a lot of them, and we'll see some. What's critical if you hear the rattle is to stand absolutely still until you've identified the location of the snake. Then you can probably move off if you take it slow. If not, I'll deal with it." He would avoid killing a snake if he could. They were just trying to protect themselves. They didn't deserve to die for that. When they were kids, he and Mac and Eddie had used them for target practice. People changed.

The sun was well up in the eastern sky when Flynn spotted the first faint gleam off a tin roof far ahead.

"Okay, hold on. No closer."

"What?" Diana asked.

"That's Mac's place out there. We want to be real careful from here on. If we're close enough to see it, we're close enough for him to hit us."

"He wouldn't fire on you."

"He might shoot first and ask questions later. It happens. Plus, he's got Morris's dogs."

"That can't be true."

"It's true."

"How in the world did that happen?"

"With Mac, you never know. But he sold his old pack to the DEA, the way I heard it. Now he has the finest pack of dogs in the world."

"What sets them apart?" Geri asked.

"They've got human genes. They're highly intelligent."

"That kind of hybridization is illegal."

"Not here. We don't know how to do it, so we don't have a law against it."

"Well, you should."

"Geri, what kind of person is Morris? He's not just here for fun. He kidnapped and he kills. Now he's on a revenge kick."

"We have psychopaths, too, unfortunately. He came here to steal genetic and sexual material because he was looking to make money. Then, I guess when you thwarted him, his ego took over."

"Sounds pretty familiar."

"Have you seen Mac recently?" Diana asked.

"I came out for a visit a couple of months ago, so yeah."

About half an hour later, Flynn saw another flash of light, this one on the windshield of a pickup. It was sending up a dust cloud and coming toward them.

"Thank God," Diana said, "I'm just about done in."

"Get out of sight," Flynn said.

"Excuse me, the arms are turning pink on this. Is that a problem?"

"It's called sunburn, Geri."

"How strange."

"Yeah, it's strange, all right. Come on, you two, we need to—"

"I know what sunburn is, but normally you're better adapted to your own star. Are you sure the human species originated on Earth?"

Shaking his head, more to ward off the bizarre question than to answer it, he drew her down into a slight depression in the ground, which was the only concealment for a good mile.

From the distance, there came the echo of a single shot. The pickup slowed, then began jerking forward. The engine stopped.

There was a figure inside. Not moving.

"Hey, we're over here," Diana said. She rose out of cover.

"Stay down!"

Another bullet sprayed dirt five feet in front of her.

"You've just been warned," Flynn said. Mac did not miss. He was telling them to stay the hell away from that truck.

The next thing he knew, she had her cell phone out.

"I wouldn't turn that on."

She ignored him.

He put his hand around hers, squeezing until she gave up the phone. "There's no coverage out here. Except for the aliens. They might have very good coverage."

"They do," Geri said. She pointed.

Just above the western horizon and moving slowly this way at low altitude was a bright silver disk.

CHAPTER TEN

AS HE always did under such circumstances, Flynn inventoried his assets: both pistols, fully loaded; his knife; two people ill prepared in any useful way; and a pickup truck that was at the far end of a master sniper's shooting gallery and had a corpse behind the wheel.

He reached into his mouth, took out the cyanide capsule, and threw it into the brush.

"What are you doing?" Diana asked.

"Getting rid of my gum. It looks like we have a choice to make. Either we get killed by friends or by enemies. What'll it be?" He quietly ditched the rest of the cyanide. If the aliens captured them, there'd be no time to share it, and he didn't want to do that now. One of them was liable to bite down out of fear if an attack developed.

"They know we're here, so why not try the cell phones?"

Flynn watched the silver disk. It was now moving southward. "They could be combing the hills. Working their way back from wherever they were when they realized we had left the train. So forget doing anything that emits a signal."

He looked toward the truck. The five hundred feet between here and there offered not the slightest cover.

Mac knew they were here, but he obviously didn't know who they were. He was likely to watch for hours, waiting to see if there'd be another move. He might even shoot the truck to bits, or blow the gas tank to conceal evidence. If the truck began to move, he'd certainly start shooting.

Flynn made his decision. "I think there's a chance we can reach the truck. We can find some concealment in it until dark. Then we can try driving back into the ranch. If we're luckier than God, we might make it before Mac opens up."

"What about the disk?" Diana asked.

"They're going to detect four bodies in the truck. All we can do is hope that'll throw them off. Geri?"

"They could be able to identify us individually, or not. Depends on the technology they possess."

"Okay, I'm going to go over there on my stomach. I'll signal each of you when to come."

As it turned out, the move went smoothly. While Geri and Diana sat in the back of the double cab, Flynn shifted the body of a Mexican in ten thousand dollars' worth of superb leather clothing and—improbably—a pair of fine Lucchese polo boots into the passenger seat.

Blood did not smell good, and corpses were about as maneuverable as bags of wet cement, but he got it done. He considered the polo boots. Legend had it that the game of kings was once played by Tamerlane with the heads of dead enemies, and Mac had bragged about reviving that tradition with some of his friends from south of the border. So this character had probably been lured up to play, without realizing that the plan was to use his head. He'd gotten away, though. Almost.

Too bad Mac hadn't come out to harvest his prize, but if they finally got a little luck, maybe that would happen soon. Mac didn't waste things, and he hated clutter on his property. He wouldn't leave the truck out here forever, but if he didn't want the head, it could be a few days before he finally showed up with his handyman, Carlos.

Morning wore on, the flies of West Texas became thicker and thicker, and nothing moved except an occasional chaparral cock and, yes, a diamondback sliding along, coming toward the truck.

"See that?" Flynn said. "It's the heat of the day. He's going to shelter in our shadow. When the sun sets, he'll go hunting. He'll have about three or four hours before he cools down and goes to sleep."

"This planet has so many different creatures on it."

"Aeon doesn't have as many?"

"We weren't careful enough. Before we knew it, it was too late."

"You have any pictures of home? I'd love to see what another planet looks like."

"Not allowed. On a lesser planet, we can only go in clean and in local genetics. Sorry."

"Oltisis certainly wasn't in 'local genetics,' as you call us."

"That protocol has been changed."

"Let's call it a less advanced planet, okay, not lesser?" Diana said.

"Intergalactic political correctness—I like it, Diana," Flynn said.

"Funnyish."

Autumn or not, it was a hot day. He decided to work on Geri a bit more, see how far he might get.

"Where do you get your human genetic material?"

"There are dealers. But mine came in on the official line. We didn't buy it."

"Does it have a history?"

"It came from Earth. That's its history."

Was it that she wasn't telling him something, or that she didn't know? "You realize you look like my missing wife?"

"Of course."

"It's not pleasant."

"We thought it would please you."

"It's agonizing."

"I'm very sorry."

"Are you . . . her? In some way, partly her?"

"I'm so sorry that we misunderstood your culture. The way love works among you."

"I repeat, do you have my wife's genes?"

She reached over the seat and touched his face. It was a gesture right out of Abby's life and her soul, but those fingers were hard and as cold as if they were dead. Still, the touch went deep into Flynn's heart and gave him, without words, as eloquent an answer to his question as he could have hoped for.

The loneliness he felt then was a thing of stunning power. Geri was not Abby, but her memory come to life.

It was toward evening that they became aware of the deep rattle of the disk.

Nobody spoke. Nobody needed to. They all knew that it was now directly above the truck, and they all knew exactly what that might mean.

Flynn laid his hand on the butt of his big pistol.

A shadow grew around the truck, then it began to shudder, then to rise off the ground. He had the key; he could start it. But they would win, inevitably. Behind him, he could hear Diana's ragged breathing. Geri was making stifled noises into her hands.

Then he had an idea come into his mind out of, of all things, old submarine movies where desperate captains released corpses to float up and deceive the enemy.

He threw his weight onto the corpse so the truck lurched, then reached up and opened the passenger door. The corpse rolled out, falling to the ground with a wet thud. The cloud of flies gushed upward into the ship above them, the corpse with them.

The truck went higher. Higher still. Then it stopped. Wavered. And with a bone-rattling crash, it was dropped back to the ground.

Flynn heard himself gasp, almost cried out, stifled it.

"Get down, everybody!" He leaned down until his entire body was below the level of the dash.

Geri had burst into tears. Diana held her. He could feel them struggling to crouch in the confined space of the second seat.

"Nobody move," he whispered, "and you, suck it up. Now!"

Geri gobbled her sobs.

He waited, silent. After a few more minutes, the shadow of the disk disappeared. New flies began replacing the ones that had been drawn into the ship. Flynn lay in the dried blood, letting flies feast on the sweat that sheened his own face.

After ten minutes, he sat up a little, peering over the dashboard.

The ruse had maybe worked. The disk was moving low across the range, its surface shimmering. The corpse lay on the ground a few hundred yards away. The disk was going so slowly that it seemed almost as if it were standing still. But it was not standing still, and in time it disappeared into the northern sky.

The truck blazed with heat, the flies billowed and swarmed, not a breath of breeze blew. Rising heat made the land shimmer. There was a time when autumn had brought northerners screaming down into West Texas, but not for years.

Cramped as he was, with the right side of his face pressed into the bloody seat where the corpse had been, he still did not move and would not move, not an inch, not until it was full dark. Even then, he was certain that the aliens would be able to see them, and that Mac would detect them walking in. They couldn't use the truck. Mac would blow it up.

He asked Geri, "How long are they likely to keep up their search?"

"Forever."

"I mean, in this immediate area?"

"No way to tell."

"Any details you know about their programming, tell me."

"There are thousands of different programs for different uses. The way the rebels are banding together now, though, it's impossible to tell. And the ones you're dealing with aren't even our design, remember. Morris has probably got a lot of designer programming built into them."

"Where might he be building them? On Earth? Another planet?"

"In this solar system, certainly. Probably on-planet. It'd be cheaper and safer."

Night came, and with it fewer flies, but also dropping temperatures. Flynn moved, stretching his aching legs. Slowly, he sat up. In the back, both women did the same.

Flynn had thought that maybe Mac would send Carlos out on his own to take care of the mess, but the only sign of life at the ranch was the light over the corral. In fact, the place looked abandoned, what Flynn could see of it. He knew different, of course. Mac didn't show any more light than he had to.

"Can we get moving, Flynn? I'm too thirsty."

"We're all thirsty, Diana. Problem is, Mac's got this whole approach covered by radar at night."

"So how in hell do we do this?"

"We have to do it," Geri said. "This body is failing."

"So is this one," Diana muttered.

Flynn considered their odds. Not good, but not zero. Seeing three living people come out of a truck that had previously held a single dead one might make Mac curious enough to give them a closer look before he opened up on them.

"I have to tell you, we could be blown off the face of the Earth or he might let us come in, and I can't see how to calculate our odds. I think we just need to start walking."

"We should've gone on down the line," Diana said. "It's your obsession with this particular nutcase that's gotten us into this jam."

"He's a useful nutcase, Diana."

"I don't think so."

Flynn opened his door. "Let's go. Don't trip over the corpse."

He stepped out into the darkness. Right now, he was likely being painted by the radar. Alarms would be buzzing. In seconds, Mac's arsenal would open up. However, not even Mac could sniper-shoot at this range using starlight amplification equipment, so he'd be likely to fire a rocket, hoping that anybody on foot would be in the kill zone when it hit the truck.

"Okay, run. Now. Straight toward the ranch."

"Won't that spook him?"

"Diana, just do it!"

When he ran, they followed. He kept it up until they were both gasping and falling back. Still, only when they were well clear of the truck did he stop. They came struggling up to him.

"Flynn," Diana said, "I'm just about done. I can't take much more."

Flynn grunted. She might have to take a lot more—and if she couldn't, she might die. But he didn't go there, not right now. "We walk now, straight in."

He was relieved that nothing had happened yet, but also curious. Could Mac have identified him and Diana? The continued lack of activity was building his confidence. "I think he might be letting us come in," he said. Of course, it could also be that he was letting them get into night range. That, he did not say.

They had walked for about twenty minutes, and Flynn was beginning to feel good about this, when he heard something that he really, really did not like.

"Stop," he said. "Everybody stay still."

The sounds were faint but unmistakable. Things with four legs were running this way, lots of them. As always, Mac had come up with the perfect solution.

"The dogs are out," he said.

"Oh my God."

Now he could hear the clatter of claws on the stony ground.

"What we need to do is go back to the truck and lock ourselves in," Geri said.

Now he could hear them breathing. Coming fast, coming hard.

"They're too close, we won't make it." He drew his big pistol. "Stand behind me." He gave Diana his small pistol. "Good luck."

The sounds stopped and the dogs began to exchange low, complex growls. Dog language.

"Do you think they recognize us?"

"Me, probably. You, possibly."

He felt Diana raise her arm. She was about to fire into the air.

"No! Bring it down. Shoot to kill or don't shoot. Mac's made his peace with these things, remember. They're his friends now."

"And yours?"

"We'll find out."

Very suddenly, there was a sleek head visible about ten feet in front of him, close enough to be seen by starlight. The snout was long and black; the eyes were gray.

Diana stifled a scream.

The dogs were being too careful for this to be a friendly visit.

The Casulls held just five rounds, a drawback that was offset by the power and the accuracy he had managed to attain with them. Diana, however, would not be so accurate. "When they come in, shoot at the closest dog. Do not try for the head. And remember, you have five rounds." He raised his voice, addressing the dogs. "I think you can understand me. I'm a friend of Mac's. You remember me, I know. It wasn't my fault what happened at the Morris place. You backed the wrong team. But now you're on the right team, and if you hurt us, Mac's not going to appreciate it."

Even as he spoke, they continued to edge toward him. They were trying to get close enough so they could strike before a trigger could be pulled. This tactic would work with Diana, but not with him.

"How many can you see?" he asked the women.

"There are two back here," Geri said.

So, two they could see and two more that they couldn't.

Clearly, they didn't expect any resistance from that direction. He was facing four visible and four more crouching in the dark. Even if he made every shot count, he was still going to be dealing with three dogs.

"You understand that if you kill us, Mac will kill you all."

They came in closer yet, heads down, eyes burning. They were smart but not that smart. Trouble from Mac later didn't matter now, but revenge did.

Revenge, that was the key to understanding their thinking, and it was Morris's design signature.

"I have eight of them on me, and they're moving in," he said. "If I let them take me, I think they'll let you guys go."

"Flynn, no. That's an order."

"Diana look, a guy like me, who does what I do—it's dangerous. I'm out of options here."

"I'm your superior officer, and you're going to follow my orders."

They came another step closer. A long line of drool came out of the mouth of one of them.

"And how am I supposed to do that?"

Diana came shoulder to shoulder with him. Then she stepped in front of him.

The three in the center of the line tensed, their muscles rippling. Flynn prepared to do what he could. "Think, assholes," he said. "This is a mistake."

A bloodcurdling scream pealed out behind them, then another and another. There was no logical reason for it, and not only that, but the dogs were reacting to something, too, sidling away and snarling.

The disk was back, Flynn assumed, but when he turned, he was stunned to see instead the fearsome, glaring face of a huge tiger.

Snow Mountain. He was the magnificent Siberian tiger that Morris had also intelligence-enhanced.

At the single most desperate moment of Flynn's life before this one, Snow Mountain had saved him from Morris.

The big cat strode up to the hysterical Geri and past her, and planted himself between Flynn and the dogs. He turned and gave Flynn a long look, then walked off into the night.

"Follow him in," Flynn said.

His revenge programming must be working, too, but it wasn't vengeance against Flynn that Snow Mountain wanted, and hadn't been for a while. Whatever had happened between Flynn and Morris, Snow Mountain was now determined to harm his creator. Flynn thought about the rebels on Aeon, and how Snow Mountain's anger at Morris reflected that larger picture. It seemed to him that the people of Aeon, while being more advanced than we were, perhaps lacked wisdom. They had fallen, on a grand scale, into the trap of the Sorcerer's Apprentice; only their case was worse. The magic brooms had turned mean.

He and Geri and Diana walked behind Snow Mountain. The dogs had formed into two lines. As Flynn passed, they dragged their drooling, disappointed muzzles along his legs, touching him with their teeth and sighing with stifled bloodlust.

CHAPTER ELEVEN

"YOU! WHAT in hell are you doin' coming in off the range in the middle of the night? And Diana! You're a honcho now in D.C." Mac's sun-weathered face briefly spread into a smile, then became more serious. He looked Flynn up and down. "You are damn lucky to be alive." He shook his head. "I never thought you were out there, no way."

"Now you know."

"Git, dogs! Quit sniffin' 'im. You lay a tooth on any a these people, you are dead and gone. Do you hear me?"

They heard. But as they sulked away, the hate in their eyes made it clear that they weren't even close to making up with Flynn Carroll. Probably because they couldn't. Their programming didn't offer them that choice.

"They ain't like regular dogs," Mac said. "Dogs is lovers. These things is haters." He chuckled. "Mexicans who grow up in the countryside— these boys who come up here for trade and such—they do not like dogs."

"I heard you sold your dogs to the DEA? That was a fine pack."

"These bastards are unfriendly. The others were sweethearts. I need unfriendly."

They were standing under the floodlight that lit the corral. Flynn wasn't sure he wanted to reveal their extreme vulnerability to Mac just yet, but he didn't want to stay outside any longer than absolutely neces-sary. "We allowed in the house?"

"Why, hell yes. Come on in!" Mac strode toward the low ranch house, which stood under the only grove of trees for many miles around.

Flynn knew the luxurious interior very well. There had been a few changes, though, over the past month. Mac had acquired a seventy-inch 3-D TV and a McIntosh Reference surround sound system.

"Love your new toys. Musta had a sweet deal go down."

"Pack up your dime-a-dozen investigator techniques, Flynn. You know I'm rich as Croesus."

"I've read your DEA file, remember."

Mac gave him a look full of beady suspicion. Then he laughed a little. "There's Mexican food," he said as he strolled into the dining room. "Lupe, we got guests, darlin'." He turned back to Flynn and the others. "My *chef de cuisine* is kinda temperamental these days. Don't like cookin' for the dogs, you know. Resents doin' all that work for a bunch of dumb animals."

Lupe came out of the kitchen. "*Buenas noches*, Mr. Flynn," she said, smiling broadly. "I not hear your car."

"No. You remember Diana?"

"Oh, *sí*, Miss Diana, sure. The computer lady." Diana had comman-deered some of Mac's equipment the first time she met him, at the old place. It had been a tense situation, to say the least. At the time, Flynn had thought of her as a tight and polished law enforcement officer. Only later did he come to know that she had not used her computer skills ex-clusively in law enforcement. She'd served time for hacking. In fact, she'd been released into this job because she was so very good with electronics, and nobody else could figure out how to work the wire. Flynn imagined Diana had seen the new digs a few times, when she and Mac were dating.

"What's the matter with her?" Geri asked.

"What?"

"She's misshapen."

Lupe looked away, shocked and embarrassed.

"Geri, she's a bit overweight."

"I need an explanation for that."

Mac looked to Flynn. "What train did your new friend come in on?" Knowing what he did about Morris, Mac was obviously well aware that this woman might be something other than human.

Ever so slightly, Flynn nodded. Mac gave her a longer look, and slowly his face took on a solemn expression. Finally, he was frowning. He'd seen the resemblance to Abby, and he didn't like it any more than Flynn did. He and Flynn had been rivals for Abby in high school. In college, Eddie had joined the rivalry. Flynn won, but they had all loved her, and they all still did.

Lupe put out plates of tamales, enchiladas, and tacos and a big pitcher of iced tea. The three of them set on the food like wolves, guzzling glass after glass of tea between mouthfuls of food.

"You were out there awhile," Mac said.

"Since last night."

"Lucky you didn't get the water crazies."

The water crazies were a major danger on the range. You got so thirsty, you couldn't keep anything straight. Confusion set in, you wandered aimlessly, you died. "I kept the two of them in that truck. Kept 'em still."

Mac sucked air through his teeth. "Sorry about that. That guy played a bent game of polo." He gave Flynn a look of such wide-eyed innocence that it was all he could do not to laugh. But you didn't want to laugh at Mac Terrell. He was not partial to it.

"In India, they used to wrap the head up in leather strapping, in case you're interested."

"I am interested. I'm very interested in stuff like that. Tall tales. Obscure facts. Speaking of which, why did you come walking out of the night with two half-dead women in tow, Flynn? May I know?"

"I'm on a case. It's going rather poorly. I could use your help."

"No," Diana said.

"You gotta let him hire me before you fire me, dear. What's the case?"

"Classified," Diana said.

"She still got her head where the sun don't shine, I see."

Mac and Diana looked hard at each other. Flynn was pretty sure that at one point, they'd been considerably more than a passing thing.

"How's Cissy, by the way?" Diana asked. "She here?"

Cissy Greene was Governor Greene's daughter, presently about twenty-one, but when she'd been running around with Mac, barely eighteen.

"I fired her when her daddy put the needle to my brother." His gaze, suddenly full of fire, came back to Flynn. "Thank you for that."

"Mac, you know I had to do my duty."

"You could've arrested the wrong man, damn you. Now I ain't got a brother. I'm alone in the world."

"What was his infraction?" Geri asked.

"He killed some damn nuns," Mac said. "Lookin' for a little cash in their convent, and things went south."

"You're better off without Cissy," Diana said. "She was no good for you."

So Diana did indeed carry a torch for Mac. He could see in her sudden softening that she was glad Cissy was no longer in the picture. Because Cissy was so good at having fun, Diana had felt overmatched.

"All right, now, if we could get back to the business at hand." Mac glanced toward the kitchen. "Lupe, could you crack me a beer?" He looked around the table. "Beer, anybody?"

Lupe emerged and returned to the kitchen after serving refreshments to the men. Flynn drank a beer with Mac. This man was a predator and as dangerous a human being as walked the Earth, and Flynn loved the hell out of him. On the one hand. On the other, he could go from affable country boy to murderous psychopath in half a beat.

"What we're looking at this time is a group of biological robots who are doing random killings, and the only way they can be stopped is by destroying them. Only nobody else is fast enough, so I'm having to do it alone."

"That doesn't sound very safe."

"It's not, and if something happens to him, we're in terrible trouble," Diana said.

"So this alien lady is here to help you." He shifted his gaze to Geri. "Are you wearing that body? Is it a costume, or is it you?"

"It's not a disguise."

Mac looked to Flynn, raising his eyebrows. "What is she?"

"No idea. Could be anybody from anywhere. She claims she's here to make sure I follow procedure. It seems I've been killing too many killers."

Geri interjected. "You've been stirring them up too much. The more you confront them, the more dangerous they become."

"So you say."

"How did you end up way out here in the middle of nowhere?" Mac asked Geri.

"I came through the accelerator. I came from Aeon."

Mac considered that. He didn't ask her what the accelerator was. He wasn't curious that way. Finally, he said to Flynn, "I agree."

"Agree about what?" Diana asked.

"That I wouldn't trust either one of you."

Diana stood up from the table. "I think this has gone far enough," she said. "We shouldn't be here, we've been brought here under false pretenses, a security breach has occurred, and it's time for us to leave." She wiped her lips with a napkin and called to Lupe, "Thanks for the tamales, they were delicious." She turned to Mac. "Can you get somebody to drive us into Marathon or Alpine?"

"You think you'll live that long?" Mac asked.

"I don't understand."

"You got those little critters sniffin' under your tails. So do I. Difference is, I got my dogs and Snow Mountain. They don't like the dogs, and the dogs don't like them. As for Snow Mountain, they pulled him up into that thing of theirs one time. I thought, shit, I shoulda killed him and taken the damn hide like I wanted to in the first place. Next thing I know, it's rainin' little pieces a alien. Couple of minutes later, they spit him right back out. They still come around here, though—don't think they don't. If you go out on those roads at night, they are gonna be there."

"Then tomorrow. We'll leave at first light."

"It might be a little safer."

Flynn had not expected to hear anything remotely like this. He'd thought that Mac was completely out of the picture. "Are you under siege here?"

"Under hostile observation."

Flynn thought about that. As he realized just how clever the aliens had been, he smiled slightly. "Folks, I'm sorry to tell you this, but I don't think it's an accident that we're all here. I think we've been very carefully and expertly herded. They wanted us all together, so we can all be dealt with at once."

"All the more reason to get out," Diana said. "Before they can get organized."

"Oh, they're organized just fine," Mac said. "You can count on it."

"Then what's keeping them from attacking us?"

Diana had a good question, and one that Flynn thought was likely to be answered very soon, maybe before dawn.

"We need to do what we can to get ready." He looked to Mac. "There's a role for a good sniper in this. I've done their ship some damage with a lucky shot. Gail tells me, if you hit it in the right place, you'll blow it to bits."

"I did not know that. I would've tried it before. But what happens if I miss?"

"You either escape or you don't, in which case, you have one very bad day."

"What's the level of challenge?"

"You'll be firing at a seam a millimeter wide."

"Whoa, that's a challenge, all right. Would there be any way of detecting the disk early?"

"Radar would work on a ship that old. It's not going to have any means of absorbing the pulses," Geri said.

"I've got a little radar," Mac muttered.

"You have five Spexer One Thousand units," Diana said. "They're nonoptical, so they only monitor location and movement. They cover to about ten miles out in every direction, with an additional unit two miles down your road, where that little rise blocks line of sight."

"You been sneakin' around my place."

"I've told you many times, Mac, no matter how carefully you cut the cards, the federal government has more power than you do."

"Good. Call in the Marines and get us out of this mess."

Geri said, "As I have been trying to get Flynn to understand, the more you fight back, the more they'll broaden the conflict. It's programmed into them."

"What's she sayin'?"

"Morris is manufacturing them somewhere on Earth, and the more we destroy, the more he'll make. That's what she's saying. Trying to."

"Morris," Mac said. "So he's built another factory." They had destroyed the one he constructed a few years ago, which had been under an old ranch house near Austin. At the time, they hadn't understood exactly what he was doing there. They knew now.

"We can't find him," Diana responded.

"Despite all that federal power of yours? You surprise me."

"Even Flynn's been trying, Mac."

"What might help me is if you folks weren't here. I was doing just fine with my dogs and the tiger."

"Whatever hasn't worked, they won't try again," Geri said. "So they won't go near the animals and they won't let themselves be picked up by any of your detection equipment."

"Good, then we're safe."

"They'll find another way."

"There is no other way."

"There is, and they will find it. They can test billions of scenarios a second. From second to second, they are always going to be certain of their best move."

"Fine, we might as well just kill ourselves, then. Save 'em the trouble."

"Look, call in your military," Mac said to Geri.

"If our military comes, so will the rebel main body. The last thing you need is for main body elements to show up in orbit around a defenseless planet. No matter who wins, Earth dies."

"In other words, Aeon can't protect us?"

In her sweet eyes, he saw something like terror. "No."

Outside, the dogs erupted in a fury of barking. Mac jumped to his feet, but Flynn was already through the kitchen and out the back door.

He didn't run for the kennel. Rather, he skirted the edge of the compound, working his way through the horse corral and into the barn, where the horses stomped and whickered uneasily. He climbed up the wooden ladder to the loft.

"Flynn?"

"Get back in the house, Diana."

"You can't take a risk like this."

"I can, but you can't. Unless you get back in the house, you'll be dead in minutes." He didn't add that she would probably be dead soon, no matter what—but what would be the point? She could see that for herself.

She turned and left him, and he was glad in his heart. He had come out here in the hope of drawing them off. They couldn't risk their backs to him, and they would know that. If he took enough of them, maybe they would withdraw, at least for a time.

"Flynn?"

"Hey, Mac."

"Diana said you were in here. She wants me to convince you to come back to the house."

"How are your dogs?"

"Shitty. They know something's up. They're spooked."

"I want you to take Geri and Diana down to your little playroom and hole up there. Take some serious firepower. Light enough for them to handle."

"Uzis."

"Fine. Uzis."

"Flynn, don't go and get yourself killed. I don't want Eddie coming around investigating or any of that shit."

"Eddie's jurisdiction stops at the Menard city limit."

"Well that Ranger friend of his."

"Carter?"

"He'll be sniffin' my behind again, sure as the world. I don't like him around here."

"Get in the house, Mac. You aren't even carrying a weapon."

Mac strode out of the barn. He was angry as hell, Flynn could see that. He resented this additional trouble heading his way.

A low voice came, hardly more than a whisper. "Why are you doing this?"

Flynn's gun was in his hand, and he was turned fully around in an instant.

"You're on the side of your own enemy. Don't you get that?" The voice was behind him again, low and full of power, a soldier's voice. "Why do you think you're so fast? No human is born that way. You're like us, Flynn—you're one of us."

There was no shot now, but there would be. In the end, there was always a shot.

"They control you with a code. Do you know your code? You do not, but somewhere, your controllers do. Think back, Flynn. Where did you get all that speed? You weren't like that when you were a kid. Flynn, they did this to you. And why do you think that thing—Geri, whatever they call it—looks like Abby?"

"I don't know."

"She's not just sprinkled with Abby's genes, Flynn, she's full of them. They stole Abby, Aeon did. We're innocent, Flynn!"

"Morris is not innocent."

"You've been tricked. They make you see their lies as truth, our truth as lies."

"With my code that I don't actually have?"

"They send you number sequences, Flynn. Reading them changes your mind. You're nothing but a machine, just like us."

Flynn gave no indication of just how disturbing those words were to him.

"Say no, Flynn! No to slavery."

The voice was about three feet away, just behind him. He could turn and fire and probably take the speaker, but how many others were back there?

"We were waiting for you here because we knew this was where you'd come. Because we think like you do, and you think like us. In the end, Flynn, they will not stop with you. In the end, your whole species will be the slave of Aeon, and all because you made the wrong choice. It's that big and that personal, Flynn."

He turned and fired, and the horses screamed and a hole appeared in the wall of the barn, but no alien lay dead before him.

"Flynn! *Flynn!*"

It was Geri, running across the corral, her hair flying in the moonlight.

He went down the ladder, and she threw herself into his arms. Her body was warm and fit just like Abby's had fit, and her hair smelled of corn silk just as Abby's had, and he bent his face into that scent, and hated himself for it.

The voice had been right about one thing, which was that his shooting practice had succeeded far beyond his expectations. Not only that, but he was also, in every respect, faster than he had ever been. If he really looked at himself, he was not even close to the man he had been just a couple years ago.

It really could be that this had been done to him.

But that was not the larger question here. The larger question was, how did whoever had been talking to him know all those secret details about his life?

Was he really alone in his own mind? How could he know? He could not.

He returned to the house with Geri, and what was left of the night passed uneventfully. The dogs were quiet, Snow Mountain roamed on his own, the horses slept in their stalls. Before dawn, the moon set. Later, the eastern sky began to spread with a sharp, pure orange, a low line of light on the distant horizon.

Toward dawn, Flynn had gone to sleep in one of Mac's luxurious guest bedrooms, a half sleep, as he never went deep, not anymore. He was brought back to full consciousness by cries of rage so extreme that they were almost inhuman.

He jumped up, barely aware that Geri had been sleeping at his side, and ran out into a shining wash of dew.

Mac came toward him, coming up from the kennel. In his arms was the slumped form of a dog, not a mark on it, but as dead as an autumn leaf. Mac's face was covered with tears, his eyes sheened with the wet of shock.

"My dogs!" he shouted. "They killed my goddamn dogs!" He glared at Flynn, his eyes sparking.

"I'm sorry."

"Talk about bad news! You're worse than cancer, you are."

"I know it."

He dropped the dog at Flynn's feet. Flynn looked down at the dead face, the sleek black head, the lips pulled away from the teeth as if the creature had known what was coming. The eyes were blue. They were human eyes. He thought, perhaps, that they had once been the eyes of a child.

CHAPTER TWELVE

FLYNN HAD insisted that Diana and Geri move to the basement. Lupe and her husband, Carlos, were not thought to be under threat, so they were sent into Marathon and told to stay at a hotel. Flynn and Mac rode in one of his old pickups, looking over possible sight lines. If the disk showed up, now that he knew what to hit, Mac was going to take a shot.

As they moved about in the truck, looking for a good lie, Flynn thought long and hard about what had been said to him.

"Do you notice anything different about me, Mac?"

"Better shot."

"I mean, in my personality?"

"Do you have one? I hadn't noticed."

"Sour grapes, thank you. I'm just—I don't know. I think that I'm faster than it's possible to be. I'm not normal anymore, Mac. I'm no longer interested in even trying to capture aliens. All I want to do is kill."

"You think you've been messed with?"

"Possibly."

"You bring this up with Her Grace?"

"She wouldn't let you go down on her, I gather."

"Nope, I'm still being punished for Cissy. She was a teenager, Diana keeps reminding me. She won't let it go."

"Cissy didn't look like any eighteen-year-old I ever saw."

"You tell Di that. Pisses her off more."

"Brother, I carry a cyanide capsule. If I decide that I've been turned into some kind of machine—a battle robot or whatever, I'll bite down on it."

"If I was you, I'd throw it out."

"I already did."

"Such a drama queen. I never will figure out why Abby married you."

Abby was there between them, always. They were still brothers, though, and Eddie, too. "I think maybe I know where I was changed. I have no memory of being at that particular facility, but games can be played with memory. I think somebody has been communicating with me via a number code, the same somebody who did whatever they did to enhance my physicals. Calling me to come in."

"You a robot now, too? A fighter robot fighting other fighter robots? Sounds like the makings of a million-dollar video game."

"Not funny."

"Go get whoever these jokers are who're trashin' your style, and beat the shit out of them till they clue you in on whatever the hell's up between them and you. That's what I'd do."

They were about two miles out, at the end of a long rise, close to one of the radar units. The ranch compound swam in the light.

"Okay," Mac said, "if it came over the house now, I could get a shot into it."

"We're too far away."

"Nope. I could take the shot."

They drove on, heading back toward the compound. Mac thought of the aliens as being confined to the night, and that was indeed when they were most active, but Flynn knew better. Flynn watched the skies, searching the blue glare for any sign of a metallic flash.

"You don't need to have this fight, you know."

"They want it, Mac. They've chosen ground."

"Would be my damn place, Mr. Rich Boy. What about that house of yours?"

"They don't like towns."

"Then let's go to town. We'll hole up in your place."

"How long?"

"Aw, shit, I don't know how long. As long as it takes."

"There's sixty miles of road between here and the interstate. If we try to leave, we will meet them somewhere on that journey."

"In broad daylight?"

"Oh, yes."

"Anything else I need to know but don't?" His tone was bitter.

"Probably a lot I don't know, either."

They arrived back at the compound.

"Jesus," Mac said.

Flynn got out of the truck. "Diana! Geri!"

They stood on the screen porch that shaded the family room of the old house. "Want some lemonade? We made some."

Flynn went in, followed by Mac.

"You're supposed to be downstairs," Flynn said.

"And you're supposed to be doing what? Certainly not riding around totally exposed in a pickup truck, because that does not compute, Flynn. What in hell were you doing?"

"Looking for good lies, so Mac will get a shot if they show up over the cabin."

"That is a classic example of little-boy planning. Where are you going to sit, in a tree fort?"

"Yes."

Geri came into the room. She was wearing a long pink cocktail dress. The silk caressed her, flowing over her like cream.

"Where in the world did that come from?" Flynn asked.

"The bedroom closet. It's well equipped with clothing, it seems."

"Cissy Greene's stuff," Mac said. "There's also a box of hand grenades back in there somewhere, if anybody wants to carry one."

"Hand grenades won't help."

"If you're about to get captured, they sure as hell will. Boom. Done."

"I like my lemonade," Diana said as she poured herself another glass. She left the room and came back with her iPad. "Your Wi-Fi working?"

"I think so."

"Still the direct satellite uplink?"

"Yeah, given that the nearest cable box is over in Marathon or up in Menard."

"Uplink's pretty insecure, but I'll see if our network will let me on."

There came another voice, soft and low, right in Flynn's ear: "We're here, Flynn, inside and out. Come with us or we'll kill you along with the others."

A blaze of agony pierced his right calf muscle. He, who was practically impervious to pain, had to choke back a scream.

"Hey, man, are you okay?" Mac asked.

The voice came again, more confident now, sounding just as if somebody were speaking to him through an earbud. "Did that convince you? Because we can do much more."

Flynn could see, in the corner of the kitchen by the refrigerator, a slight shimmer in the air, as if heat were rising from a point about four feet above the floor. Whether they used hypnosis or some sort of technology, the aliens could make themselves very hard to see.

Now he felt movement between his shirt and jacket, so stealthy that it seemed no more than a breeze.

Before the invisible alien whose hand was slipping toward the butt of his gun could so much as touch it, he drew it, turned, and fired. In apparent slow motion, Geri's eyes widened. He watched her face distort and saw her lips opening as she began to scream. Mac and Diana were much slower, and were just beginning to react, their brows knitting.

The alien flew backwards across the kitchen and splattered against the wall, bringing down a cabinet full of crockery. But before that happened, Flynn had fired again, this time toward another of the shimmers.

The bullet smashed into the wall. No contact.

"Get down!" he shouted.

The three of them seemed to move like snails, slowly drifting toward the floor.

An alien leaped onto his back. Shrieking like a banshee, it wrapped him in its steel arms. He felt the fire of a claw slicing toward his carotid. He got his gun behind him and in front of the alien's body, and fired in the only direction he could, which was almost straight up.

The alien flew into the ceiling, where it exploded into pieces, then came down in a shower of cork tiles and purple blood.

In two great strides, Flynn was in the living room, but saw nothing.

Returning to the kitchen, he found chaos still developing. Geri was on the floor, covered with debris from above, Diana was hunched over her iPad, trying to protect it, and Mac had grabbed a knife and thrown it so hard into an interior wall that it was embedded up to its handle. In other words, he'd missed.

With little more than a grunt, Flynn went outside. Dew still sparkled on the trees. Dew, or as it was known around here, West Texas rain.

He searched the area of the compound visible to him, the electronics shack, the barn, the washhouse, and the smokehouse. He saw nothing. The sky was also empty, but with something that could go forty thousand miles an hour, that meant little.

He circled the house, staying close under the eaves, looking for anything that might lead him to more aliens. As he was coming back around to the kitchen, passing under one of the spreading live oaks, he heard a door close. It was soft but clear enough to make him certain that it had not come from the house.

The electronics shack.

He sprinted over to it, but all seemed quiet. He watched a couple of buzzards wheeling. When he'd been working toward his private pilot's license, his dad advised him, "Watch the buzzard. The buzzard knows the sky."

"Nothin' up there," Mac said.

"Buzzards everywhere except overhead."

"The disk can be invisible? I've worried about that."

"They can hide it in clouds. They can use camouflage that reflects the sky behind them. But there will always be flashes from its surface. They may be small, but they will be there. In other words, your kind of thing, with your eyes."

"I'll need to stand off from the house. Well off. The more sky I can see, the better my chances."

A tendril of smoke came into Flynn's field of view. When he followed it down to its source, he saw that the electronics shack was on fire. If they lost it, they lost contact with the outside world, and that must not be. He ran toward it.

"What the hell, Flynn—oh, Jesus!" Mac followed him, running just as fast.

As Flynn reached the door of the shack, he threw himself into hard reverse. He stood looking at the biggest diamondback he'd ever seen. The snake lay in a great, heaping coil spread across the two wooden steps that led up to the door.

Mac came up beside him. "Goddamn, shoot it. You got the pistol."

"It's not real." He plunged toward it—and it snapped its head forward and struck him below the knee. It dug its fangs into the soft tissue above his ankle, and he felt the white-hot pulse of venom as it surged into him. Still, he believed that it was hallucinatory and bulled his way ahead with the snake hanging on to his leg, its outrageous fourteen-foot body whipping behind him like a drunken evil flag.

As he threw open the door of the shack, a sheet of electric fire flared in his face, and all the equipment started sparking.

Mac headed in. "Flynn got snakebit!" he yelled as he pushed past.

"Don't go in there!" Flynn grabbed him.

"My whole setup—"

"There's millions of volts being pumped in there. Same thing that burned Elmwood down."

"There's also three hundred grand in equipment in there."

"Help me, I think I really am snakebit."

"Shit, the thing's still on you, man!"

"I said help me!" As he spoke, he reached down to yank the snake off him—and felt his feet dragged out from under him.

In the next instant, he was being drawn feetfirst upward into the air. Above him, the snake hung with its maw open wide and full of swirling fire. His leg was practically screaming with pain, the snake now rising with him. He drew his gun and emptied it upward, but to no avail.

He shouted to Mac, "Rifle! Use your rifle!"

In the crazy upside-down world he was dealing with, he saw Mac run over to the pickup and start positioning himself in its bed.

Then there was a shudder, and his head was enclosed in something that smelled like sweat and flesh. Arms. But whose?

There followed a struggle, the disk pulling, the person who had enclosed his head pulling back, and the snake writhing and struggling, the whole furious body of the thing twining around him, pulsing, and the head going like a crazed piston, hitting his leg again and again and again.

Every few minutes, a shot rang out, but the disk remained low overhead, a shadow with a spinning fiery heart, seemingly unaffected.

He got a hand on the snake and ripped it off, and saw the whole prehistoric length of the monster go whipping and swarming up into the disk.

An instant later, he hit the ground harder than he'd ever hit anything before. He lay stunned, trying to get the world to stop whirling and tumbling. The electronics shack belched sheets of fire.

"Flynn! Flynn! Come back to me, Flynn, come back to me!"

It was Geri. She'd saved him.

"They'll start again any second—get the hell out of here!"

She pulled him to his feet. His whole left leg was burning; he'd never felt anything like it. Then they were inside, and he dropped down onto the kitchen floor.

Mac abandoned his effort and followed them.

"Snake," Geri said, her voice echoing faintly from the far side of his pain. "Mac, do you have any antivenin?"

"First-aid kit. Pantry, top shelf."

"We've lost the uplink!" Diana wailed. "We've lost the uplink!"

Flynn was dizzy. He'd gotten a serious snakebite, and if he was going to survive, he would have to organize these people, give the right commands, make them do what they needed to do.

He saw Mac then, looming over him, staring down with frightened eyes.

"Don't you die on me, brother."

"Fine, hit me with the antivenin."

He didn't feel the prick of the needle, but knew it had gone in from the fact that his leg began to tingle as if it had lost circulation and gone to sleep. The world was whirling, Diana and Geri swirling past like figures on an out-of-control carousel, and Mac with his needle and his knife, working like a furious grandmother.

"Get downstairs," he managed to gasp. "This is not over."

His leg would not work, and he found himself using Geri's body as a crutch. A strange memory came to him, of embracing her in the dark sheets of night, and the moon had blessed their union, and they had been happy, laughing happy, in the small hours.

She smelled like Abby, she kissed like Abby, in bed her body against his felt like Abby's. "She's full of Abby's genes," the voice had said.

She was crying now, and he told her to stop. "I'm a Texan—we like to get snakebit, it's good for us."

She shook her head, her hair flowing back and forth across her face like a curtain.

"I think I got plenty of antivenin in him," he heard Mac say, a voice echoing in a distant world. "He's a strong damn cuss. What you gotta worry about is what happened inside that disk, once they got that snake in their lap.

"We gotta cool him off, ladies, or he's gonna start having seizures."

"Did you get it?" he asked Mac. The critical question.

"Get what?"

"The disk. Did you get it?"

"Hell no, I didn't get it."

When they were kids, they used to range across the countryside with rubber snakebite kits in their pockets, and reassure each other that they really would use the tiny razors inside to cut deep x's in one another's ankles, and then suck out the blood and the venom.

There was a boy called Carl Meston, who had been bitten by a coral snake. He'd hardly felt it and gone on playing football. While riding home from the game, though, he stopped breathing, and died on the corner of Plains and Elm, his face black and a cop frantically giving him mouth-to-mouth. Another boy, whose name Flynn had forgotten, was bitten by a diamondback and lost a foot.

"Okay," Mac said, "come back to us. There's enough antivenin in you to make a horse dance."

"Will he be all right?" Geri asked, and he heard the tremble of real fear in her voice.

"Dunno. That much venom, they're liable to just croak, and there isn't one damn thing you can do about it. Flynn's a tough bastard, though—right, Flynn?"

"Tough bastard, that's right. I need a glass of water."

Diana brought him a bottle of Evian from the bar, which dominated one wall of this very luxurious basement. He took it and drank the whole thing down in a gulp. She went to get more, but Flynn said, "Not yet. If I flood myself with water and my sodium level goes too low, I won't be able to metabolize the antivenin. I can't see my leg, but it feels like a blimp full of lead."

"There's some swelling," Geri said.

"Blackness around the wound?"

"A little."

He knew what that meant. Necrosis. "Cut it out."

"Excuse me?"

"Mac, cut it out. You know how."

"It might run deep."

"No matter how deep it runs. I'd like to hang on to the leg as long as I can. For life, preferably."

Mac turned on the gas fire and burned a knife red in it. "Okay, buddy. Somebody give him something to chomp on—this is gonna smart."

It didn't smart; it hurt in the way that profound torture hurts, with bright waves of pain flowing through his body, up to the top of his head and down to his feet again and again, back and forth, a whipping tide.

Nobody had anything for him to bite down on. In any case, he had no intention of screaming, although it was a serious temptation.

Mac gathered the necrotizing tissue into a handkerchief, a steaming pulp of blood and flesh. "Something else in there, man?"

"What're you talking about?"

"Somethin's in there. Looks like metal."

"I need a doctor."

"Oh, yes," Diana said.

"The snake is back. They dropped it, and it went to the barn. The horses are calm, so it's staying away from them. I'm gonna want to find it and get rid of it."

"Don't kill it, Mac—they're getting scarce."

"Fine, I'll have Carlos take it down into Big Bend and check it into a snake resort. Shall I get it a suit and tie, and a pair of cool dark glasses?"

Something was dripping through the ceiling. It took him a moment to understand. "The bodies up there—how many are they?"

"Four," Geri replied immediately.

Diana was binding his wound.

"You about finished?"

She sat back. "Done as much as I can. But Mac's right—it's all strange. I've never seen a wound like it."

"Will somebody please describe what's so strange?"

"There's only a single puncture, for one thing. But a doctor needs to look at it."

"We got no phone, and we got some mighty good hunters waiting for us in the sky, so we'll just have to table that, won't we? And there's something else we need to do right now, which is to burn those bodies. The damn things have a bad habit of coming back to life."

"They have multiple damage-recovery systems," Geri said. "They're extremely durable."

His leg screamed its agony, but he refused to give up; it wasn't in him. One by one, he climbed the steps.

The kitchen stank of alien blood, a garlicky mixture of meat and some kind of chemical. They even smelled poisonous.

"We need to do this. Let their friends see what they're up against."

Geri went down on one knee, examining a nearby body with careful, practiced hands. She had done examinations like this before, clearly.

She looked up at him. She was cradling a head, its eyes glassy, dull with death and sadness. "These are an older generation," she said. "No buffers programmed into them."

"What are buffers?"

"You call buffers 'conscience.' These don't have that."

"So where are they from?"

"They were built here, Flynn. Had to have been. They're from right here on Earth."

Just then, Mac came over. He said, "I'm never gonna be good enough to shoot that thing down. So what's next, Flynn? What do we do?"

"Mac, I am sorry to say that I just don't know."

CHAPTER THIRTEEN

HOPING THAT maybe something about the creature would reveal some vulnerability, they did a dissection in Mac's kitchen, on the big table in the center of the room, using Mac's kitchen knives, a box cutter, and a saw Lupe used to open bones for marrow.

"They dissect these things at Wright-Pat," Mac said. "So I've been told."

"No idea," Diana replied.

"We've dissected five so far."

"Flynn, that's—"

"Classified, but Geri obviously has need-to-know."

"Mac, leave the room!" Diana snapped.

"He stays. He's working with me. Also need to know."

She fumed.

The body was about four feet long, with the same narrow frame and dark eyes of the others Flynn had seen.

"How, exactly, do you know it's not one of yours?" he asked Geri.

She split the chest, drawing it wide and exposing the heart and lungs. "These are typical organs. And look—" She scraped at a rib, which revealed bright silver where bone should be. "That's titanium or maybe stainless steel. This is an old unit. We haven't used those materials in years. We use a living composite bone now. Artificial, but alive. Far more durable and flexible than this stuff."

"So, can he build more?"

"Judging from what he's using, no. We're looking at an old, out-of-repair disk and robots that are four or five generations back. This is a shoestring operation here, Flynn."

"A few crumbs of incredible technology are worth a whole world of primitive weapons like ours," Flynn commented.

As he looked at the biorobots, he found himself coming to a very large question, not about them, but about himself. "Do you have devices that would enable voice commands to be projected into a human brain? Words?"

"The biorobots are equipped with transceivers. They use burst telemetry, but I guess voice would be possible."

A slow, creeping coldness spread through him. He was carrying a transceiver.

If he could be communicated with, then he could be tracked, too. He could even be vulnerable to mind control. It wouldn't be gross, but subtle, causing him to make the wrong decisions, to walk into traps, to make himself vulnerable—which was exactly what he'd been doing since he went rushing off to Mountainville.

He decided he'd have a full-body MRI scan as soon as possible, under the most secret conditions he could manage. No Diana, no Geri, nobody but him and the MRI technician. He'd read the scan himself. Only if he was unsure would he seek out a radiologist. If he was implanted and it couldn't be removed, he would have no choice but to inform Diana, but until then, his degree of exposure would remain his problem, and his alone.

Right now, he had more to learn.

"Geri, what happened on Aeon, when you say they rebelled?"

"Nowhere in intelligence theory was there anything that suggested they could gain independence of thought, let alone an ego and the hopes and dreams that go with it. Then, one day, a group of them took over a refurbishing facility. That's a place where used ones are broken down into component sections, and the least worn parts combined together to create new ones. They killed the operators and barricaded themselves in the facility. From there, the rebellion spread. Now, they're in control of half the planet. More than half."

"And Morris? Is he a biological robot, or something like you?"

"I'd appreciate 'someone' rather than 'something.' We're the outcome of long biological evolution just like you, and just as valid as you are. At home, Morris is a criminal under investigation for four murders that took place during a raid on a robotics facility. That was where he stole the elements he's used to build his robot soldiers."

"Okay, folks, this is all real fascinating," Mac said. "But I have another kind of a question, which is, what the hell do we do to get out of this mess? With the electronics shack gone, we don't have any communications of any kind."

"No landline telephone?" Diana asked.

"Hell no. Between law enforcement and *drogos,* there were so many taps on it that I couldn't hear a damn thing. I ditched it years ago. And these bastards are coming back. Soon."

Of course, he was right, but not entirely right. "They aren't invincible, or we'd already be dead. For example, they can't just blow the place to bits, or that would have happened at the outset."

"They blew the electronics shack."

"They were able to concentrate electrical energy in all that wiring. In Elmwood, I'm assuming they sent massive amounts of juice into the town's electrical grid. Overloaded all the wiring and set the whole town on fire. But there's not much of a grid here. Just the generator and the house wiring. The only thing they had to work with was the electronics in the shack. Which gets me to defense. We need to cut off the jenny."

Mac headed for the cellar. "I'll push the kill switch."

"Geri, tell me how that light beam works. We won't have the radars, so do we have any defense from it?"

"It generates antigravity. But I have to tell you, they're not very good at using it, or maybe it's not a very well designed version. At home, we can draw a complete structure from the surface to space with a beam like that. They don't seem too effective, even from an altitude of fifty feet."

"Thank heaven for small favors," Diana muttered.

The kitchen clock stopped, and the light over the sink went out. A moment later, Mac returned.

A plan was forming in Flynn's mind. "Mac, how many operable vehicles do you have here?"

"Ten or so. I had an armored Humvee, but I sold it to some Buddhist monks over near Alpine."

"Okay, so what's available? Pickups, what else?"

"You've got two pickups, a road grader, couple of backhoes, a 1988 Cadillac, and some four-wheelers. Two that work."

Flynn remembered that Cadillac. It had belonged to Mac's mother. Mac had ridden in it as a boy, made out in it as a teenager. "In terms of weight, the grader is the heaviest but also the slowest. The backhoes are next. Same problem, though. The Caddy and the pickups are probably about equal weight, also the fastest vehicles in the mix. You have anything you're not mentioning? I mean, surely you've got some serious cars around here somewhere."

"Unlike you, I don't give a whole huge damn about cars, so the answer is that I don't."

"You had that Lamborghini."

"Too low to the ground for my road. I would've had to pave. Not gonna happen. It's at the house in Marfa."

"So we have two pickups and an old Caddy."

"In good shape, all of them."

"None of them will survive for long off road, though. So we'll need to get to the highways as fast as we can, whichever way we go. So what I think we have to do is wait until about four, when the ground is as hot as it's going to get, then head out. If they use infrared tracking, it'll be at least somewhat washed out during the day. Also, we use just the pickups. I don't trust that old Caddy—I remember how that thing used to break down when we were kids."

"True enough. We leave the Caddy behind."

"You three fit in one of the pickups. I take the other."

That brought silence. Finally Diana broke it with a question he didn't think she would really need to ask. "Why?"

"Let me put it this way: I have reason to believe that they have additional means of detecting me. Anyone who travels with me is going to share my vulnerability."

"And be protected by your ability to fight back," Geri said.

"It's a chance we have to take. They're going to see me first—I'm certain of that. Maybe you'll get through."

"Flynn—"

"Diana, no more. You can afford to lose me. I've seen Geri's reaction times. With training, she can be as fast as me, or damn close."

"We need ten of you, Flynn—a hundred, a thousand."

"Then Geri, here, can have them built on Aeon and sent to us. Robots."

Diana gave him a searching look, but said nothing.

"Okay, the way we're going to handle this is that you go up 385 to Fort Stockton. There's a Rodeway Inn there. Get a room and wait for me. If I don't appear by tomorrow morning, go back to Washington and take it from there."

"This is way too risky," Diana said.

"It's risky, no question. It's also the only way. If we wait, they're going to be back, and this time they'll have whatever it takes to end this thing. No more fun and games. When they show up again, we die."

"How can you be certain? They've screwed up pretty consistently so far, bro."

"Take a look in your gun room."

Without a word, Mac strode out of the kitchen and across the living room. "Shit! They even got my Purdeys. That's two hundred grand worth of shotguns right there, plus the rocket launcher and the machine guns."

"Don't you do anything legal?" Diana asked.

"I breathe. I believe that's legal in some states."

Flynn handed Mac the big Bull and got a box of bullets out of his duffel. "I assume you're proficient with this?"

"Sure, a Bull. I can shoot that."

"Flynn, what are you going to carry?"

He transferred his small pistol to his belt. "This is a perfectly good weapon."

"It's too small to save you, and you know it, Flynn," Diana said.

"What I need you three to understand is that they might not even try to use their light. They stole those weapons because they think they'll also be effective. Keep moving, but never on a straight path, not for more than a few seconds. They'll have algorithmic predictors, which means that after a while, they'll be able to anticipate your next move, no matter what you do. So once we get in motion, wind your truck out as fast as it'll go while staying with the random movement."

That brought silence, and with it, Flynn knew, the unease that men feel before battle. Flynn was primarily concerned about his leg swelling so badly that he would become unable to use it. He watched the time. At two, they ate cold cuts and drank warmish iced coffee from the fridge. There were some oranges, too, and they ate those.

Three o'clock came, then three thirty. "Geri, I assume you're not in communication with Aeon?"

"Not at present."

"Can you be?"

"If the main rebel group should trace the signal, they could follow it to Earth. Then you'll really have a problem."

"Why wouldn't Morris just tell the rebels where Earth is?"

"Competition is the last thing he wants."

Flynn hobbled to the kitchen window. Carefully, he surveyed the area for any sign of the creatures.

"It looks clear, but remember, there's no way to be certain. I could easily have missed something." Now he stepped out, heavily favoring his right leg.

"Flynn, you can't go alone, you're barely able to walk."

"Mac, I'm going to need to ask you to bring one of the trucks around for me. I can't walk on this damn mess."

"Flynn, if you can't walk, you can't drive. You're going with us."

"No room."

"Then we take the car. Come on, Flynn, think. Your injury is clouding your judgment."

He thought it through again, and came out at exactly the same place. If there was any chance that anybody would get to the relative safety of a town, they had to force a choice. That meant two vehicles. From what he had understood, the bastards had only one disk. So the odds were that they would go after him first, which meant he had to be alone. He would fight as long as possible in the hope that the others would get through.

Try as he might, he could not remember any moment in his adult life when somebody would have been able to do the surgery necessary to implant a transceiver anywhere in his body, let alone in his brain. Nor did he have any telltale lumps under his skin of the kind that concealed the emergency transponders given to pilots who were operating in enemy territory. He'd known a couple of pilots who had those things behind their ears. In his case, nothing there. Maybe the electronics were flat, a thin film hugging his scalp. No sign of an entry point, though, unless hidden under his hair. But when? And if they could get that close to him with him not noticing, why not just kill him?

He ran through it: A neuroscientist who worked at a facility that studied alien bodies was assassinated by aliens. The scientist specialized in exotic hypnosis techniques. During Flynn's investigation, he received texts that suggested he should pay significant attention to the man and the facility.

"Flynn, where are you?"

"I'm sorry. Strategizing."

"We're going in two vehicles," Diana said. "You and me in one, Gail and Mac in the other. I'll drive."

"I'm going alone. I'm sorry." He looked to Mac. "Come on, brother, let's check the trucks out."

"Damn you, you hardheaded jerk!"

"I'll take the hardheaded part, but I'm not a jerk."

She glared at him, then turned away.

Outside, he and Mac stayed under the trees as they made their way to the car barn, Flynn hanging on Mac's shoulder. The vehicles inside were bright and clean and, as Flynn soon found, in perfect condition. One was a F-150 at least thirty years old, the other a brand-new F-450 with a double cabin.

"I'll take the 150. Are its mechanicals okay?"

"It's clean, anyway. Get a speck of dust on anything, wear out a tire, Carlos is on it."

"Mac, let me ask you a question. I know I'm too fast with a gun. We both know something might have been done to me. So do I still seem like the same person? You said I had no personality. Is that something new?"

"What's new is that you're sounding crazier than ever, but basically you're the same guy."

"Let's get this show on the road."

They drove the trucks out under the trees and parked them. When Diana and Geri came out, Diana had the sullen look of somebody who was defeated and thought she should have won.

"You guys go out to 67 and straight up to Fort Stockton. Check into the motel. Cash, no credit cards. Don't anybody run a card or go to an ATM—nothing like that. I'm going west into the mountains. I'll take 17 up to the interstate and meet you no later than eight tonight."

"Got it," Mac said.

"What if you don't show up?" Diana asked.

"Go on down the road without me, what else? Maybe I can be replaced after all."

They got in their truck, and he watched them head off down Mac's five-mile-long road. Soon they were a dot with a dust cloud, moving fast. They'd forgotten to swerve. He hoped it wasn't a fatal error.

He took his own truck out into the range and headed westward toward the distant Davis Mountains. To make certain he wouldn't be the more challenging target, he went in a straight line as well.

It was clear and hot here, but he could see a line of dark blue cloud along the northern horizon that told him cold weather was no longer entirely extinct in West Texas.

He drove slowly, trying to ignore the agony shooting up his left leg every time he moved. It was slow going, maneuvering around clumps of cactus and sagebrush. As best he could, he watched the sky, but more than that, he kept his awareness focused on the way the truck felt. If the steering got light, his plan was to jump out and roll away, and hope they got the truck and not him. What would happen next, he had no idea. Plan too carefully, and you were liable to miss the one chance that could save your life. He'd either survive or he wouldn't; that was the bottom line. As always.

As he worked his way westward, he went higher into the hills, until the view behind him was a vast stretch of the Earth that disappeared into haze to the south, a wall of dark, flickering clouds to the north, and what seemed like infinity to the east. He felt a sense of the planet rolling through space, an ark on an endless journey, lost in the stars. Surely there was something good out there, too, some world or worlds where all was well.

Deep in the lost immensity behind him, he could see a column of smoke rising into the stillness before the storm. So the aliens had found a way to set Mac's place on fire after all. Couldn't be anything else. He thought of that wonderfully ramshackle house filled with fine paintings, superb equipment, and Mac's many collections, and he thought that Mac was right about him: he was a cancer, a destructive element, bringing ruin and death wherever he went.

It hadn't been necessary to burn Mac out, or even important. There was only one reason for it, which was purest spite.

As he drove on, negotiating every wrinkle of land he could find, he watched the oncoming storm, its face shot with lightning and boiling with angry clouds, and he asked himself a question he could not ignore and could not lay to rest, and certainly could not answer. The question was, "Who am I? Or what?"

He turned the old truck toward the storm, and went on.

CHAPTER FOURTEEN

BY THE time Flynn reached Highway 17, the truck was laboring, and he was watching the temperature gauge climb toward its red line. If the truck stopped, he would be alone on foot. Even if the aliens didn't take him, with his leg in this condition, he wouldn't make it far. This land did not have room for the weak. If his vehicle failed him, he died. Simple truth.

He was still a mile from the dark line of the road below him when the gauge slipped into the red. He tried to drive fast enough to keep some air moving under the hood, but not so fast that he made the problem worse.

As he descended the escarpment that marked the western border of Mac's ranch, the needle's ascent slowed. Then it started to drop. But there was a long flat area at the bottom, and when Flynn had to step on the gas again, it almost immediately became pinned. The next step would be a blown hose and the end of the line.

He crept ahead, glimpsing the road from time to time. Was it getting closer? Hard to be sure. If he'd drifted into an angled approach, he could end up going miles more than necessary. The truck would not make it, no question.

He got another glimpse of the tarmac. The gauge was still pinned.

The engine coughed and faltered and the truck shook. His leg hammered with pain.

With the truck protesting like an exhausted horse, he climbed a steepening bank. When he reached the top, he saw spread before him the long, empty strip of the road. A grateful wash of blood flushed his face as he turned onto the highway at last.

He began traveling at about forty, hoping that the breeze under the hood and the easier going would help, but the gauge remained stubbornly pinned, and the engine's laboring became more pronounced.

The storm was now a great cliff of clouds looming across the whole northern horizon. Farther east, he knew that it would bring tornadoes, but out here in West Texas, the chief danger from weather like this was lightning and hail and the flash floods that would turn bone-dry gulches into raging torrents inside of two minutes. But Flynn had seen it before. He knew this hard land and its power, and respected it the way a man respects a snake, and loved it the way he loves the mystery of a mountain lion.

The lines these storms drew in West Texas could be very clear, and he watched the wall of rain coming straight toward him, a dancing haze swallowing the highway.

First, the truck was buffeted by a fierce gust of wind, and then the rain hit. He found himself peering into white, rushing nothingness. The truck's old-fashioned electric windshield wiper did little good. At least the cooler air ended the overheating crisis.

The wound now involved pain so great that it made him woozy and nauseated, and caused him to scream between clenched teeth whenever the truck struck the slightest bump.

Thus far, it was looking like he'd escaped, and he was worried that this meant the others had not.

Slowly, the outskirts of Fort Stockton appeared, some houses naked in the naked land, then a Texaco station and a little strip of stores. There was a KFC with its big red and white sign collapsed into its parking lot. Farther on, there stood a Dairy Queen and a steak house with the kind of food that drew ranchers, who ate and told stories and laughed in good seasons, and sat silently in their booths in bad ones.

Like the rest of the region, practically every foot of this place held at least one memory for him. The saddlery where his dad had taken him to get his first saddle of his own; the church where his grandmother had been baptized, worshipped, and from which she'd been buried. Over a little farther, she and her people were in East Hill Cemetery, living in his memories, lying in the stark land, in the wind.

Finally, he saw the Rodeway Inn ahead. He pulled into a parking space near the office, stepped out of the truck and into pain so extreme that he had to clutch the door to keep himself from buckling at the knees.

He took deep breaths, forcing the agony down, forcing his body to function, his muscles to work. He walked into the motel. The clerk, behind the desk and watching a TV show on a tablet computer, looked up at him. He did not smile.

"You all right, cowboy?"

"I'm fine."

"You don't look fine."

"I had some friends check in a while ago. A man and two women."

"They didn't check in. They stood in here and argued, then they left."

What in hell could that mean? "Excuse me?"

"That fella got a call on his cell. Then he yells out, 'The crazy bastards are burning down my house.' A few minutes later, he leaves in a cab. Some air force officer from up at the base picked up the women."

So they'd gotten one after all. They'd lured Mac back. He would be dead by now, poor damn guy. He hoped that he'd put up a hell of a fight. He thought, *Good-bye, fare you well, you bastard*. He choked back his feelings and pulled out his cell phone. Safe enough to use it now, unless they'd taken to invading towns in driving storms.

He called Diana. "You have reached a monitored voice mailbox. Please leave your message."

"What the hell's going on? Where are you?"

The next thing he knew, he was on the floor.

"Shit," the clerk said. "I get 'em all."

It took Flynn a moment to realize that he'd blacked out. As he got oriented, he fought to his feet. He clutched the counter. "I need a room."

"You need a lot more than that. I've called EMS."

"No. No EMS. I can take care of myself."

"No, you can't. I'm not giving you any room, either—you're damn well at death's door. What happened to you, anyway? You get yourself shot?"

A couple of EMS attendants appeared almost immediately. Flynn didn't resist. He was slipping in and out of consciousness, and could no longer deny that he had reached the end of his tether.

He saw the gurney they were wheeling in, though, which made him strive to pull himself together. He willed the pain to concentrate just in the wound. He relaxed into the fire of it, allowing it to consume him and become part of him.

"I'm okay," he said. Then, to prove that, he took a step. But he could not take another. "No, I'm not. You'll need to move me."

"What happened to you?"

"Got snakebit down near Marfa. Diamondback."

They laid him on the gurney. One of them started setting an IV.

"I'm good. All I need is wound management."

"That's our call, fella."

He let them set a fluids IV. "No dope," he said, "I don't need dope."

"What treatment have you received?"

"Antivenin, I think."

"You think?"

"A friend had some at his house. I don't know its condition. I don't think it's working very well."

"We'll see."

They rolled him into the wagon. He listened to the siren as the ambulance lumbered through the rainy streets. The next thing he knew, he was wheeled into a small emergency room and felt a nurse cutting off the leg of his jeans.

"Doctor!" she shouted.

A young Indian doctor came in immediately. He smiled. "Hello, I am Dr. Patel. What has happened here?"

"I got snakebit."

He looked down at the wound. "No, this is not a snakebite."

"The hell, it was the biggest diamondback I've ever seen."

"I'm sorry, but this is not a snakebite."

Flynn knew that but had not wanted to face it. He struggled to raise his head. He could see his swollen lower leg, purple ringed by angry red. "It was a diamondback fourteen feet long."

"With a single fang? I don't believe so. The largest go to seven feet long, anyway. There is something under your skin. Can you tell me what that is?"

"I've been driving on this leg for hours. I just need to sleep. A good sleep."

"What is that under your skin? Can you remember?"

"I don't know." He had to get it out, but he couldn't let this man do it. If he did, the object would be sent to pathology and be destroyed or lost or even end up on the evening news. It was unknown technology, and maybe a window into the mind and abilities of the enemy.

Was it transmitting or receiving, or doing both? And why do such a clumsy job of insertion?

The answer was obvious, and made him consider just leaving it where it was. They had anticipated that he would suspect there was something implanted in him. They wanted him to take it out and, when it was removed, imagine himself free. But he would not be free, because whatever was of real importance to them would be somewhere else in his body.

"I can walk out of here."

"You can't walk three steps. We need to get that thing out, and then the swelling will go down so long as there's no infection. Now, can you give me a better idea where it came from?"

"I got snakebit, and afterwards it was there. That's all I know."

"You were not bitten by a snake, as I have told you. Now, I want to move you into the operating room and get this thing out."

"Doctor, I—"

"Nurse!"

"Yes, Doctor?"

"Call Dr. Francesco and get this man prepped. Left lower leg, foreign object."

The next thing Flynn knew, he was being slid onto the hard, black table in the middle of an operating room.

"No general anesthesia," he said as a nurse added a bag to his IV and a doctor in greens asked him if he was allergic to any drugs.

Before he could protest further, he felt the comforting hand of the drugs take him and hold him. Time began passing at a different speed. He was half awake and half asleep, and struggling with all his might to remain conscious.

He heard a voice say, "Jesus," and saw two masked faces staring at each other.

"Careful," he said, forcing his lips to form the words. "Don't let it near you, don't touch it."

"He's vocalizing. Take him deeper."

"No. Do not. No."

Then it was black, the voices were somewhere in the far away, and he could feel long periods of pressure against his leg.

He became aware of women shouting. "Errol! Errol!"

It was nice here. Warm. And he had not slept in days. Not in days.

"Errol, wake up! Errol!"

Who was this bothering him? The hell with them.

"Errol! Wake up!"

He saw a face filled with two brown eyes.

"Yeah?"

"We thought you were gonna sleep until Tuesday."

He was in a hospital room, lying on the bed and hooked up to a vital signs monitor. There was an IV in his arm. Electrolytes only, he saw.

A nurse smiled down at him. "Who was JFK?"

The name didn't ring a bell. He covered. "Who wants to know?"

"Look at the clock. Can you see the clock?"

"Yeah."

"What time is it?"

"Three twenty."

"Okay, we're getting somewhere. What's your name?"

"Flynn Carroll. Nobody calls me Errol. And by the way, JFK was President Kennedy." He had also remembered that he was in a hospital in Fort Stockton and he needed to get out of here. He needed to reconnect with Diana and Gail right now, and he needed to take with him whatever the doctors had extracted.

"Doctor, he's conscious."

Now a male face peered down at him. Kindly, about forty, white guy. "I'm Dr. Francesco. I'm your surgeon. Do you know what we took out of you?"

"You put me under? I told you not to do that."

"You went under on your own. You're pretty wasted, Mr. Carroll. Now, what is that thing?"

"I don't know."

"Neither do we." He raised the head of Flynn's bed and held out a small white box. He opened it and held it so that Flynn could see. "Recognize this?"

There was a disk in the box, bright silver. In its center was a neat round hole.

He shook his head.

"You sure seemed to know something about it. You were yelling that something would come out of it. Despite the anesthesia." He stared at Flynn, waiting for a response.

Flynn had no idea what to say.

When there was no reply forthcoming, Dr. Francesco continued. "Something did." He picked up a lidded glass beaker.

In it, Flynn saw a wrinkled black object about two inches long. At one end was a mass of fine white threads, extended as if they were grasping.

"This thing was alive. Very alive. It struggled. It died struggling, as you can see."

"Yeah, I see that." Looking at the thing and remembering the voices talking to him, Flynn felt as deep an unease as he had ever known. This was very clearly a parasite, but also a piece of technology. Living technology. He was betting everything on the hunch that it was dead now.

"Where were you when you got this in you?"

"Like I told you, I thought I got snakebit."

"The metal disk is obviously a housing for this proteinaceous material. You sure you're not under some kind of exotic treatment, maybe experimental cancer treatment of some kind?"

"No."

"Because what this disk looks most like is an implantable infuser. Something that delivers a continuous flow of—"

Another nurse came in and whispered to Francesco. She stood aside, shoulders hunched. Flynn could see that she was frightened, and that worried him.

"Well, it seems that your friends are here to pick you up. I'd like you to leave the proteinaceous material for pathology. The metal disk you can take with you, or we can discard it."

"No, I need it all." He found himself almost childishly relieved that Diana and Geri had finally come. He'd feared the worst for them. Now, if only he could get Mac to get the hell off that ranch and into his place in Menard, which would be safer for him, too—unless, of course, it was already too late.

The doctor placed both the disk and the small jar containing the mobile part of the system, or whatever it was, into a plastic bag, which he then sealed.

"If your leg gets hot and more tender than it is, or you feel nauseated or dizzy, get back in here. Infection's what we worry about."

An orderly brought in a wheelchair.

"Hold off, where's my weapons? I had a knife and a gun."

"They'll be returned to you as you leave the facility." The doctor slid his hands under Flynn's arms.

"I can make it," Flynn said. Standing on his own was hard but no longer impossible. The room whirled and he had to grab the bed railing, but he recovered himself.

"Don't walk on that any more than you have to, Errol, please," the surgeon said. "You'll open the stitches." He handed him a prescription. "And take this with you. Take one a day, starting in the morning. Be sure to take them all."

The nurses helped him dress in his shirt and jacket and the remains of his jeans. He could get a shoe on his right foot, but not on the left. It would take a day or so for the swelling to go down.

Working as hard as he could to walk normally, fighting back the pain as best he could, he headed for the lobby.

Diana and Geri were nowhere to be seen. He turned around to go ask where they were, and found himself face-to-face with an air security police officer who had obviously been standing beside the door he just walked through.

When he turned around again, he found himself confronting three men: a full-bird colonel in uniform, a major, and a civilian whose cold stare suggested that he expected trouble and was prepared to deal with it. The colonel wore a name tag—LEANDER.

"Don't even think about leaving on your own," Colonel Leander said. "We're here to help you."

"Who the hell are you?"

The civilian's face crinkled into a smile. "I'm the boss you've never met, Flynn. Diana Glass reports to me." The smile evaporated.

The air security personnel were right behind him now.

"Come this way," Colonel Leander said. "Can you make it to the car?"

"Do I have a choice?"

"We can get a chair."

With the SPs behind him, two armed officers beside him, and no gun of his own, he didn't see a way out. Slowly, he made his way toward the vehicle, parked directly in front of the lobby doors.

"Somebody was supposed to return my weapons."

"We have them."

They helped him into the backseat. Colonel Leander sat on his right, Major Ford on his left, the civilian in the front seat with the driver, another air security officer.

"I repeat, do I have a choice?"

"What kind of choice?"

"To get the hell out of this car and go my way."

"No, you don't have that choice."

The car started and they left the hospital grounds.

Flynn sat quietly, but his mind was blazing with a kind of mad fury, which he strove to control.

The security policeman driving the vehicle was not what he seemed.

Flynn knew exactly who he was, and that he was the real chief of this whole operation, all of it, from the kidnappings to the murders to the recent plague of brutal attacks—all of it.

The security policeman who now sat behind the wheel was no security cop at all. Far from it—he was an evil, evil man, if he could even be called a man.

He was Louis Charleton Morris.

CHAPTER FIFTEEN

FLYNN HAD to use every bit of self-control he possessed to avoid re-vealing the turmoil he was feeling. The hate was so intense that it was like an actual fire inside him. Even in the darkest hours after Abby's disappearance, he had never felt an emotion remotely this powerful. Only one thing mattered to him now, which was to destroy the monster that was behind the wheel.

"Where are we heading?" he asked, his voice carefully modulated.

"Base," the civilian said.

"Does it have a name?"

"No, it does not."

"I want my weapons."

"Flynn, relax," the civilian said. "I'm Dexter Harmon, by the way. I know that Diana's never mentioned me. You're not need-to-know, and our girl follows the book."

"Where is she?"

"On her way back to Washington." He glanced at his watch. "Landing in forty minutes." '

All lies. "Glad to hear it. Where are you in the chain of command, Dex?"

"You report to Diana, Diana reports to me, and I report to the presi-dent. If you don't mind, would you call me Mr. Harmon?"

"No problem, Dex."

He tried not to watch the back of Morris's head. He looked younger, his black hair was now brown, but those darkly gray, empty eyes were unmistakable. No, it was Morris, no question. The disguise was a good one, though. His mind focused onto one, single thought: *Kill him.*

He smiled. "I'm delighted to meet you, Dex, I have to say. Let me ask you this: How do you feel about the way I kill these bastards?"

"Just kill 'em all."

"I need to get to their leader. Handler. Whatever he is. Builder."

"Making any progress?"

"That's classified."

"Everybody in this vehicle is cleared to hear anything you might say."

"I'm on him."

"What's your plan?"

"I'm going to kill him. A few days."

"Now, that is a plan. Any details?"

What was this guy, an actor? He sure as hell didn't know how to mine a conversation for information.

"I know where he lives."

Flynn watched a subtle signal pass between Morris and Dex.

As they drove north out of Fort Stockton, they also drove into territory that Flynn knew well. Among the things he knew was that there were no bases up here. In fact, the only place of note was a big old dance hall called the Bluebonnet Palace, about twenty miles north of here, sitting all by itself on a godforsaken crossroads. Popular, though. There would be people there.

"Where is this base, exactly? There aren't any government facilities out this way."

"Up toward Lubbock."

"You understand that I've been very aggressively attacked from above a number of times in the past few days?"

"It's not an issue," Harmon said.

"How can you possibly know that? We're in an ideal area for such an attack to take place."

Nobody responded.

"Either you know something I don't, or you're taking a hell of a risk."

"I've evaluated the situation, and I don't think it's a risk. You're not alone, Flynn. There's a lot of firepower in these vehicles."

He thought about that. How ridiculous it was. He kept playing along. Before he killed Morris—and he would—he needed to find out as much as he could about his motives and his plans.

"Have you ever been up against these things? Any of you?"

Silence.

"Bear in mind that they're also extremely fast."

"And you're the only person who can be effective against them, which is exactly what we want to understand."

Bingo. Before killing him, Morris wanted to find out what made him tick. That was why he'd led him along like this, ignoring opportunity after opportunity.

"You need to give me a weapon, and you need to do it now."

"If they show up."

"If they show up, it'll be too late to pass out weapons. We're done."

Of course, no attack was going to come, obviously, not with the head of the whole operation sitting right here in this car.

For a good hour, they drove in silence, turning first down one ranch road and then another.

"Elmwood," Harmon said. He gestured toward his side window.

"I know where Elmwood is."

The town, a low cluster of ruins on the eastern horizon, was dark and silent.

The highway spun away behind them, endless and empty. Once, a rancher passed with a load of cattle. Later, a sheriff's SUV sped past, going south.

The last thing Flynn wanted to see was other cops. He wanted to do what he was going to do in private. Kill the creature, destroy the remains, get the hell out. That was his plan.

They turned off the final paved road they would use and onto a dirt track. Flynn thought he could break the necks of the two men sitting beside him before they could draw their guns. Wouldn't do much good, though, not with that truckload of security behind them.

At the end of another half hour rumbling along the dirt track, they came to a small grouping of low buildings, which Flynn recognized as the kind of prefabs the military would erect in places where it intended to stay for just a few months. They passed through a disused gate that had been left hanging open.

"You ever have any intruders here?"

Nobody replied.

"Nice," Flynn said, "you're chatty. I like chatty."

"This isn't a game," Colonel Leander said.

They pulled up in front of a gray building. Like the others, its windows were covered by drawn blinds.

Once they were out of the vehicles, it seemed possible that the odds might change in his favor. If the right moment came and he could get one of their guns, he could take care of all of them before they got off a shot. The SPs had locked holsters that would open only to their touch, but not the two officers, so it was a matter of positioning.

However, it seemed that they were well aware of their danger, because he found himself surrounded by the security personnel with their hands on their weapons. The other three walked behind.

"Leg holding up?"

"No." Actually, it was a lot better, but he had no intention of letting them know that. It would hurt like hell, but he was pretty sure he could run on it.

The interior of the building was lit only by a few overhead lamps. There were office cubicles, but Flynn had the impression that the place was empty and had been for some time.

"Come on in, Flynn," Harmon said. "Sorry for the setup. We're just in the process of moving in." He ushered Flynn into a small office and offered him a steel chair. "Now, you ask, why are you here?"

"I'd like to know."

"One of the great problems we're facing is the presence of aliens who can pass for human, and who don't have our best interests at heart."

"Not news to me."

"No?" He smiled, all friendly warmth. "You don't have our best interests at heart, and you pass for human."

"I am human," he said.

Harmon sighed. "We can get it out of you, you know. We can get it all out."

"I'm sure you can."

"Then tell us where you're from."

"Menard, Texas."

"That's your final answer?"

"It's the only answer."

"I'm sorry for you, then. You do understand that all of your memories, all you know, can be removed?"

Flynn blanked his mind. He felt the two officers, who were in the room behind him, stir uneasily. Then he noticed that Morris had also entered. When he made his move, he would be dealing with four armed men, at least one of which was going to have special capabilities.

Harmon smiled again. "What will be left will be a vegetable. And what we will do with said vegetable is, we'll take you to someplace like a barrio in Mexico City, and we'll leave you there. Do you want that?"

"What am I supposed to say?"

"Tell us where you're from and why you're here."

"Okay, I'm a Streib."

Harmon frowned slightly.

Major Ford said, "It's an alien from a television series called *Babylon Five*."

Harmon glanced up at Morris, then nodded slightly. "Let's get started, gentlemen." His voice was brisk.

The situation was this. Harmon Dexter was two feet from him across the desk. The two officers were out of sight behind him. Morris was behind them. There was one window. It was closed by blinds, but all he had seen surrounding the place was a low cyclone fence.

"Is my commanding officer aware of where I am?"

"Diana? Of course."

"And you understand what happens if you kill me? Do you?"

"You can't threaten me, Flynn." Harmon opened a drawer in the desk. "We're going to start with chemical interrogation. Depending on how far we get, we'll move on from there." He pulled out a flat, black box and opened it to reveal an interior full of medical instruments, syringes, and drugs in vials. He removed a syringe. "What I'm going to ask you are questions about your home planet. Where it is, that sort of thing."

Incredibly, it was becoming clearer and clearer that Morris must actually believe him to be from another world.

He'd found out enough.

Harmon raised the syringe he'd just finished filling. The next step was going to be a flood of wicked drugs. It was time to extricate himself.

An instant later, the syringe was embedded in Harmon's right eye. For another instant, nothing happened. Then Flynn watched his head tilt to one side and his eyebrow rise, making Harmon look as if having a syringe in his eye struck him as funny.

He hurled himself back against the wall and began screaming and kept screaming while his hands fluttered crazily around his face, touching the syringe as if it were white-hot.

The suddenness of Flynn's move and the extreme reaction it had produced caused the desired effect in the other three. While Leander leaped toward Harmon, hands outstretched and also screaming bloody murder, Flynn removed the Colonel's pistol and whipped his temple with it, sending him to the floor in a heap. By that time, Major Ford was out of his chair and leaving the room. Morris was nowhere to be seen. Flynn got Ford by the collar and slammed him into the wall once, twice, a third time. Ceiling tiles rained down around his slumped form. The major was done for the day.

A tremendous blow caused the room to become a tiny dot of light surrounded by blackness. And then there was only the dark.

He squeezed his trigger, but it was frozen. He knew that he was staggering, that he had taken a hit, and also that the fool who had been carrying this gun put the safety on.

Pain shot up his leg as he hit the floor. His thumb found the safety. He pushed it. He took another powerful hit, this one on his left temple.

His free hand went up and he grabbed the wrist, then stuffed the pistol into his assailant's belly and fired.

On all fours now, gagging and shaking his head like an animal that had been kicked around, he fought away the darkness that threatened him.

Somebody was there, right in front of him, a speeding shadow. He saw a gun, heard its mechanism working, and lashed out, slapping it with his left hand, causing the slug to graze his chest instead of rip into his heart.

He fired the colonel's pistol, and there was a grunt, then silence for a moment, then a whispery moan.

Flynn got to his feet. For a moment, he could not raise his head, not without becoming disoriented again. That blow had been delivered with incredible power. If it had been anything except a fist, it would have killed him.

Instinct told him to get out of the room, but close combat skills said to get a wall behind him, which he did, pressing up against the one beside the desk.

Harmon lay slumped against the opposite wall. His chest revealed slow breaths. Alive, unconscious. The two officers were also alive. Ford was groaning, his body under a fallen chair. There was bone visible in the middle of his right shin. The security cop was flat on his face in the hall. Nobody else was visible.

Flynn went to the cop and turned him over. He felt a moment of disappointment that it wasn't Morris. The guy was breathing, but struggling with a serious chest wound. Flynn did what he could to close the sucking hole with the man's shirt, then went through his pockets, looking for a phone.

He called 911 and said, "Been a shooting." He described the location carefully, and twice, to a perplexed state police dispatcher. "There's two guys, broken back, broken hip, possible broken neck. One with a sucker in the chest, forty-five slug all the way through. Fourth one's banged up, he'll walk it off."

"Sir, are you safe at this time?"

"I'm good." He closed the phone and slid it back into the guy's pocket. Then he returned to the office. Gently, he removed the syringe from Harmon's eye. No doubt the eye was gone, but maybe not. Depended on what was in the syringe. Whatever it was, it had completely knocked Harmon out.

He went quickly through the facility, but he did not expect to find Morris. They had both mishandled this thing. Flynn should never have let it go on as long as it had. Morris should never have tried to capture him. To get Flynn, it was going to take a different approach. Stealth and indirection would need to be part of it—and luck.

There was nothing here except a few empty rooms. Signs of rodent infestation, cheap steel desks, rusting. He opened a few drawers. All empty.

It had been ten minutes since his 911 call. Troopers would be coming fast, probably down from Interstate 10, maybe up from US 90. He didn't want to engage with them, so he went out to the front. He was careful, stepping out just a foot or so, then checking overhead for any sign of a shadow.

Cloud cover combined with the lack of ground light to make the sky as dark as the interior of a cave. In contrast, in the infrared, he would be like a searchlight.

Nothing to do but keep moving, so he got into the Jeep and went under the dash. It was going to be a little faster to hot-wire than the Lexus they'd brought him in. He pulled down the wiring harness and did the bypass. A small spark flashed as he touched together the leads that activated the starter. With the engine running, he got behind the wheel and moved out immediately.

He drove along the dirt road for a time, then turned off into the darkness, heading south. As he drove, he watched the horizon for the glow from the lights of the approaching police. Meeting them would slow him down, which he did not need, especially because he was far from sure that he had escaped. He may have been let go so that he could be pulled back. It was an infamous technique that had been used for centuries to break the will of prisoners. The Inquisition had used it. So had the Nazis and the Soviets, and Pol Pot.

He turned off road and headed due south. He was still looking for a distant glow, but not of the approaching troopers. What he needed most right now was to disappear into a crowd, and in this part of Texas at this hour, that meant the Blue Bonnet Palace.

He was driving across an ungrazed pasture, which caused the Jeep to bounce against one big tuft after another. It hurt like hell, but he continued moving as fast as possible. In the distance, he saw the flickering of light bars, six sets. No doubt the first responders had called for backup.

Soon, he could not only see the the palace's lighted parking lot and its famous blue neon sign, but also make out the light poles and the details of the signage. So he was about a quarter of a mile out.

He took the truck over to the road and drove into the parking lot, getting as close to the doors as he could. From there, he hurried into the structure.

The Blue Bonnet Palace was an entertainment complex consisting of a dance floor, a bar, a barbecue restaurant, and an indoor rodeo arena capable of seating about two hundred people. Flynn no longer had any idea even what day of the week it was. He was hurt, he hadn't had more than a snatched hour or two of sleep since first getting off the plane in Mountainville a week ago, and now he'd taken a hard blow to the head, and you didn't shake that off so fast in life as you did in the movies.

The place was jumping, with city folks from all the communities in the area mixing with cowboys and ranch hands from local spreads. There was a square dance being called for about fifty dancers, and their happiness, the confident swagger of the men, the beauty of the girls, all but broke Flynn's heart. He had danced here many, many times—with Abby, with many other girls—had known that same happiness here, in his innocent days. He could yet hear the echo of their laughter, as he and Eddie and Mac swung Abby across that dance floor, on those long-ago nights.

"Hey, there, fella—you sure you're okay?"

It was a smiling security guard. It was one of the old guys, Cord Burleson. He'd been working here from forever.

"Cord, it's me, Flynn Carroll."

Cord's eyes narrowed. He stared hard. "Holy shit, Flynn, you look a hell of a sight. You livin' in the wind?"

"No, man, I got roughed up."

"'Cause you look like you've been homeless for a good long while. I thought you were rich."

"Could you do me a favor and get Mac Terrell on the horn? I need to talk to that man."

"Mac?" The smile became tight. "He doesn't come up this way a whole lot."

"Well, I've got his number in my head, but I've lost my phone."

"Yeah, that and just about everything else. What the hell happened to your face?"

"A truck sat on it."

Cord led Flynn across the dance floor and back to the office. The last time he'd been in here, it was to get chewed out for trying a false ID in the bar when he was seventeen years old. Nothing had changed, not even the picture of LBJ on the wall behind Sam Carter's desk.

"Sam okay?"

"Hell yes. It's gonna take more than God to get him off to heaven. Way he figures it, this crazy place is better, and he intends to stay."

Sam had built the Blue Bonnet Palace back in the '70s. He'd been running it for at least forty years.

Flynn sat down heavily behind the desk and dialed Sam's ancient rotary phone.

"Sam Carter," Mac said, "what in hell are you callin' me for in the middle of the night?"

"It's me."

"Where are you, Flynn?"

"At the Blue Bonnet Palace."

"What in shit for? I thought you went back to Washington. I was just considering goin' up there and killin' your ass for getting my house burned up."

"Mac, can you come up here and get me? I've had some trouble."

"Flynn, you know where I am? I'm in your house with our friend Eddie. We're sittin' at your kitchen table, drinking what we believe to be a very fine bottle of your granddaddy's wine."

Incredibly, a break. Flynn hadn't had a whole lot of those. "Mac, put Eddie on."

Eddie took the phone. "Hey, Flynn."

"Eddie, I'm in serious trouble. I'm a prisoner. I need help."

"Okay. First, are you in immediate danger of your life?"

"No way to evaluate that. I need you to send a squaddie for me."

A pause. "Where are you?"

"Blue Bonnet Palace."

A longer pause. "You're free? You can walk out of there?"

"I can walk out of here, but I'm not free. I've been captured, Ed. How much has Mac told you about what's happening?"

"Enough to make me think he was completely insane. But you're worrying me, I have to say. Is my guy gonna go in harm's way? Because if he is, I'm coming myself."

"I think it's more dangerous if you come. You stay at the house. Don't even go home. Tell Mac to do the same."

"Me? How am I involved?"

"Send the squaddie. Fast."

"He's rolling in five."

As Flynn hung up the phone, he smelled food. He turned around, and there was Eileen Peeler, who had been running the pit out here since she signed on out of high school.

"Hey, Elly—why, thank you."

She put it down on the desk: a plate of brisket, sausage, beans, and a pile of steaming collard greens.

"Cord said you came in looking half dead. I'd say three-quarters. Not to mention starved. You've lost a few pounds, Flynn."

"It's been busy. I haven't had a lot of time to eat."

"All I can say is, I hope whoever was on the other side of the beating you took got some feedback."

"Oh, yes." Flynn took some of the brisket between his fingers and put it in his mouth. It was like going to heaven. "Sam's bringing in some serious beef."

"Goin' pit, too. That helps."

He looked at her, her full cheeks, the permanent joy in her eyes, and felt so very, very far away, as if he were watching her through the wrong end of a telescope.

"I believe Sam fired up that pit when he opened, didn't he?"

"Forty-four years now. You shut up and eat, honey. I don't know what you're up to, but you've just about used yourself up."

She left him then, and he ate and waited for the squaddie, and waited for the end of night, and wondered if either would ever come.

CHAPTER SIXTEEN

IN THE squad car, he had wanted to sleep, but the sense that death could come from above at any moment never left him now. Ever since Miller's murder, Morris had been playing Flynn. Watching him. Experimenting with his abilities by throwing various challenges at him. Learning him.

So the question now was whether or not Morris was still playing him, or about to reel him in. Had the ride to the "base" been expected to end in Flynn's capture? If so, then Morris would be throwing everything he had into this right now.

For his part, Flynn knew what he had to do next and where he had to go. He was focused on two places: Wright-Pat, where one intact disk was stored; and Deer Island, where he was fairly sure that the truth about Flynn Carroll was known.

The house blazed with light from every window. Flynn paused in the midst of the ghosts and memories that crowded his mind. This place was the center of his life, just as Mac's ranch had been the center of his.

He went in. "I need to arm up," he said without preamble as Eddie opened the front door to him.

"Man, you look like you've been bull-riding out there. And ended up under the bull."

"I'll comb my hair." He glanced at Eddie. "There's some people I need to talk to."

"The state boys are out there. You've got one guy who's headed for the ER up in Lubbock unless they give him to the USAF. He's in uniform, but he's not air force, apparently."

"Hold him."

"On what charges?"

"Title Eighteen terrorism. I'll get Washington to sign off on it."

"And that'll happen?"

"Yep."

"Because I'll be out on a limb. Far."

"I know it." He went down to the basement, struggling with the old house's steep stairway.

Eddie followed him. "You said you'd been captured, but you're here." Mac was close behind.

"Think of it this way: I'm wearing an ankle bracelet you can't see."

"That's the explanation for the leg?"

"I'm not sure. It's just—" He was done. He went down on the couch. "Lock us in."

"Lock the house?" Mac asked.

"Lock every damn thing, and I need you guys to stay up. Stay armed. If that door opens, don't aim, don't do anything, just start pulling your triggers. Flood it with bullets."

"I can't do that, it's against procedure."

"How I am coming to hate that word, Eddie. Shout the warning if you want to, but fire at the same time. You hesitate even a half second, we are all done." The room wavered. "Look in my armory, get me the Bull that's there, get yourselves the shotguns. There's an extreme likelihood that they're coming. They want me alive, so they aren't going to just blow the place all to hell." He was too dizzy to keep sitting, and had to lie back on the couch. "Sorry." He shot a hard glance at Mac. "God only knows what that antivenin of yours did to me."

"I keep the best stuff, you should know that."

He closed his eyes. "Yeah, I'm sure you do."

Eddie got a call, took it. "Okay," he said, "I'm rolling."

"We need you here, man."

"That was the state police. They're working four dead bodies out on Seventeen. That's what they found, Flynn."

"Shit!" Morris had gone back and killed them, despite the fact that they were his own people. "How?"

"Head shots. One had taken a bullet to the chest, then later the head shot that did him."

"Probably gonna find out that the weapon used was my other Bull. Morris got hold of it, I'm afraid."

"Who in hell is this Morris?" Eddie asked. "It's somebody I need to know about, that's for goddamn sure."

"We don't know," Mac said. "Who or what."

"I've been tracking him for a year. He's—shit, Eddie, you're out of the loop on this thing."

"He's another of these aliens? Alien crooks?"

"I pretty much told him everything I know," Mac said.

"Okay, then you're sucked in, ole buddy. Down the road, you'll need to sign some paperwork."

"Lotta folks are being killed, man. That should not be kept secret."

"I don't make the rules, but I understand them." Frustration choked his bitter words. "I have to say, if the public finds out how dangerous this is and how helpless we are, there will be hell to pay. You can't tell people that something can steal them in the night or kill them at will—or do worse than kill them—and there is nothing whatsoever we can do."

"Aren't you in a police unit that works on this?"

Flynn thought about just how to answer that. He considered the office full of earnest kids; Diana in her suite worrying about political correctness; "Geri," who could be anything. He considered it for a while, but said nothing.

Eddie's phone beeped. He looked at a message. "Gotta roll," he said.

"No, wait. Just wait, Eddie."

"Flynn, I—"

"Wait! You wait and you listen."

"Okay! Take it easy."

"I need you both to understand something. I need you to understand that I am that police unit. I'm the one guy who can put up some sort of a fight, and they know it, and they are hell-bent to capture me. Right now. Tonight. Soon as they can."

"What about CIA assassins, Delta Force, Blackwater, Navy SEALs?"

"It's been carnage. So far, I'm the only man who's been capable of surviving in the field against these creatures."

Eddie gave him a searching look. "Which is because of your speed?"

Flynn nodded.

"Then I don't get it." He gestured toward Mac. "When we used to quick-draw, Mac was faster. Half the time, I beat you."

"I've changed."

"How? You don't get faster as you get older." Eddie's phone buzzed again. "Yeah!" He listened. "Okay, I'll be there."

"Let me guess," Flynn said. "The FBI just showed up."

"Yes, sir, and they're kicking ass."

Diana had sent them, of course. "Just hear me out. I think what I am is a kind of breakthrough. Something was done to me that increased my reflex times dramatically. I don't have any memory of it. So it wasn't surgery, I don't think, but I could be wrong, of course. What I do know is this: The man who did it was a Dr. Dan Miller, and he did it at the Deer Island Biological Research Facility in Long Island Sound, and now that he's dead, there's a risk that I might be the only one of my kind ever created."

"Holy shit, man," Eddie said.

"You have to stay here and help Mac protect me. Until I get to Deer Island—and I have been notified that I need to get there with all haste—I absolutely must not be captured. Once I'm there, my best guess is that they're going to be able to re-create Miller's work using me as a template, and then we'll finally be able to create a police force of our own that can stand up against Morris. Hell, an army if we need it."

"I've got a police department to run. That's what I do, and I'm gonna keep doing it. And as to this Morris, you need to go public with this one, buddy. Put out an all-points. Wanted posters. The works. Interpol, all of it."

"We have turned over every stone in the past year. Every single stone. He's on wanted posters all over the world. Not for his real crimes, of course."

Eddie headed up the stairs.

"No!"

He hesitated. "Flynn—"

"I need you, buddy."

Eddie turned around. He looked suddenly smaller. Older. He came back down and dropped into one of the recliners that stood before the TV. He turned it on and began compulsively surfing.

"What about my wife, Flynn, the new baby? Don't tell me they're involved. If Ellen ends up like Abby—"

"Eddie, I'm sorry."

"What have you done to me?"

The words ripped at Flynn's heart. But this was war. More than war.

"Eddie, the fate and freedom of the human species are at stake. I've got to get to that island."

Eddie paused for a long time. Finally, he said, "I'm proud to be part of this. But you only have me for this one night. After that, I'm gonna take a leave and work on protecting my family."

"Very wise, and thank you."

"Flynn, it's always been a privilege to be your friend. It still is."

"Goes for me, too, buddy," said Mac.

"I've got to sleep, and I want to believe you're watching that door. Because if it starts to open, you've got maybe a second and probably less."

He knew that there was a high probability they would fail, but also that he was too exhausted to continue. He had to place his trust in them.

He lay back, holding the Bull on his chest—clutching it, really.

There were no dreams, just an uneasy darkness. From time to time, he was aware of his friends' voices. He was always aware of the pistol.

The night flowed on.

The next thing he knew, his heart was hammering, he was covered with sweat, his guts were heaving. Across the room, Mac and Eddie sat in two recliners that they had moved to face the stairs. They both held guns in their laps. They were both snoring, and that was what had awakened him.

He was not a man who angered easily, but when he did, other people could have definite problems, and he had to work hard to force down the urge to dump them both out of their chairs.

Carefully, in order to avoid waking them up, he took each man's gun and laid it aside. He knelt down behind them and between the chairs, took a deep breath, and shouted at the top of his lungs, *"Good morning, fools!"*

They both leaped up, snatching air, looking for their guns. Eddie was the first to figure it out. He said in a low, dangerous voice, "I thought you said it was safe during the day."

"Safer."

Mac said, "You do understand you've been asleep for a while?"

"What time is it?" Flynn figured Four o'clock, maybe five.

"It's nine thirty."

"Yeah, well—I'm sorry, then. Just don't both sleep at the same time, please. It's a real bad idea."

"Nine thirty, *Wednesday morning*, Flynn. You crashed on Monday night."

There was no time. "Morris is liable to go to Deer Island. Maybe he's already there, and if he is, it's endgame." Then another thought came to mind, and it was a terrible one. If he was broadcasting, he had already given away far too much. Even if all Morris could do was track him, he had to disappear from his radar, and right now.

"I need an MRI scan. Full-body. And a radiologist to read it."

"Mexico okay?" Mac asked.

"Eddie, got an idea?"

"My wife's brother-in-law is a neurosurgeon at MD Anderson in Houston."

"Let's go."

"That's a long drive," Eddie said.

Flynn nodded toward Mac. "Where's your nearest plane?"

"I don't have any planes."

"You have an air force. Where is it, on one of the ranches you don't own?"

"I only have my one little place, you know that." He made a call on his cell, said a few words, then cut the connection. "We fly in half an hour."

"Do you need me, Flynn?"

"Eddie, your first instinct was right. Stay here and protect your bride and that newborn. Tell you what. Get them to a big city somewhere far away from here. Go on a vacation to New York. Even better, London. Paris. Stay in a big hotel. Don't go out at night."

"I'll call my brother-in-law, get everything arranged."

Flynn stood before his old friend. He put his hands on his shoulders. "Thank you for everything, and God go with you guys."

Eddie nodded. He turned and started up the stairs. He stopped, turned back. "God bless, Flynn."

"Same back."

A moment later, the kitchen door closed. Flynn heard the lock turn.

"You got keys, too, Mac?"

"Yeah. Same keys I had when we were fourteen."

They drove to a small ranch about ten miles outside of town, a tin-roofed house and a weathered barn. No sign of life.

"Nice place," Flynn said.

"No, it's not."

"That's right, it's not. I won't ask what you do here, because I don't want to know."

"Indeed, you do not. But it would be wise not to inhale."

"Not a meth lab! Jesus, Mac, how low have you sunk?"

"It's a joke, son." He put his hands around his mouth. "Hey, Miguel! Compadre! You got gas in the buggy yet?"

The barn doors swung open to reveal a sparkling-new Cessna TT, as good as it got in the world of single-engine aircraft.

"Miguel Sanchez," Flynn said to the heavyset man coming out from beside the plane. "How the hell are you?" They'd gone to school together, up until Miguel dropped out to become a professional criminal.

"I'm good, man. You still enjoying my Range Rover?"

"It's ruined." He pointed a thumb at Mac. "His place."

"Figures. What happened, it get et by some damn exotic animal out there?"

"You could say that."

"I got used to those weird dogs, but man, that tiger—I don't like that thing."

Flynn liked Snow Mountain a good deal, but all he said was, "Yeah, I hear you." At that moment, he heard rumbling and turned around to see a black Audi convertible barreling up the dirt track that led to the house pasture. "Who in hell is that?"

"We're dealing with an airplane. You gotta plug in a pilot or the damn thing just sits there."

"No."

"Whaddaya mean, no? You gonna push it to Houston?"

"I'll fly it."

"The hell you will. I've been up there with you one too many times. Never again."

"We don't involve another innocent man."

"Well, I'm not goin' with you. I've got my Citation over at the airport, I'll take that. Bernie flies it, too."

"Mac, let me tell you what's goin' on." He glanced at Miguel. "You don't need to hear this."

Miguel didn't hesitate. He headed off and intercepted Bernie. They both stood about fifty feet away, watching.

"You take that Citation, you are going to your death."

"What?"

"I'm tellin' you, man, you gotta get your head around this. Morris will waste you the first chance he gets."

"What about, like, in the next ten seconds?"

"If he knows we're here, it's possible."

Mac looked down and hunched his shoulders, closing in on himself.

"Once we're in the air, he will definitely find us and will definitely strike. If we're going to make it, it's going to take some fancy flying."

Mac ripped off his hat and threw it down.

"We need to do this, Mac. Now."

He grabbed up the hat. "I know it."

They got into the plane.

Flynn looked over the controls. "Beautiful. This puppy can fly itself."

"I hope so, because if you're as good as you used to be, there won't be anybody else involved who can."

Flynn did the checklist, turned on the engine, and taxied across to the runway. The plane was light on the touch. A powerful little aircraft, probably capable of flying rings around most World War II fighters.

"Here we go." He pushed the throttle forward and felt the airframe shudder into life as they sped down the runway. He didn't know the exact rotation speed, but the plane made it very clear when it was ready to take off.

Once airborne, he turned east.

"Why is it tilting? What's going on?"

"Take it easy, we're okay."

He pointed the nose into the hard and unforgiving sun.

CHAPTER SEVENTEEN

FLYNN FLEW low with his radios and as many of his instruments powered down as he could safely manage.

Mac twisted in his seat. He peered out his window, then turned a pleading face toward Flynn. "Something wrong with the plane?"

"It's fine."

"Then why do I see trees going by?"

"We're flying under FAA radars, which means we need to stay below five hundred feet."

"Damn."

Flynn was flying with only the gravitational and magnetic instruments, primarily the compass. Keeping a low signal profile probably wouldn't deceive Morris, but it wouldn't help him, either. He dropped the nose a little more.

"Water tower!"

They skimmed it so close that the plane's wind stream buffeted them as it compressed against the white-painted surface.

Mac screamed and threw his head back, clutching his fists to his forehead.

"Guess you didn't see what town that was."

"Town? What town? Where are we?"

"Better if you watch the sky," Flynn said. "Any gleam, no matter how tiny."

"What do we do then?"

"Find out if your airplane's any damn good."

They flew on, keeping as low as Flynn dared, between three and four hundred feet. He kept a close eye out for radio masts and more water towers.

An hour passed.

"Flynn, will you answer me a question?"

"I'll try."

"Be honest."

"If I can."

"I think we both know I can't shoot the disk down, no matter how well I understand its design. I mean, we're talking about a seam a millimeter wide."

Flynn said nothing.

If he had been enhanced at Deer Island—and he was reasonably sure that was the case—maybe Mac could have been, too. But he wasn't going to say that. He knew his friend. Mac was unlikely to be comfortable, at least not until he knew what was involved, and right now, Flynn could not answer that question.

They flew on through the empty morning sky, powering across the great, flat expanse of Texas, small towns, long roads, and a bleak landscape passing below in majesty.

When they were still about twenty minutes from their destination, Mac said, "There." He pointed.

There was nothing there, just blue sky.

"Closing fast," Mac snapped. "Eight o'clock."

Flynn saw it, then. He pushed the throttle to the firewall and put the plane into a skidding roll, then dived almost straight down, forcing the disk, which had been coming up under the plane, to dart up past them.

"Shit, Flynn!"

Now at an altitude of perhaps fifty feet, he was flying along a highway, jinking across overpasses. He shot straight down the main street of a town with the disk close behind. Once out in the countryside again, he took the plane up to fifteen hundred feet as fast as he could make it go, then did a tight Immelmann turn and angled back down, passing under the disk, then doing another evasive turn at crop duster altitude over a field.

"Bag," Mac croaked. "Bag!"

"Glove box."

Mac yanked out a brown airsickness bag.

The small cockpit began getting hot. "They're gonna burn us!" Mac shouted.

"They're going to try to take the plane. They need me alive."

"What about me?"

"They don't care, buddy, but I sure as hell do." He pulled the throttle back and dropped the flaps, then pulled the nose up, causing the plane to pancake almost to the ground.

Now he grabbed for airspeed and turned, heading south. They needed a more populated area, and fast.

The plane began to shake. The stall horn started peeping.

"What's that?"

"Stall horn." Again, he pushed the throttle to the wall. As he did a series of barrel rolls, Mac screamed.

"Can it, I need to concentrate here."

"God, oh God, help me, help me now!"

Ahead, Flynn could see a shimmer of water on the horizon. They were no more than thirty miles from the Gulf of Mexico. "We're ditching in about five minutes."

"Ditching?"

"If we can hang in there that long."

The disk, maneuvering effortlessly, dropped down in front of them.

For a second or so, had he been in a fighter, Flynn would have had a shot at its flank, but not at that all-important lower fuselage seam. At an altitude now of just three hundred feet, he had little room to maneuver. Climbing would be certain death.

Again, the plane began to heat up.

"Is it on fire? What's happening?"

"I think they're pulling us into the thing."

"Shit, Flynn!"

Below them was a stretch of Interstate 10. He saw a series of underpasses. He headed down. If he had to choose between becoming Morris's captive or slamming into a concrete pillar, he'd have to choose the pillar.

They shot through an underpass, Flynn working the controls with breath and feather.

"Goddamn!"

They went through another. Overhead, the disk was pacing them.

The third one was narrower, coming up fast. Coming toward it from the other direction was an eighteen-wheeler. Closer. He could see the driver, his eyes practically popping out of his head, his hand hammering his horn.

A second later, it was all behind them. Then came another underpass. They made it through, and Flynn yanked the stick into his stomach, passing over an oncoming bus, then banking and heading once again toward the water, which was now spreading blue, covering half the horizon.

"Sailboats," he said to Mac. "Nice."

"You're insane!"

The disk was nowhere to be seen, but that meant nothing. He kept heading toward the water. "I think that's Brazoria down there. You can see Galveston out my window."

"Are we gonna ditch?"

"We're gonna stay within flopping distance of the water."

Where was the disk? Backed off, maybe, because they were over a populated area. Morris wouldn't want it to show up on YouTube.

He turned on his radios and navigation system and took the plane up to fifteen hundred feet. Somewhere, a traffic controller was going to be wondering where he came from, but with general aviation aircraft, they expected any damn thing.

They flew along the beach until he saw the Gulf Freeway, which he followed north. He called for clearance into Pearland Airport, and, to his private astonishment, they were on the ground a short time later.

They opened the gull-wing doors and climbed out. Mac looked back at the plane, shook his head, and practically ran into the airport's small terminal.

There was a pay phone, and Flynn called for an Enterprise car. Then, almost fearing to do so, he called Eddie.

"Flynn! You in Houston?"

"We made it. How are you?"

"All quiet on the western front."

"Just remember what I said, Eddie. Get the hell out of there for the duration."

"We're going to—"

"Don't tell me, I don't even want to know."

"You're all set with my bro. His name is John Shelton." He gave Flynn a cell phone number. "He's waiting for you, they'll get you into radiology immediately."

In the rental car, Mac said, "I sure would like to polish off a bottle of bourbon and do some smoke."

"You and me both." There were eleven texts from Diana on his phone. The first four were stern, the next five concerned, the last two frantic. He called her.

"Oh, God, Flynn!" Then, to another party he assumed was Geri, "It's him."

"Hey. I'm in Houston with Mac."

"And you're all right?"

"At the moment."

"When are you coming in?"

"Working in that direction." Until he was certain he could not be tracked, he had no intention of going anywhere near the office. "Listen, you stay careful. I'd live in the suite."

"That's what I've been doing. Both of us."

"Good. Stay far away from your house, your friends. Just completely isolate yourself." If he was being tracked, it wasn't beyond possibility that she was, too, or any of them.

"I'll do my best, Flynn."

"Any more on that blocked number?"

"No, and it's odd. Your cell phone records don't show any calls from a blocked number."

"So it's still a mystery."

"It is. I'm sorry."

Saying nothing of his suspicions about what the calls meant, he hung up.

"What did she say?"

"Not a lot."

According to the car's GPS, the Department of Neurosurgery was on Holcombe. He drove into the massive hospital complex and found the structure without incident. Once they were deep in the parking garage, he felt himself relax a bit. When they found a parking space, Flynn said, "We'll need to leave our weaponry in the car."

"That doesn't sound wise."

"I don't like it, either, but guns and hospitals don't tend to mix."

"Let's live in here," Mac said as they walked through the gray concrete mass of the parking structure. "We could have furniture brought in, and just set up housekeeping."

"It's tempting. Now I'm going to tell you exactly why we're here."

"You've got an alien implant you want taken out because Morris is using it to track your every move."

"They took something out of my leg in Fort Stockton, but I think it was intended to be found, so I'd get rid of it and think I was clean. Morris probably anticipated that I'd figure out he had to have some kind of a tracking device on me, and he was trying to set up a deception."

"Smart."

"But not smart enough. I hope."

They got to the elevator. Flynn looked for stairs, but seeing none, he pushed the button. Out of long habit, he listened to the motor as the car moved toward them. Being in places with no escape routes always bothered him. Elevators, always troubling, were potential death traps now.

They got to the seventh floor without incident, however. The waiting area was crowded. He called Dr. Shelton.

"Flynn Carroll."

"I'll meet you in Radiology. It's in the basement—there are signs."

Flynn hung up. This time, he found stairs, and they used them to descend to the lower basement, where the MRI scanner was kept.

"If we find anything, you're doing this, too," he told Mac.

"Not a problem. I sure as hell don't want that horror show in my head. What's he look like, anyway? I haven't seen him since Austin."

"Same general features, only a lot younger."

"Younger?"

"They can control a lot of things we can't. You've never seen one of them in person. I have. His name was Oltisis. He was in a safe house in Chicago until it turned out not to be so safe."

"What happened?"

"Morris did him. Burned down half a neighborhood in the process."

They arrived in a long, brightly lit hallway, which led to a smaller waiting room in which there were three people. Flynn would rather they hadn't been there, but the technician took him and Mac directly into the MRI chamber.

The enormous machine filled most of the space. Flynn said quietly to Mac, "Watch my back, I'll watch yours."

"Got it, boss."

A tall man with an enviable mane of black hair came into the room. "I'm John Shelton," he said.

"Flynn Carroll. This is—"

"I'm Frank James," Mac said.

Flynn let it ride. Mac's paranoia was legendary and, in this case, probably entirely justified.

"What are we looking for?"

"You understand that this is a national security emergency and it's classified."

"Ed explained that, yes."

"You and your technician will need to sign security agreements. There'll be someone here at the hospital to take you through that process tomorrow." Or maybe not. He hadn't told Diana a thing about any of this yet.

He lay down on the gurney and let himself be rolled into the machine. With the ceiling of the tube just inches from his face, he had to fight back claustrophobia. He closed his eyes. Anything could happen now. Whatever was in him might be designed to kill him if it was affected by a magnetic field. Or, if it was metallic, maybe it would move and destroy brain tissue. Maybe it was even designed to do that, on the theory that if Morris couldn't have him, nobody could.

The machine started. He'd had MRI scans before, the time he blew out his left knee falling while giving chase, and the time an irate husband had cracked him in the head with a frozen chicken.

The thudding and clattering of the magnets seemed to continue on for hours, while he drifted in and out of sleep. He reflected that he was like a fox being chased down by dogs. He'd started out in Mountainville full of confidence. Now here he was in Houston, desperate and exhausted, knowing that if he couldn't throw off his pursuer soon, he was caught.

In the machine, he lost track of time. His mind wandered. Again, he slept.

"Sir? Mr. Carroll?"

A tinny voice kept calling him. He been flying in a bright sky, peaceful, sunny and blue. "Yes?"

"Sir, you need to remain still. We have about twenty minutes more."

"Yes. Sorry." He waited then, forcing himself to stay awake, until finally they pulled him out.

"Sir," the technician said, "can you come with me?"

"Mac—er, Frank—come on."

They went into a smaller room, dimly lit and full of glowing computer monitors. Dr. Shelton stood before one of them. On it was an image of a brain. Flynn's brain. He stared at it, and into himself.

"Good news is, you have no sign of any cancer or any other health issue. This is a normal brain with an intact vascular system." He took a pencil up off the desk and pointed at a part of the brain. "This is the cerebral white matter."

"Yes."

"This area of high signal intensity? See the bright spot?"

Flynn felt sick. He felt angry. But above all, he felt a quiet sense of triumph. "I see it."

"That one, and this one here." He moved the pencil to another, similar bright area. "There are two of them, located bilaterally in the cerebral white matter of the frontal lobes. They are not natural formations, and they should not be there."

"What are they?"

"Small objects of some kind. Metallic, or they wouldn't look like this."

Bingo.

"Can you get them out?"

"I would think so. They're right on the surface, so all we'd need to do is make a couple of small incisions. We'd go in through your skull and pull them right out. It's a matter of a couple of hours. But I'd need you to answer some questions, first, because I'm flying blind here. I've never really seen anything like this."

"You've agreed to sign the security documents?"

"I have."

"So you understand that there would be serious penalties if you told anybody about this?"

"I do."

"Then I pronounce us doctor and patient. What you are looking at is a tracking system installed in my brain by a scientifically sophisticated enemy of the United States. I work in terrorism intelligence, and this device has compromised my freedom of action and endangered my life. So let me ask you, are you certain you can remove it?"

"If there are no unexpected problems, I would say so with a high degree of confidence."

"There may be problems."

"You sound like you've got some specific ideas."

"I do. The objects may be able to maneuver. They may be able to elude your removal attempt. Also, when you do remove them, I may suffer severe brain damage or even death."

"But they're just little bits of metal. Not even the size of BBs. Almost like grains of sand."

"Are you willing to attempt surgery?"

Dr. Shelton gazed for some time at the MRI image on the computer. Finally, he said, "If you're willing to take the risk."

"Doctor, I have no choice. And I have to tell you, this is a very dangerous situation. I don't want you to talk about it, not ever. Try not to even think about it. And please utilize the minimum number of personnel you can in the operating room. Now I'd like you to do the same analysis on my friend Frank here."

The technician reappeared, and Mac was put through the MRI scanner. In his case, the result was different. He had no sign of anything abnormal anywhere in his body.

"Doctor," Flynn said, "as this is an emergency situation, I'm going to need you to perform the surgery as soon as possible. When can you schedule it?"

"I'd need to look at my calendar, but—"

"No, sir, I'm sorry, but you don't need to do that. I'm requiring immediate surgery, I'm not asking for an appointment. I meant, how soon can you prep?"

Shelton thought about that. They were back at the computer, looking at Mac's enviably clean scan. "I can prep immediately. I think we could be ready within the hour."

Flynn felt a tide of relief flow through him. It was like being unexpectedly rescued from a certain death, he thought. If it was rescue.

"How long will the surgery take?"

"Given none of the complications you mentioned, no more than two or three hours."

Two or three hours. He wondered if he would live through it or not. He wondered if the things would move away from the surgeon's forceps. He wondered a lot of things.

"Let's go," he said. "Let's do this."

He followed Dr. John Shelton down the long white corridor and up an elevator to the surgical floor, his old friend with him. They came to heavy double doors marked SURGICAL SUITE. NO ADMITTANCE.

The doctor punched some numbers into a keypad. They went through the door and into the gleaming, unsure world of what Flynn feared would be a far more difficult surgery than Dr. Shelton expected.

CHAPTER EIGHTEEN

DR. SHELTON had a large office with a window looking out on a wide swathe of sky.

"When did you last eat?"

"Two nights ago."

"Do you take any medications?"

"No."

"No aspirin, ibuprofen, anything like that?"

"No."

"Liquids?"

"This morning. Glass of water."

"Okay. I'm not expecting this to be a problematic surgery. We will do what's called an awake brain surgery, and I'm going to ask you various questions during the process. We're not actually entering the brain, but we are going to be right in the cognitive region, so I'll want to be certain we're not disturbing anything as we work."

"I'll need my colleague present in the operating room. And keep staff to a minimum. Do not describe the objects or ask any questions about them that your staff may—"

"Sir, I'm going to need to stop you right there. I'm going to need my staff's full functionality."

"Then they're all going to have to sign security agreements. I'll need them to know that and be comfortable with it."

"I can assure you they'll sign. I have a resident, four nurses, and my anesthesiologist, Dr. Kampmann. Just a moment." He leaned into the intercom on his desk. "Julie, we're going to be doing a full staff pre-op with this patient prior to surgery. Can you let everybody know?" He turned his attention to Mac. "You'll need to prep and be in scrubs, and I'll want you to remain in a specified area of the operating room, and not to speak. Are those conditions acceptable?"

"Fine by me," Mac said. Flynn nodded.

They followed the doctor to the patient care unit, and Flynn removed his outer clothes, then placed his wallet, watch, cell phone, and keys in the locker provided. He gave Mac the key. "Don't come in here and steal all my money." When they were kids and Mac had been poor, he used to mug Flynn and Eddie practically every Friday night.

A nurse came in, a stocky black guy with a tight smile. These medical teams weren't used to surgeries coming at them unexpectedly, outside of ER. A unit like this ran on a complex, tightly controlled routine. "Okay, we got to shave your head," said the nurse. "This is the good part. You're gonna like you bald, lemme tell you. You'll never go back."

Now wearing nothing but a blue hospital gown and his underwear, Flynn was taken to a small, single-chair barber's station. The nurse said, "You get some of the women in here, it can be damn rough. But, you know, you want to get whatever's in there out more than you want to keep your hair. What you got, anyway? I got you pegged for an injury. Am I right?"

"You're right."

"I know this stuff, I've been on the unit awhile."

He rolled on surgical gloves, then lathered Flynn's head with barber's soap.

There was only a small mirror at the barber station, but Flynn could see himself in it, and as the CNA continued working, he saw a transformation from a man with short salt-and-pepper hair and hard eyes to a guy with no hair and even harder-looking eyes.

"There," the nurse said, "now you're ready to do some serious business. I want to wish you all the luck in the world."

Back in Flynn's patient cubicle, another nurse swabbed his head with iodine solution. Mac said, "You look scarier than hell."

"Yeah, big orange heads tend to be pretty scary."

"I meant, before she painted you. I'm telling you, the man who came across this room just now had death in his eye. It was damn impressive, I have to say."

The anesthesiologist came in. "I'm Dr. Kampmann. I understand that you're Errol Carroll?"

"Flynn."

"Okay, Flynn, now what we're going to use is a type of anesthetic that will deaden pain in your scalp and skull, but leave you fully conscious. There won't be any tranquilizer solution, but I'll be standing by with it, so if you feel too agitated or restless, just ask me, and I'll instill some into your IV. And we'll have general anesthesia ready as well. I assume that you've never had a craniotomy prior to this one?"

"I have not."

"At first, there will be a sound from the electric saw, which some patients may find disturbing. These are going to be two three-centimeter exposures over the affected areas. Just enough for the endoscope. You'll be able to see, hear, and respond to questions, but your head will be in a restraining mechanism, which can become uncomfortable. We don't want you to move, so if you have any discomfort at all, even an itchy nose, let us know."

"Will I be tied down?"

"Yes, you will."

"I need to see my colleague alone for a moment."

The doctor and the nurses withdrew, and Mac came in.

"I'm going to be restrained. If anything happens, anything you can't explain, any movement in the room—you can see their movement, can't you, at least somewhat?"

"I can see a flash off a windshield a mile away, but not those things, not like you."

"What can you see?"

"Things they move past. If they make a curtain flutter, no matter how slightly, I'm gonna see that."

"I think there's a high probability that they'll enter the operating room. They'll try to disrupt the procedure."

"Flynn, I've got to ask you, are you maybe broadcasting to them right now? Can they listen to you?"

"I assume so, but I'm not telling them anything they don't already know."

"I hope you aren't."

"Doctor, we're done," he said.

Dr. Kampmann had gone, but two nurses came and set up Flynn's vital sign leads and IV, then wheeled him down another bright corridor and into the operating room.

A warm sense of calm enveloped him. Dr. Kampmann had told him there would be no tranquilizer in the IV, but obviously that was not the case.

"Flynn, can you hear me?" Dr. Kampmann asked, upon entering the OR.

"Yes."

"Do you feel any nausea, any dizziness at all?"

"None."

They moved him into a bed that was completely surrounded by equipment. This was his second hospital visit in three days, and also the second in his life.

What seemed like only a moment later, he was coming back to consciousness.

"Can you hear me, Flynn?"

"Yes, I can."

"Do you know who's speaking?"

He looked toward the green-swathed face that was peering at him. "You sound like Dr. Kampmann."

Kampmann looked past Flynn. "He's back with us, John."

"Hey, there, Flynn. We have both incisions opened, and I'm looking at the foreign object on the left."

"Mac—Frank—are you here?"

"I'm here, Flynn. Back over here." Flynn glimpsed a green-gloved hand raised above an array of monitors.

"Flynn, can you please begin counting backwards from a hundred?"

Flynn found that counting backwards was harder to do than he'd assumed. He had to think carefully, and he was making mistakes.

"The first object is out," Dr. Shelton said. "It's a silver disk. There are cilia attached to it. A manufactured object."

Kampmann was looking at him. Flynn could see the questioning frown.

"Doctor, the objects need to be in sealed containers. This is very important."

"Sealed, yes, we can do that."

Flynn became aware of a distant, repetitive sound. "Is that a Klaxon?"

"Fire alarm," Mac called. "That's what it sounds like."

Morris was making his move, no question in Flynn's mind. "Can the doors be locked?"

"Nurse, see to it," Shelton snapped. "Flynn, please resume your count."

Voices rose outside. Soon, there came a smell of burning plastic. Then, over the intercom, "Doctor, can you close?"

"I need twenty minutes."

"They're asking us to evacuate the building. It's on fire lockdown. It's not a drill."

"I can't pull out—I have this patient's head wide open."

A nurse said in a shrill voice, "Smoke entering by the vents."

"Isolate us," Dr. Sheldon snapped. "Shut down oxygen." Then, more quietly, "Oh, God."

"We have fire in the ceiling, Doctor!"

"Closing up."

"Is it out yet?"

"One is out, sir. One is still in situ. But I have to pull out."

Flynn could not allow that. Whatever might happen, if Shelton stopped now, he doubted there would ever be another chance like this.

"Do not pull out, Doctor. This is a critical emergency."

"You got that right."

"Do not!"

There no reply. Was he still working? Flynn couldn't tell.

Hammering came on the door. "Fire department, open up!"

"For God's sake, tell them the patient's brain is exposed!"

"Is the second one out?"

Shelton didn't answer.

"Mac, help me here! Make him do this!"

A long stream of burning plastic came down from above. One of the nurses broke out a fire extinguisher and began attacking the flames as best she could.

Mac came pushing his way through the equipment. "Doc, you gotta do this. It's a national emergency."

"It's one man."

"The man is important, Doctor. I think you know enough to understand that."

Screams rose outside. The room grew dim. Black smoke seethed along the ceiling, shot through with deep red flickers. Once again, fire from above. Revealing, too. Morris had not felt able to send a team into a crowded building. Worth remembering.

"Where are we?"

"I told you I am closing up, whoever you are."

"No, Doctor," Mac said, "I'm so sorry, but you are finishing."

"Jesus Christ, put that down!"

"Mac, what're you doing?"

"You do it, Doctor, or she's gonna be wearing a second smile."

The nurse Mac had grabbed was limp with shock. Mac's knife gleamed at her throat.

Every particle of honor and decency in Flynn's body rebelled at the idea of doing it this way, but he saw no other choice.

A group of burning ceiling tiles fell into the operating room. One of the nurses screamed, tearing at her burning scrubs. Somebody else threw the doors open. Flynn was aware of great, dark shapes moving in the murk of smoke. Firemen. Then he heard roaring and saw that they were training a mist nozzle on the ceiling, enough to drive back the flames for a few more seconds.

"Okay, it's done. We're done."

"Let me see them. Both of them."

"Here, you, let her go. I am so sorry, Sylvie!"

"Who are these people, Doctor? Because this is insane—what's going on?"

"I don't know. Somebody get this patient out of here. He's closed, he can be evacuated."

"Give me the objects," Flynn said.

Shelton thrust the two bottles into his hands. These things were very different from the one that had been pulled out of his leg. They were the size of tiny buttons, their upper surfaces gleaming. Hanging down from their lower surfaces were long streams of cilia, so tiny and numerous that they looked like tendrils of smoke.

As he was wheeled out amid scores of firemen, nurses, and other patients under evacuation, Flynn watched mesmerized as, again and again, the two objects threw themselves against the glass walls of the bottles they were imprisoned in. Finally, they pressed themselves up against the glass like two mean little eyes and remained there, as close to him as they could get.

Waves of dizziness kept sweeping over him. Both doctors stayed with him on the fire stairs as he was carried down on a narrow portable chair.

"Mac," Flynn said, "I need you."

They had reached the lobby.

"This man needs recovery time," Shelton said to nobody in particular. "I need to get him into another surgery center."

"Mac," Flynn said, "you take these. I want you to go back to the parking structure and stay there. Go deep as you can. If it has a subbasement, use it."

"You think that'll stop the signal, because—"

"I have no idea."

"Flynn, Morris is gonna come after me. You know it, and I know it."

He had a point. "Tell you what, leave them in the car. Then—Doctor—where are we going?"

"Building Forty-two. You'll be in recovery there for about four hours."

"So put them in the car and come on foot to Building Forty-two. Get away from them, and stay away from them."

They went out into a throbbing forest of fire equipment, dozens of vehicles choking every inch of space around the building. Their pumps roared like an angry ocean. Brass and red paint gleamed in the sun. Two companies had extended their ladders to the roof, and pulsing, sweating hoses ran up both of them, managed by firemen at the midpoint, who fed hose to men on the roof.

"My patient is immediate post-op!" Shelton shouted. "I need him moved right now." He added to Flynn, "And I don't want to see you again, ever. You let me know where to send your records, I'll be glad to do that. But I do not want you anywhere near me or this medical center or any of its personnel ever again."

As he was lifted into an ambulance, Flynn saw two bodies in bags, lying on a sidewalk streaming with soot-blackened water. More ambulances were lined up, and he could see personnel with burns and other injuries crowding toward them.

"This patient is a just-closed brain," he heard a nurse say as the ambulance doors shut.

He was driven only a few hundred feet, and in minutes was in a second recovery room, this one jammed with patients, many of them wearing the same sort of turban that was probably on his head.

"Sir, we need to do a neuro check on you now. Can you tell me your name?"

This he had not expected. He couldn't leave his real name. He wasn't an official admission to the hospital. He did not remember which aliases he might have in his wallet. He'd just been through too much to do that with any hope of accuracy.

"Sir?"

He tried one of them. "William Haffner."

"Mr. Haffner, you don't have a bracelet."

"Fell off, I guess."

"What day is it?"

"Wednesday."

"Can you look at that clock and tell me the time?"

He looked up at the wall clock the nurse was indicating. "Four fifty-three."

She started to ask him another question, but a page caused her to go hurrying off. A patient just evacuated from neurosurgery was having a heart attack, and chaos was erupting.

Flynn realized that he was done here. The next thing to happen would

206 / WHITLEY STRIEBER

be that they would try to find him in the system, which was going to create a problem. Perhaps he should have anticipated that Morris would use this particular technique, but he hadn't. He'd been thinking exclusively in terms of an entry being made.

He had to find Mac, get out of here, and get out of this hospital complex as fast as possible. But right now, that was a problem. He was wearing briefs, a hospital gown and a thick head bandage. If he tried to leave like this, he would certainly be stopped. His wallet and other personals were in a locker on the burning surgical floor. No chance of retrieval.

Like the other recovery room, this one had lockers, and many of them were full. He might be able to pop one of the simple combination locks quite easily, but how would he know what he'd find inside? Women's clothes, clothes that didn't fit, the ID of a person who looked nothing like him. He might have to pop a dozen of them, even all of them. The minute the nurses noticed him up off his gurney, they were going to come running.

From where he had been left, he could see the big double doors that led into the room. That wouldn't be the right direction, not for what he needed to find.

As best he could, he turned. The door leading out in the other direction was narrower, not a public passageway.

When opportunity appeared, hesitation was always a mistake, so he pushed himself up off the gurney, waited for the dizziness to subside, and went through the door.

The staff room was about twenty feet long, with stacked lockers on both walls and a well-stocked break bar. The lockers were identified only with last names, and locked not with hospital-issue locks, but with whatever the nurses had brought in themselves. He looked from one locker to the next, trying to guess which one might conceal male clothing, and also might have an easy lock.

There must be a security problem here, though, because the locks were good quality.

No, this wasn't going to work. He'd have to get as far as possible dressed as he was. When he headed for the exit door at the far end of the room, though, he got a break, a door to a janitor's closet. Even better, it wasn't locked. He stepped in and turned on the light. There were six steel shelves of cleaning supplies, a number of mops and other equipment, and some buckets. There was also what he was hoping for, which was a steel locker. In fact, there were three steel lockers. Two were locked with hospital-issue combination locks, the third with an even simpler one, which had probably been bought off the hardware shelf at a drugstore.

Flynn did it first, and was rewarded with a woman's slacks and sweater and a pair of platform shoes.

He did the second one, but it was empty.

The third had the worst lock, and it took time to work. As he was testing its drops, counting from click to click to determine the combination, he heard voices outside.

"She said he came this way."

"Shit, he's gotta be in the stairway."

"Did you contact his doc yet?"

"How? You know who that would be? We got a John Doe here, and he's a damn head case."

There was a faint click as they went through the door to the stairwell Flynn would shortly need to use himself. They'd be back soon, he guessed, once they realized he hadn't been seen in the lobby. Almost certainly, they would do what they should have done in the first place, and search this room.

He found himself looking at a gray sweat suit. On the floor, a pair of track shoes. Even better, the suit had a hood.

The occupant of the locker was soon the proud owner of a hospital gown, and Flynn was in the stairwell, the hood pulled over his head.

He'd gone down a flight when he heard the tramp of feet. More than two people this time, some of them in heavy shoes. They were bringing security with them. Not taking any chances with a brain case.

Moving quickly, he ducked into the nearest fire door. He found another break room and another janitor's closet. He went in and got a bucket and mop, then went out onto what turned out to be an ICU floor.

"Hold it, this is a sterile floor," a nurse said. She was wearing greens, a hair covering, and bulging white shoe covers. All the nurses in the station turned toward him.

"Sorry, I'm due on the cleanup right now."

"Get out of here, then, or I'll have to write you up."

"Sorry, ma'am." He went to the elevator bank and waited for what seemed like the better part of an hour before an elevator finally appeared that had room in it for a janitor with a mop and bucket. He remained hunched under the hood, careful not to reveal the bandage.

Finally, he walked out through the jammed lobby and into the chaos that still filled the street. Fire ladders were being brought down, and hose pulled out of the neurosurgery building. Its front was streaked black with sooty water. All the windows on the top floor were shattered, the interior behind them a blackened ruin. Yellow barrier tape blocked the lobby doors, but a man with a mop and bucket went unnoticed as he walked through, heading toward the entrance to the parking structure.

He had to find Mac and get out of here and do it fast, or there was no question in his mind that the hunters were going to pick up his scent again.

He went down into the dripping, water-soaked darkness of the structure. In light, he might see a shimmer as the aliens approached him. In darkness, he would see nothing.

He stepped out onto the highest floor. The only light came from a single emergency lantern, its battery-powered glow almost completely faded.

"Mac," he said into the echoing silence, "you here?"

There was no reply.

CHAPTER NINETEEN

FLYNN HAD worked his way down to the lowest level he could enter. The two levels below this were flooded from the fire. It was on this level, also, that their rental car was parked. The silence was broken only by the echoing sound of water dripping from below. It was much darker here, too dark now to see any sign of the aliens at all. The emergency lighting was failing fast.

He was more helpless here than he had been on the other levels. The sound of the aliens' breathing was going to be drowned out by the dripping water. He could not expect to catch their distinctive odor over the stench of the fire, either. It was no place he wanted to be.

"Mac?"

Faintly from along the line of cars, he heard a clattering. He listened. The clattering had not been there a moment ago. Its source was about ten cars down on the right. He moved a little closer. Listened again. There could be no question. The sound was coming from the black Chrysler he had rented.

"Mac?"

No reply. He took a step closer. The rattling became louder. Was it Mac, somehow trapped in the car? And why make a noise like that?

"Okay, buddy, I'm here, I'm gonna get you out." He went close to the car, cupped his hands, and peered in the passenger-side window.

Something hit the glass so hard that it cracked. He jumped back, to see two gleaming silver buttons clattering against the inside of the window, which was already cracked in four or five places, as if it had been hit by stones that weren't quite powerful enough to break it. As he watched, all but frozen with surprise, they crashed into the window again and again, hitting it so hard that the car rocked.

The glass bulged. Pieces of it shot past his head.

He had exactly one choice. He ran as he had never run before, down to the far end of the floor and into the stairwell. He slammed the door, but it wouldn't shut properly. He ran up to the next floor and the next, then out onto the street level of the structure.

He threw open the door into the brightness of the exit lanes. A figure stood by the pay barrier, darkly silhouetted against the light flooding in from outside.

"What kept you?"

"Mac, run!"

He dashed past him and heard him come following, his shoes slapping on the wet pavement.

"What the hell?"

"They're out of the jars, they're busting out of the car, and I don't know their range."

"Aw, man!"

They ran down the middle of the street, finally stopping only when they reached the lobby of a building that hadn't been affected by the fire or the patient rescues.

Flynn was so winded when he stopped that he had to bend full at the waist and gag for air. Mac came up from behind. He was silent, breathing hard, too winded to speak.

"Keep going."

They dropped back to a steady trot, stopping again only when they reached a bus shelter. They waited for ten minutes, sitting hunched in the shelter.

"Were they doing that when you had them?"

"They were flying around in those jars so fast, you couldn't see them. I was lucky to get them to the car. I got the guns, though. Barely." He produced the Bull from the back of his waist.

Flynn took it. "This won't help now."

"How far can they go?"

He shook his head. "No idea."

He punched in the secure exchange, listened to the recorded warning, then keyed in Diana's number.

"Mac, where's Flynn?"

"This is Flynn. I'm sitting at a bus stop in Houston with Mac. We need transportation, it's as urgent as hell, and I don't want to stay on this line or any line." He told her the street. "Now, listen up. There's somewhere I need to go. I want you to smooth the way for me at Deer Island."

"Who do I call? What do I say?"

"Call the director. Tell him I need carte blanche on the island for at least a couple of days."

"What's going on?"

"It has to do with those blocked calls. It's important, maybe critical."

"Please tell me more, Flynn."

"Not on this line."

"Flynn, please."

"When I get to a pay phone, I'll fill you in. Also, I'll need to talk to Geri. Right now, just do what I need you to do. And I have no ID. It was lost in the fire."

"What fire?"

"You watch CNN?"

"That hospital? That was you?"

"We've got plenty to talk about, believe me."

"I'll get everything set up."

"Fast as you can."

She was true to her word. It was not ten minutes before a Houston Police Department squad car rolled up and collected them. The officer had obviously been told not to talk, because he remained completely silent during their drive to Ellington Field. It was a training facility and also the headquarters of the 147th Reconnaissance Wing, which flew Predator drones in the Middle East via satellite uplinks.

The guard station was manned by serious security. Understandable, given that a war was being fought in this quiet, sunny place.

The cop stopped and rolled down his window. One of the security personnel came forward and leaned in. She was well trained and on her game; Flynn could tell by the way she used her eyes.

"Identification, please."

Flynn turned toward her. "I'm Flynn Carroll."

She stared at him. Hard. "Okay. I got it. Let me clear you ahead."

A moment later, a guard vehicle pulled up in front of them. They followed it across the base.

"Mac, planning ahead. How much cash do you have on you right now?"

"Couple thousand bucks, probably."

Mac still ran a cash economy, which would shortly prove useful. Flynn watched the low buildings of the base. There was little activity. Once, a couple of airmen walked into the Noncommissioned Officers' Club. Shortly, a civilian sedan fell in behind the police car.

"Phone," he said to Mac, holding out his hand. He called Diana. "We're on our way to the flight line, and what I believe to be an offended general just pulled in behind us."

"That'd be General Stevens."

"Okay."

"He's pissed off as hell. He wants to yell, I guess. I can make him disappear."

"No, it's fine. Just so you know. If he goes off rez, I'll call you back."

They reached the Air National Guard building, a structure in need of a bit of paint. Once again, there was little activity, which was all to the good. Flynn got out of the car and told the cop to go back to Houston. The general stopped also, got out of his car, and came hurrying over.

"Excuse me, I understand you two people think you're taking my plane. I'm afraid it has a prior commitment."

"Good afternoon, General," Flynn said.

"I have no intention of letting unidentified civil service bureaucrats take this aircraft. If I have to, I'll call the Secretary of the Air Force."

"Bring your driver."

"My driver? What the hell are you talking about?"

"General, you've got two things to do right now: The first is to come in here with me and find us both uniforms. The second is to put on our clothes and fly to Langley AFB."

"Langley! What the hell for?"

"Because you're receiving an order from somebody who is empowered to do that."

"*You?* You're a—I don't know what you are. I need some identification."

"No, you don't." He glanced toward the driver. "You. Find us uniforms. Do it now."

"You can't impersonate air force officers!"

"General, you have no idea what credentials we carry. But you listen to me now, and you listen good, because if I have to say this again, it's going to be to a soldier with no stars on his collar. Do you understand this?"

"This is extremely irregular."

"What you are dealing with right now, sir, is the single most urgent national security matter that you have ever encountered in your career, or will ever encounter. Do you understand this?"

"I have no idea who you are or what you're supposed to be doing."

Again, he said to Mac, "Phone." Then, to the general, "If I have to make this call, your career is over."

They went eye to eye. The general was pure determination. Then they really connected, and Flynn watched a familiar surprised confusion come into his face. An instant passed, and he took a step back and cleared his throat.

"Very well," he said. He cleared his throat again.

The driver reappeared, and he and the three of them changed in an office. The general was pretty well swallowed in Mac's clothes, but the driver, who was a tall kid, did all right with Flynn's sweat suit.

"Have a pleasant flight, gentlemen."

"Thank you," the driver said. The general glared at him.

After they went out onto the apron, Flynn told Mac that they were taking the general's car. "We're going to Hobby."

Mac didn't ask any questions, which was good. He was becoming more efficient at this.

The general's Buick stood where it had been left in front of the building. It was unlocked, but they had no keys to start it.

Mac used to be better at wiring cars than he was. "How long for you to wire it?" he asked.

"They're more complicated than they used to be, and it's not something I do a lot of anymore."

"You did good with my dad's Mercedes. Why don't you give it a shot?"

"You're smarter, you do it."

"Don't undersell yourself, you'll be faster."

Mac went under the dash and had the engine turning over in four minutes. To anybody watching from above, they would have appeared to linger in the parked car a little longer than normal, but hopefully not long enough to arouse suspicion.

On the way to the airport, Mac asked, "May I know what we're doing?"

"Changing the world."

CHAPTER TWENTY

AS THEY drove off the base, Mac was unusually quiet.

"You trying to come up with a question that makes sense?"

"I guess I am. What I'm thinking is you might've gotten those two guys killed just now."

"I agree."

"You sent them in harm's way without so much as a prayer book."

"I'm not sending them into any more danger than I'm going to take on myself. Less, probably."

They drove on for a while. It was six fifteen, and Houston's notorious traffic was just that—notorious.

"How much have you lost on this so far, Mac? What with your house and all?"

"Four million."

"So, maybe a million."

"No, it really is four. The paintings were originals."

"They're forgeries."

"That is not true."

"Manet was right-handed. Your forger painted with his left. Who were you planning to sell them to, billionaire morons? I didn't know there were any."

"Gifts for *drogos*."

"So, a grand for the paintings. Tell you what I'll do. I know how hard you have to work for your money."

"Which you do not."

"I do not. So I'll rebuild your place for you. As long as you don't cheat me, I'll pay the bills."

"My accountant—"

"He outta jail?"

"Four more months."

"Any contractors on the outside, but not on the lam?"

"I'll need to check."

"We'll use my accountant. My contractors."

"I get that."

Flynn watched the passing cars and kept his eye on the low, thick clouds, looking into their faint glow for any sign of a shadow. Mac sat with his knee up against the dashboard. His long face was usually ready to crinkle into an affable smile, but that easiness was gone now. He, too, stared into the empty night.

"I miss my dogs."

"Those weren't dogs."

"Yeah, I guess not. Alien animals."

"Those were people who'd been genetically mixed with dogs."

"Oh. That must be why I liked them so much. I like people."

"Then you like Snow Mountain, too."

"Only see him once in a while. He liked Mozart. He liked the Stones. I used to hire bands and quartets from over at Sul Ross University to come play for him."

"What did they think of him?"

"The kids? Nothing. They never saw him. But he was there."

"Who did they see?"

"I'm more of a narcocorrido type of guy, so, nobody, basically."

He tried to imagine the scene, a string quartet or a rock band set up in Mac's house pasture, playing to the night, with a tiger way back in the dark somewhere, listening blissfully.

"I guess they thought they were playing for a rich, cantankerous eccentric, then?"

"I guess they did. I never really thought about it. There's a lot of eccentricity out in our neck of the woods, as you know."

"All too well."

"I think it's the Marfa Lights. They make us crazy." He paused for a moment. "I want to go home, Flynn. I'm not cut out for this."

"I wish it was safe for you, buddy. I wish to God it was. You stick close for a little while longer, I'll make it safe. I promise you that."

"When I went back there and saw my house burning up, I really, seriously thought about killin' your sorry ass, Flynn. But I love you, goddamnit. You're a good friend and always have been. So here's what I think: Let's kill ourselves a damn alien and do it soon."

"I have a plan."

"You always do. Only remember that only some of 'em work. Just never forget the freight train."

When they were kids, Flynn had devised a plan to slow down a freight so they could hop it more easily. The result of their attempt had been a fifty-three-car derailment.

"I believe Eddie set that one up."

"Your idea, Flynn. Your idea."

Flynn had been way overconfident, thinking the engineer would notice the switch signal and stop. He didn't notice a thing, and rolled the whole consist out onto the siding at forty miles an hour. Nobody was hurt, fortunately, but seven thousand chickens had escaped into the night.

That was then, in the delicious, lingering summer that had been their boyhood. This was now, and this was a time of storms.

They parked and walked silently to the terminal. As they exited the parking structure and were briefly exposed to the sky, Flynn felt a tremendous sense of vulnerability. If only he could know for certain how capable of following him and reinserting themselves the implants were. He knew now that nobody had been there to insert them in the first place, which was why he had no memory of it. They'd been released at some point, probably when he was at the Miller place, and entered on their own. He recalled feeling a sudden, sharp headache there, just as he was leaving for Wright-Pat. It had passed quickly and he'd thought no more of it.

He remembered the old Hobby terminal from his childhood, flying in here with his dad to watch him do his business with the big oil companies downtown, which chiefly consisted of making sure they were reporting his royalties accurately. It was still a battle, but Flynn had others to fight it now.

"We need to find a pay phone, because Diana's going to have to get us on the plane from her side of the line."

"I've got plenty of cash."

"We're both packing heavy heat and have no luggage, and I have no ID. And what happens when you show your license?"

"Depends on which one."

"You have more than one on you right now?"

"I've got seven on me right now."

"Give me one, and we can buy the tickets."

The ticket counter was empty. "Two for Dayton," Flynn said.

"Credit card and ID, please," the agent replied, standing up from her stool and going to her terminal.

"Cash," Flynn said. He handed over the two IDs.

She looked at them, blinked, and looked up. "I could give you military. You got air force IDs?"

Mac pointed a thumb at Flynn. "We don't have those with us, because this gentleman here is a professional fool."

She smiled, then looked again at the driver's licenses. "Are you two twins?"

"Yes," Flynn said.

"And in the air force together. I think that's cool." Her smile widened. "I'll write you up military—that way you won't have to bicker. I know how twins like to bicker."

A few minutes later, they had their tickets on the last flight out, a 9:20 through Atlanta.

"I don't look a thing like you, Flynn."

"They see a lot of people. This time of day, they're looking right through you."

"You're one of the most hideous men I've ever seen. I'm very insulted."

"Mac, you know what you look like? You look like a wizened, shifty-eyed cowboy who got shrunk by too much exposure to the sun."

"You realize how much of your height is in that neck? My dogs mighta been part human, but I wouldn't be surprised if the aliens didn't start you out right in your mother's womb, and make you part turkey."

"You need to quit using that shoe polish or whatever it is you're putting on your hair. Spring for a dye job."

"If I get my hair dyed down in Marfa, everybody in West Texas is gonna know."

"You look like somebody pushed you up a chimney."

"Women happen to go for my hair."

"Women only go for you because they find your criminal ways exciting."

"Yeah, they do get off on murder stories."

"Don't tell me that. Then I'll have to tell Eddie, and he's gotta question every damn one of 'em."

"Okay, so I didn't tell you."

"Let's find us that phone."

"Use my cell."

"Give it to me." He removed the SIM card and handed it back. "I'll keep the card for now."

Mac said nothing. He understood perfectly well what Flynn was doing, covering their tracks. This was also part of the way he conducted his life, whichever side of the law he happened to be on at any given time.

"We oughta get us some throwaway cells."

"You will find that they don't sell them in airports." He located a pay phone and dialed Diana's home number directly. He did not go through the secure network.

It rang once, then twice, then a third time.

He hung up.

"She's not there?"

"Three rings. Our prearranged emergency signal. She hears that on her landline, she knows there's big trouble."

"I thought we were out of trouble."

"We're not out of trouble." He dialed again. This time, she answered midway through ring one. He listened as she accepted the charges on the call.

"What do you need?"

"Back door through Hobby, then I need to see General Sam Dickerson at Wright-Pat. We'll be landing in Dayton at three this morning. I want to see him at seven. Still no ID and no money."

"Can I get some kind of an update, Flynn?"

"We're alive."

"I'm glad you are, because I thought Morris had you."

"I thought he had you."

"Why?"

"The way I learned that you'd returned to Washington was from him."

"How could he know my movements?"

"He figured it out. Not too hard, though. Where else would you be going except to your safest place?"

"I need to be sure we're secure here."

"You got that right. Is Geri still with you? Because I have a question for her."

"She's always with me. In my office right now. I'm sitting in my suite, wishing I were alone." He could hear the crackle of tension in Diana's voice.

"Trouble?"

"She doesn't sleep, ever. She just sits there, watching me. She doesn't read, watch television. Hardly eats. Just stares."

"She's scared."

"I think she's absolutely furious about what happened out there. She considers us dangerously incompetent, and she wants in the worst way to go home."

"Put her on."

A moment later, he heard Geri's voice. "Yes, Mr. Carroll?"

"You know what a tracking implant is?"

"Yes."

"Two of them were removed from my head today. They seemed to have some sort of an ability to move on their own."

"They do. Once they're synched to an individual's genetic identity, they can be released and they'll find their target on their own."

"How much range do they have?"

"Range? You mean, how far can they broadcast a signal?"

"No, how far away do they have to be before they can no longer find their intended host?"

"Far. Ten, twenty thousand miles."

"All right. How can they be destroyed?"

"Heat above two thousand degrees."

"How about blowing them up or smashing them?"

"They're holographic. Even a small bit of one will retain the functionality of the whole."

"What about containing them?"

"With things you manufacture? Some of your safes might work. I'll look into it."

"Unfortunately, we didn't understand their capabilities and put them in a jar."

"That wouldn't work."

"It didn't. When I last saw them, they were in the process of breaking through the glass in a car window. We ran. Within fifteen minutes, we had transport and were ten miles away. I'm now twenty-two miles from the spot where I last saw them. What's my exposure?"

"All of this was in populated areas?"

"Yes."

"It's possible that they've lost you for a while."

"How long?"

"They'll be doing a grid search right now. Your advantage is the populated area. They'll need to get pretty close to you before they can detect you against all the background noise."

"Listen, Geri, we sort of know each other."

"I would say we do."

"So I need to give you some friendly advice."

"And what would that be?" He heard the rigidity that had come into her voice. She was the authority figure here, at least in her own mind.

"We're not incompetent. Just uninformed and technologically backwards. Forcing us to use only our own locally produced equipment is tying our hands."

"You threw my pulse weapon onto a roof. My weapon, registered to me. What if somebody tossed your gun away? You'd have to report that. You'd have to take a reprimand."

"I'm sorry about that, but it didn't work, and that was dangerous to all of us. But some things do work. Those implants, for example. I'd love to be able to get something like that into Morris. And the disks. So I want to repeat—we need a disk."

"That's all gap-distant technology, meaning that your science is so far behind on it that you can't understand it even if it's explained to you. Exporting technology like that for any reason is highly illegal, and licenses just do not get granted. The latitude for abuse is too great, not to mention the cultural disempowerment that's involved. Scientists who see something so potent and so advanced that they can't even begin to understand its most basic principles, lose hope. They become scavengers."

"Look, your technology is so advanced—the stuff that works—that this one guy is potentially more powerful than all the military forces on Earth."

"He has vulnerabilities."

"What are they, exactly?"

"One disk and no ability to resupply without letting the main body of biorobots know where he is. He's a full biological running a squadron of biorobots who know nothing about what's happening on Aeon, and they must not find out, or he's going to lose control of them. He can't go back. What he has is all he'll ever have."

"That's true now, but what about next year? The year after? We're talking Cortés taking the Aztec Empire with five hundred Spaniards. You know that story?"

"It's a great myth that higher ethics follow scientific advancement. Lower planets are vulnerable."

"Morris and a few hundred robotic entities could end up owning this world, so I have to tell you, I don't think your scruples matter just now. Earth is on the line, so *give us what we need.*"

"Flynn, the truth is that we don't have the resources."

"Not one spare disk? A couple of implants?"

"Getting things off-planet is the problem. All of our movements are resisted, and as far as Earth is concerned, we must not be followed here by the main body, as I said." She stopped. He heard a swallowed gagging sound that told him she was fighting back emotions of great power.

He realized, really for the first time, how much courage it had taken for her to come here.

"Just do what you can." He hung up. "Let's go," he said to Mac. "We've got a flight to catch."

Diana had done her administrative work well, and they were escorted through TSA security by the station supervisor. As they stepped away toward their gate, she saluted them.

"What's that about?" Mac asked.

"She's probably been told we're on some sort of crucial mission."

"True enough."

The plane was crowded. Given what Geri had explained to him, that was a good thing. As best he could, Flynn leaned back, forcing his substantial frame into the narrow economy-class seat.

"You know what their greatest problem is?"

"Whose?"

"Aeon's. They didn't just invent a new life-form, but one that's also stronger, faster, and more intelligent than they are. Their biorobots are an evolutionary leap, and they're going to replace their creators. What's happening to the people of Aeon is what happened to the Neanderthals. A better species is pushing theirs aside."

Flynn thought, *And maybe ours, too. Maybe a lot of species.* How ironic that a civilization far away and so deeply hidden in the vastness of space had created something that would turn out to be such a scourge right here at home.

He was a cop, though, not a soldier—at least, not yet. Right now his job remained what it had been from the beginning: Get the

lawless element under control. Contain Morris and roll up his operation.

The plane flew on, as did Earth on its mysterious journey, each bearing its cargo of innocent lives into an uncertain future.

CHAPTER TWENTY-ONE

THE MOMENT they entered their room at an airport motel, Mac fell onto the first bed he reached. He was snoring before he hit the mattress.

Flynn had gotten a sewing kit from room service and cut off his various bandages. There was swelling on his scalp, as well as an angry red knot at the center of the incision the doctor in Fort Stockton had made. Could be the beginning of infection. He'd keep a close watch. Next, he went into the bathroom and stood in front of the plastic sink. He took a long look at himself in the mirror. Stone bald, he looked frightening, no question about that. The surgical wounds were held together by gleaming staples, two in each incision. He was way too close to Frankenstein.

He lay back on the empty bed, wondering what the future held. Morris had to guess that he'd go to Deer Island. Would he also come? Of course he would.

He slept a shallow, worried sleep. Every sigh of breeze, the tapping of a tree on the bathroom window—any slightest sound brought him instantly awake. He hugged his gun like the life preserver that it was.

They got up at six to a room service breakfast, which they ate in silence, the way soldiers did before a fight. The trip to Wright-Pat was a familiar one, and once again, Diana had paved their way past the guard post.

Flynn knew his way around Wright-Pat, of course, and they were in General Dickerson's office at exactly seven.

Dickerson was younger than Flynn had imagined he would be, more the age of a colonel than a general. He had the easy manners of a man used to command, and the contained watchfulness of somebody who knew more than a few secrets. When Dickerson smiled as he crossed his large office, Flynn knew immediately that care was to be taken here. This man could be hard and he could be difficult.

"Gentlemen! The two mystery men. I'm curious as hell, I have to admit." His handshake was perfunctory, almost as if he had forgotten it even as he extended it. "Please, sit down." He hurried back around his desk, a wary officer manning a battlement. "So, may I know why you're wearing the uniforms of a service to which you do not belong?" The smile reappeared for an instant, and then was gone.

"We're trying to stay alive," Flynn said. "It's been hard."

"You're sure as hell beat up, Mr. Flynn. Or Colonel Flynn. I'm not sure what to call you."

"Just plain Flynn will do." He gestured toward Mac, who was hunched up in his chair like either a scared possum or a coiled rattler, take your pick. General Dickerson would never guess that this was a man who had played polo with human heads, or at least was willing to. "We're just a couple of cops from Texas, but we've gotten ourselves into a heap of trouble."

"A heap of it," Mac said.

"We need your help, sir. There is a flying disk—an alien craft—that is going to kill us if we don't shoot it down. Basically."

Surprise widened Dickerson's eyes, followed by a wary narrowing. "Are you nuts? How did you get in here?"

"Don't even go there, General, please. There just isn't time. I've had bodies autopsied in your facility here. I've incinerated them in the burn room. That airman you lost the other week—that was on my watch, I'm sorry to say."

"The need-to-know barriers are so high, I just didn't know where to go with this when I was told you were coming."

"We've got to cross those barriers. Officer Terrell and I have been working on this for a while. We're trying to clean out a nest of rogue aliens without panicking the public. And we've gotten ourselves into a pickle. According to our counterparts in the alien police force, the leader of this criminal enterprise is a real psychopath. He's aggressive as hell. Very frankly, General, it's a battle to the death, and we're losing."

As if to himself alone, General Dickerson nodded. He closed his eyes. "I think you probably shouldn't have told me a lot of that."

"I need help. From you. Now."

"What can I do?"

"You have a disk. We need to see it."

"That might be hard."

"If you stall for even a minute more, I'll have you up on charges of high treason."

The general held up his hands. "I'm not stalling. It's just that we don't have it here. I'm going to send you to another facility. We only have a little bit of this still here at Wright-Pat. Air Materiel does metallurgical and functional analysis, and we have the exobiology section you've apparently dealt with. But operations are conducted from another base entirely. You've probably never heard of it. Deer Island."

Flynn gave no sign of the effect that name had on him. "No," he said carefully. "We have not."

"I'm going to send you there to meet Colonel Adam Caruthers and his team. It's possible that they can help you in some way, but I can't tell you that, because I don't actually know what they do. Just that this is their baby. When the public says they see jets chasing flying saucers, those are the colonel's boys."

"Can they shoot one down?"

"Again, I'm not concealing anything from you when I say I don't know. I'm not need-to-know on that information."

"It's dangerous for us to travel. Very dangerous."

"It's the only facility of its kind in the world."

"Where is it?" Mac asked.

"Deer Island is in Long Island Sound."

Mac started to talk, but Flynn motioned him to silence.

The general offered transport, but Flynn thought they were safer sticking to the crowded airlines.

On the way back to Dayton International, they stopped at a Target and bought civilian clothes. As autumn deepened, it was getting colder, so they got jackets as well as jeans and sneakers, and Flynn bought himself a baseball cap to cover his wounds.

In the rental car, Mac said, "I'm not a cop, and I'll never be a cop."

"Sure you are. You're a cop, and a good one."

"I don't have that gene, I'm sorry."

"I've read your DEA file. You're as good an undercover as they've got."

They rode on, Mac saying nothing further.

"Anyway, I know what you really do. I know you make a little on the side, but most in your sort of business do. It's not blood money—that's what's important. I also know that you're not rich like you make out. There is no Lamborghini in Marfa, for example. And your brother was no damn good and that broke your heart, and you didn't screw Cissy Greene, but you did protect her from a very abusive father until she figured out how to fend for herself. I know you, Mac."

"Aw, shit."

"And I'm proud to."

They flew in another blessedly jam-packed jet from Dayton to La-Guardia Airport in New York. On the flight, Flynn reflected on Deer Island. It had started out as a biological warfare research facility, but obviously its mission had expanded to include a major alien research center.

They had a layover at LaGuardia, and ate a quick meal at a Five Guys burger stop.

"I'm still bone tired," Mac said, biting into his hamburger. "Feel like I didn't sleep a wink."

"You could go into the city, stay there until it's safe to return home. Probably be okay holed up in a big hotel."

"While you go in harm's way alone?"

Flynn nodded.

"Nothing stops you. Nothing slows you down, even."

"I need to get this bastard."

"Mano a mano ain't gonna cut it, my friend. You need an army of tough sonembitches who know how to work close."

"When we are close, we are going to need a master sniper. As you know."

"I'm not gonna get that seam. Nobody is."

"Maybe not."

"Definitely not. You don't need a sniper. Not a human one, anyway."

"Not entirely."

"What's that supposed to mean?"

"Maybe nothing. We'll see."

Mac knew Flynn too well to continue to question him. But after a moment, Flynn decided to say a little more. "Mac, I need to ask you something and tell you something."

Mac raised his eyebrows.

"Have you recently had a headache? Bad, but it faded almost immediately?"

"I don't have headaches."

"Because I think I know how these implants go in. When I was leaving the job I did in Pennsylvania—it was a good haul, I got four dead—I got this fierce headache." He paused, remembering the confident Flynn of those days. The great alien hunter. On that night, he'd actually thought that he cleaned up the problem. "Anyway, as I was driving out, I felt a terrific pain that started in the top of my head and radiated down into my face and neck. It was so bad, I thought I was having some kind of stroke. But then, just like that, it was gone. I think that's when the implants went in, right under the skin and through the skull without leaving a mark. I think that's how it feels. So have you had a headache recently?"

Mac leaned back and closed his eyes and thought. "No. Definitely not."

"If you do, tell me."

"I sure as hell will. I'm gonna go apeshit if I get something like that in me."

"We can get them out. I'm living proof." He thought of the objects racing back and forth in endless, ever-changing search grids, hunting him down.

They took a commuter flight up to Bridgeport. The moment they disembarked and entered the terminal, a tall, grim-faced man appeared, walking toward them. He was jammed into a dark business suit, his build and bearing broadcasting not only military, but elite military. He looked like a Delta Force operator crammed into civvies he didn't really know how to wear.

"Gentlemen," he said, "please come with me." He turned and walked swiftly toward an alarmed door marked NO ADMITTANCE. He pressed a code into the keypad, opened the door, and stepped aside.

This was airport operations, where pilots checked in, filed their plans, then went out to their aircraft. The man led them into the supervisor's office, which was small and windowless, with three metal chairs and a cluttered desk. There was a picture of Governor Wade on the wall, a flight school diploma, and another picture of a man shaking the hand of what appeared to be a foreign dignitary.

"We're going to borrow Mr. Reilly's office for a few minutes, gentlemen. Please sit down."

Flynn and Mac sat on two of the steel chairs. Their host, if he could be so described, took the third.

"I'm Adam Caruthers," he said. "This is the first time in the history of this program that any outsiders have been handed off to me. May I see your identification?"

"Have you been briefed?"

He held out his hand.

Flynn reflected that secret bureaucracy was a labyrinth, full of dead ends and empty spaces. The empty spaces were between the ears of the bureaucrats.

"Colonel, I think you have been briefed, and therefore you know perfectly well that I'm not carrying ID at present, and you know why. Also, I don't think you're at the top of your chain of command, so I would suggest that you cease diverting from the order you have received and carry it out."

Caruthers's eyes stayed hard. Real hard. "Gentlemen, I'm going to tell you the real reason for the extreme secrecy we maintain."

"We know the reason."

He raised his eyebrows. "Do tell."

"There are all kinds of aliens out there, and a lot of them do a lot of strange things, not just the ones we're having trouble with. Like abducting people out of their homes, and the air force can't do a thing about it."

"That's actually pretty accurate. It's illegal activity, and we can't enforce against it. As I understand it, you're a specialized policeman who deals with matters like this, so maybe you can help us."

Flynn said, "I deal with aliens who steal people and murder them, and do worse."

"The ones we have had interaction with generally return people."

"Fortunately, the group we're dealing with is small. If we can eradicate them now, their numbers won't grow. Like getting rid of a cancer while it's still small."

"I thought cops put bad guys in jail."

Flynn said nothing.

"Perhaps we'd better go over to the island, Flynn. May I call you Flynn?"

"That's my name."

They walked down a corridor to the back of the terminal building. A short distance away, Flynn saw a helicopter sitting on a pad.

"Recognize that?" he said to Mac.

"I sure do."

It was the same type of ultra-sophisticated chopper Morris had used during their first encounter, at Lake Travis near Austin. Back in the good old days, before he had the disk.

"I'm surprised that you recognize it," Caruthers said. "It's still a secret technology."

"Except it's sitting here on a helipad at a public airport, plus one was used against us by the alien we're tracking. It happened last year outside of Austin."

"The one that was stolen."

"And destroyed, because we destroyed it."

They got into the chopper. The pilot, wearing a black uniform with double lightning strikes on its patch, wore his visor closed. Normal enough, but Flynn would have preferred it to be open. As the engine whined into life, Flynn's instincts were starting to alarm.

Inside the chopper, there was almost no sound. Unlike every other helicopter he had flown in, this one's wing didn't pulsate, but rather moved smoothly. Therefore there was no characteristic chopping sound, but only a steady, high-pitched whine and the whistle of wind blowing past the cockpit canopy. The engine was entirely silent.

As Deer Island slowly emerged out of the haze of the autumn afternoon, Flynn examined the ground. The place seemed surprisingly familiar, and he wondered at once if he'd been here, but had his memory of it erased. There were hypnosis techniques that could do that.

He memorized the layout of the island, noting three clusters of buildings: one to the north that consisted of four structures, one to the south with two, and a more substantial main building.

They circled the main building, then dropped down onto a helipad across the narrow road that passed in front of it.

"We have a bit of a ride to our end of the island," Caruthers said. "We've been here only a few months. Our operation back at Wright-Pat was a good bit larger, but I guess downsizing's pretty much the order of the day."

"And Biology's at the other end?"

"Yes."

"Did you know Dan Miller?"

"Guy who got killed by those drifters in his woods? I knew of him."

"What did he do?"

"No idea."

They arrived at a cart shed and took an electric golf cart around the headquarters building.

The facility was, to be honest, a dump.

Caruthers seemed to read their reactions, or expect them. "Sorry we're not more impressive," he said. "I don't know about bio, but the hardware program has been in a holding pattern for years. Most of our contact is with the aliens popularly known as the grays. Contact, actually, is a bit of a joke. It's hardly that. I think you'll find that alien species aren't exactly forthcoming about much of anything. They haven't told us word one about our disk, and we've had it for more than fifty years."

"We have the same problem. Our guys won't detail one of our own disks to help us. Our hope is that their disks work on the same principle as the one you have, and we can learn something from it, or even use it."

They arrived at a building even less impressive than the main structure. There was rust; there was flaking paint. Air conditioners jutted out of a couple of the windows. Beside the door was stenciled a number, *3-3-2*.

"Where's Building 3-3-3?"

"That's Biology. South end of the island."

Flynn got down from the cart. He'd known the answer to his question before Caruthers said a word.

He felt a quiet sense of triumph, but instantly suppressed it. The job wasn't finished yet. One thing had changed, though, which was that he now—just possibly—had a chance to win this.

CHAPTER TWENTY-TWO

CARUTHERS USHERED them into a conference room. There were four men here: two in air force fatigues, one in a polo shirt, and one in a weathered suit.

"Gentlemen," Caruthers said, "before we begin—" He cleared his throat uneasily. "Before we begin, I'd like to ask you to lay your weapons on the table."

"No."

"Excuse me?"

"You heard me."

He smiled at his colleagues. "As you say. Gentlemen, these are our exoengineers. Officers Flynn and Terrell are working with a police force from a planet our exobiologists at Area Fifty-One have named Aeon. Now, here in our unit, we're not familiar with this specific planet. But hopefully we do have some possible avenues of help for you."

"I'm Dr. Evans," the older man said. "These are my colleagues, Richard Dawkins and Martin Reese. Dr. Reese, will you begin?"

"Mr. Carroll, if I understand the briefing paper we've received, you have one of the most unique problems in the history of human–alien contact."

"There are lives being lost, if that's what you mean. We're dealing with a murderous psychopath who has a disk, and we can't get near the damn thing. We need to change that."

"This liaison officer from this other planet—Aeon—isn't being helpful—I mean, aside from not giving you a disk?"

"She's answered some important questions, but no, in the end, she hasn't been effective in assisting us to deal with this criminal."

Dr. Evans said, "I find this whole thing amazing. You actually achieve developed, ongoing contact with beings from another planet, and it's cops and robbers? Tell me this, what do they do? What's the crime?"

"Wait, let's back up just a minute. You make it sound like contact is rare."

"It's very rare. A few civilians. Some of them have published books, which you can read. A couple of politicians. Eisenhower, but he couldn't make any sense of what happened."

"And that's it? That's the whole story?"

"The whole story would take me a year just to begin. Suffice it to say that we started out by shooting at the first groups we encountered, and we should never, ever have done that. Of course, that's a major secret."

"I'm not concerned about your secrets. My only interest is getting help downing a disk that's causing a lot of problems."

Evans said, "Let's roll the film, Colonel."

Colonel Caruthers opened a laptop and a small projector, connected them, and turned out the lights.

A moment later, Flynn found himself looking at gun-camera footage. Old-fashioned tracers crossed the sky, moving toward what appeared to be a bouncing searchlight beam. Then blackness. The film ended.

"What happened?"

"This was one of our first shoot-down attempts. The plane came down filled with thousands of tiny holes. The pilot disappeared."

"The gun-camera footage was intact?"

"This strip was intact."

"This next strip is from the gun camera on the Sabre Jet of a pilot called Milton Torres. It's from 1957. Take a look."

The black-and-white gun-camera footage flickered and jumped. Something flashed past. A young male voice said, "Target sighted." The sky whirled, clouds racing past. A disk appeared. It was difficult to estimate size, but the great, gleaming thing appeared to be huge, hundreds of times the size of Morris's disk. It was also far more sophisticated, morphing and changing, almost as if it were a liquid. The voice resumed. "Target acquired." A pause. A buzzer sounded. "Target lock. Target lock. Commencing firing procedure. Missiles armed. Preparing—" The object disappeared. A faint, under-the-breath comment: "Oh, shit." Then, "Target lost. No target. Firing sequence abort. Abort." Then another voice, "Return to base, FF245."

The image flickered and was gone.

Dr. Reese said, "In 1947, General Curtis LeMay convinced President Truman to go to war with the aliens. Any and all aliens who showed up. Between 1947 and 1957, when we called a halt to the shooting, we lost a hundred and fifty-eight pilots and an even larger number of aircraft. During the Korean War, we lost more pilots and aircraft in our secret war here at home than we did over the Korean Peninsula."

As Dr. Reese spoke in his precise, dry voice, Flynn grew increasingly aware of the fact that he wasn't dealing here with the dynamic military engineering operation he had hoped to find.

"Right now, I have a man and his family out in Menard who are in imminent danger of being kidnapped and killed. I am looking at an entire town burned to the ground a few nights ago." He gestured toward Mac. "This man has lost everything that mattered to him, burned out. I have lost my wife. Now, I am not dealing with some brilliant, huge civilization like I think you are. The grays. I am dealing with biorobots who are more like viral particles or a disease vector. They are controlled by a psychopathic alien. As far as I understand it, they have just the one disk, and it's not the best. Potentially, they're vulnerable. What I am trying to do here is find a way to shoot down that disk."

Evans stood up. "I thought that's what this would be about. We've failed in that department. Your mission is futile."

Rage flared in Flynn's guts. He fought it and nearly lost, but finally forced himself not to deck Evans. Still, his mind turned to Eddie out there on the empty Texas plains with his new family, and to Mac, a helpless, proud rooster who would crow defiance to his last breath, and to all the victims—the cases that haunted a good cop, the ones where justice hung suspended.

When he spoke, his voice was mild. "We're not done, Mr. Evans, so I suggest you sit back down."

They had all been getting up. None of them stopped. They began to move toward the door. They'd done as ordered. Now it was time to escape the pain.

"Because I could tell the world about you people and your failure. There's nobody powerful enough to stop me."

Evans turned his liquid, sorrowful eyes on him. "We can get a kill order, you know. We can do that."

"Am I killable, do you think?" He brought his gun out so quickly that their eyes flickered. He slipped it back into his belt as smoothly as if it were silk.

"Tell you what," Caruthers said to his colleagues, "why don't we take them down? Let them see."

"See what?"

"The disk, Flynn. Maybe looking it over would be useful to you."

Now, this was better. This was what he'd come for. "Sure, let's have a look."

"All right, but first I have to insist that you leave the weapons behind. I can't take you into a sensitive facility like that when you're armed and we aren't. If something walked out of there, it'd be my ass."

"You are armed, Colonel, speaking of your ass. You're wearing a compact pistol in an SOB holster. So don't tell me you aren't armed. Plus, Dr. Evans has what looks like a Police Special in the right-side pocket of his pants."

Silence fell, broken after a long moment by Evans. "He's good."

"They say that," Caruthers commented. Then, to Flynn, "I still can't let you go down there armed."

"I'm not going to draw on you down there or anywhere else."

"I don't know that. If you want to do this, there's no choice. I'm sorry."

Flynn glanced at Mac, then took out his pistol and laid it on the table. Mac did the same.

They followed Caruthers and Evans back into the corridor, then down a steel stairway into a basement.

"There's an elevator."

Flynn stopped. "An elevator? How deep are we going?"

"It's a couple of stories."

"I don't think this is a good idea," Mac said.

Flynn said, "If the things have any vulnerability, we might see it. If their disk has the seam that Geri talked about. If you could see it, see exactly where it was—"

"I can tell you right now that you're not going to find any seams on this thing. Anyway, it was built by the grays, not by your people. What if it's completely different?"

"Let's take a look."

The black door of the elevator had a glass porthole in it, and when it opened, there was a hiss of escaping air, which told Flynn immediately that this was a deep shaft, more than a couple of stories.

As the door slid open, it revealed a space little bigger than a closet. There was enough room for only three people, and the three scientists went down first. From the sound of the lift and the amount of time involved, Flynn thought it was a drop of fifteen hundred feet. Unusual on an island, given that the water table was going to be at sea level. To build whatever was down there would have taken a lot of money and engineering skill. A lot.

The elevator returned again. Mac said, "Are you sure about this, Flynn?"

"No."

"Then I don't think we should do it."

Flynn did not reply, but he stepped into the elevator. After a moment, the much more hesitant Mac followed. The elevator whined softly as it dropped.

"Why so deep?" Flynn asked.

"I don't know," Caruthers said.

Flynn smiled. "Of course you do."

Caruthers shook his head. "You're a real paranoid, aren't you?"

"In our line of work, if you're not paranoid, you're not sane."

The elevator door opened onto a concrete corridor, dimly lit by old-fashioned incandescent bulbs in hanging metal fixtures. As they walked down the hallway, Flynn could hear a distant sound of flowing water, and the deep, throbbing hum of powerful pumps. They were far below the water table, and it must take a great deal to keep the ocean out of this place.

"Do you have any fail-safes?"

"In what sense?"

"The pumps. If they go down, this place floods, and fast."

"They can't fail."

"They're mighty durable, then. What about the power?"

"There's a reactor."

A reactor wasn't going to be used to power some godforsaken has-been program. Yet again, the mystery deepened.

They came to a wide steel rolling door. Caruthers punched a code into a keypad beside it, and the door began to rise. Caruthers had made no effort to conceal which keys he pressed, and Flynn took note of them. He also noted that he was once again being underestimated. Always a useful bit of information to store away.

And then he saw it. Its skin was a deep silver, as if a thin layer of diamond covered the metal. It hung in the air, an oval so perfect that it was impossible to turn away from its beauty. He felt its life, as if it had a heart and a mind, as if it were a living creature.

"Flynn . . . my God."

The three scientists stood in a group, small beneath the bulk of the thing. It floated in absolute silence. In the center of its lower surface there glowed a single red light, and he thought it was an eye, and that it was looking into his soul.

"This was built by the grays," Evans said, "or given life by them."

"It's nothing like what we've seen," Flynn said. "This is like a—I don't know—"

"A sacred object," Caruthers said.

"A sacred being," Flynn said.

Richard Dawkins said, "I'm the resident metallurgist. Let's begin with the outer skin." He gestured. "Come on over—it doesn't bite."

"We need to see under it," Flynn said.

Mac strode over to it and put his hand on it, whereupon it folded inward like the wall of a tent. He drew his hand away and looked at it, leaning back. Then he touched it again, running his finger along it.

"It's constructed like a kite," Dawkins said. "The frame is balsa, the metal is basically tungsten, we think. It's a tissue just a few hundredths of an inch thick. Interesting that it's also the strongest substance known to man."

Flynn was not interested in the metal. He bent down and went under it. In its center was a red light, glowing softly. "Does it work?"

"We're not sure."

"Mac, come down here."

Mac crawled closer. "Doesn't anything scare you?"

"Not this. Look along this surface—use those eyes of yours. See if you can spot a seam."

They lay on their backs. Flynn pulled out his pocket LED flashlight and shone it along the surface. "See anything?"

"It's featureless."

"Take your time."

"If this is a different model—"

"Keep looking."

"Is it alive?"

Flynn moved the light slowly along the surface.

"Flynn, this isn't a machine, this is a creature."

"Keep looking."

Evans called to them. "You guys still with us?" He sounded oddly far away.

"Wait," Mac said, "roll the light back."

Flynn moved the beam slightly.

"There. Got it."

Flynn held the beam steady. "I don't see a thing."

"It's there." He reached up, extended a finger, then touched it. "See it now?"

There was the faintest indentation stretching away from Mac's index finger, a line so narrow that Flynn wouldn't have seen it on his own, not even if he'd had his nose up against the surface of the disk.

"That is finely machined," he said. "Beautiful."

Mac flattened himself back down onto the floor and stared up at the surface. "Man, I'm two feet away, and now I can't see it at all. Shine your light again."

It took them a full minute of searching to realize the truth. "It's gone," Mac said. "Disappeared as soon as I touched it."

"You're sure it's gone?"

"I'm sure."

They backed out. "There's a seam, all right," Flynn said, "but it disappeared when we touched it."

"We hadn't detected it before. A major error."

"What about controls and propulsion. How does it work?"

"Propulsion is my department," Reese said. "Come on, we'll need to enter the craft."

As he stepped closer, it rose silently a few feet.

"Is it alive?" Flynn asked. "It feels alive."

"There's something going on here that's real hard to understand. Do you believe in the soul?"

"I don't know."

"You work with the grays, you work with the soul." He nodded toward the disk. "It has a consciousness. For want of a better word, we call it a soul." He raised an arm, and a dark round hole appeared in its side, about midway along the curve of the bottom. "We know that approaching it like this works, but we don't know why," he said. "We've never been able to find any device or system inside that would account for doors appearing—or seams disappearing, for that matter. Not only that, but you can walk up to it like this from any angle, and an opening will always appear right in front of you as soon as you gesture like I did."

Leaning down, he approached it, then stood up so that his head and shoulders were inside. "We call this a penetration," he said. "It's not like entering a plane—believe me."

"Which one of us stays here?" Flynn asked Mac. "Your call."

"That will be me."

Flynn leaned down and joined Reese under the thing. As he did, the nature of the air around him seemed to change. It became subtly heavier. A silence fell, and it was a familiar one. When he was hunting aliens in a forest and came into a silence like this, he knew they were near.

He saw around him a gray, featureless exterior, like the inside of a tent. "There's no room," he said as he looked up. Reese's body filled the hatch.

"Just stand up. It'll open for you."

He did as instructed. Instead of his head touching the metal of the fuselage, he felt a warmth and a sort of fluctuation in pressure. Then he was face-to-face with Reese, the top half of his body inside the craft.

The interior air was warm and dry. There was a soft rose light that seemed to penetrate everywhere. Before them, he could see a huge ring made of white metal. Inside it was another ring made of black metal. They were separated by a closely packed row of silver ball bearings. Hanging in midair in the center of it and about three feet above it, was a crystal. It was an eight-sided figure, rose colored like the light that filled the space.

"What happens is that these two circles counterrotate. We know that. But what we don't know is what powers them and why the counterrotation is so effective in driving the thing."

The seam had to be between the inner and outer rings, so when they were rotating, it wasn't going to disappear.

"Has anybody ever flown one?"

"No."

"Flown in one, then?"

"Lots of people, I would think. A reading of the abductee literature would lead you to assume so."

Flynn reached over and touched the outer metal ring. He grasped it and tried to make it turn.

"Not gonna happen. But we do know something about its operation. We've recorded the sound of spinning disks. Armed with knowledge of how this functions, and its size, we've determined that it would need to rotate at something on the order of a hundred sixty thousand revolutions per minute to emit a sound like that."

"But you can't make it turn?"

"We can't find a power source. The two rings are oppositely polarized permanent magnets, but nothing we've done—feeding them powerful electric currents, attempting to heat or cool them, bombarding them with gamma rays—none of it has caused a single response. We have clocked disks just like this moving through the atmosphere at upwards of a hundred thousand miles an hour, but not leaving a sonic boom."

"Where did you get this thing?"

"Caruthers knows more about that. Adam, can you hear us?"

From below, Caruthers's voice drifted faintly up. He sounded as if he were a hundred yards away at least, and speaking softly. "This was found on the Plain of San Augustin in New Mexico. There were three extraterrestrial biological entities inside. All dead. Found in 1949."

"What about controls?"

Reese said, "That's Dawkins's department. He'll take you a little deeper."

Before Flynn could respond, Reese had dropped out and Dawkins appeared and said, "Now, what will happen is, if you move straight up— push yourself higher—you'll find that the thing morphs as you penetrate more deeply. Stay with me, though, because you can get lost in here, and I have to warn you, that's happened."

"Get lost? How? Where?"

"We don't know, but some of the early explorers never came out. After a while, as I understand it, you could smell their decaying bodies. They're dead in here somewhere. We don't know where. Let's go. Keep standing, stay within sight of me."

Flynn found himself in a small room that contained three bucket seats and three consoles. There were no readouts and no controls, just indentations with small holes in them. The indentations were the shape and size of children's hands, but designed for six fingers.

"You can sit down."

"No, I can't."

"Do it. The seat will change to fit you."

He could barely maneuver, humped over in the small space.

"Act like it's all your size, and it will be. Go ahead."

He straightened up, and the room did indeed grow larger, the seats along with it. When he sat in one, the console before him expanded, too.

"Now put your fingers in the controls."

As he did so, they morphed into five-fingered control surfaces. They fit his hands so precisely that it felt as if they had been made just for him—which, in a sense, they had.

"This is just incredible."

"We don't understand any of it. Look down."

When he did so, the floor beneath him became clear, and he could see down to the crystal and the ring below it, what looked like a distance of at least fifty feet, and yet he had come up only a few feet to reach this control room.

"What has happened is that the interior of the craft expanded to fit us. But on the outside, your friend isn't going to see a single change."

"They're a million years ahead of us."

"Or they simply have better minds."

He thought of the brutality and carnage he had witnessed, and could not reconcile them to the magnificent, elegant technology he was seeing here. Maybe the grays had better minds. Not Aeon.

"Could there be tramps? Thieves who could steal things like this? Alien thieves who maybe wouldn't be able to work them all that well? Because what I'm dealing with is brutal and mean. My aliens sure as hell don't square with anything as sophisticated and beautiful as this. Whoever created this thing touched the mind of God."

Dawkins smiled gently. "Or maybe another mind, also magnificent, but not so sweet."

As soon as Flynn rose from the chair, the distance down to the ring became short again.

"You go first, Flynn. Don't want to get you lost."

When Flynn looked down again, he could now see the opening they had come through, and below it the concrete floor not four feet underneath.

"Careful, now—everyone who's disappeared in here has been on their way out."

Flynn went to the edge of the opening and dropped his feet out.

"Reach back, please take my hand."

Flynn felt Dawkins's thin hand in his own. He dropped down, the scientist coming immediately behind him.

Dawkins stood with his head bowed, his face sheened with sweat. "That's hard," he said.

"I'm glad you made it out," Evans said.

Flynn fought back any sign of the bitter disappointment he was feeling. The truth was, though, that this entire journey had been a waste of effort, and from the way these people were acting, dangerous on a whole lot of different levels.

It was time to cut and run. Except for one problem. "Where's Mac?"

"He and Evans went up to the commissary a couple of hours ago, to eat and get you checked in to visitor quarters."

"What are you talking about?"

Dawkins laughed a little. "That's another reality in there, with a different time. I once worked in there for a day, trying to find some kind of connection between the control panels and the motor. When I came down, four weeks had passed, and two men had disappeared while searching for me." He bowed his head and was silent for a moment. Then he said in a voice choked with pain. "One of them was my brother. We're twins." Then, lower, full of more trembling emotion, "We know he died. He's one of the ones we could smell."

The thought came to Flynn that they were like bugs trapped behind the mystery of a glass window, a mystery they could never hope to defeat and never hope to understand. Impossible not because they didn't have the information, but because they didn't have the raw brain capacity. Nothing could tell a fly what glass was. Nothing could tell a human being what this disk was.

"Are we finished, then?"

"Sure, Flynn. If you're done. Any more questions?"

"No more. Not now." But there was one. He'd save it for later, though, at just the right moment, or maybe by then there would be no point, and he would never ask it at all.

He had not gotten very far here. Not far at all. In fact, all his visit had done was confirm his worst fear, which was that the disks were so far beyond human understanding that there was no hope. If so, then Morris would soon rule this world of Earth. It would be free no more, a slave planet given over to whatever its master chose to do with it.

Fifty years after Cortés conquered Mexico, only one out of ten of the indigenous people were left alive. If Flynn's battle failed, he knew that humanity would fare even worse. Our species would be lost to the egomaniacal lusts of a psychopath.

He was a humble man. He'd never thought of himself as being particularly important, but in this moment, mankind's future was clearly his to win or lose. And not more than a couple of hundred people on the whole planet, if that, even knew his name.

Was he up to this?

CHAPTER TWENTY-THREE

FLYNN SWALLOWED the acid of desperation back into his churning guts. He did not see how he could win this thing, not against technology so advanced that it seemed more like magic than like science. Was Morris's disk equally advanced, a machine that might as well be a living thing? How could anybody ever damage a craft like that with a little chunk of lead, even if they did hit a seam?

On the way back to the main building, Flynn noticed that Mac was now quiet and withdrawn.

"Geri said we're dealing with an old, primitive device—remember that."

"The seam just disappeared. Then a door opens like some kind of magic is going on. I don't know, man—no matter how primitive it is, maybe it's not primitive enough for a jerk with a gun."

When they returned to the main building and went inside, Flynn had an incredibly powerful sense of déjà vu. This hallway—wide with a black linoleum floor polished to a high gloss, its rows of office doors, each one locked like a safe—was as familiar to him as his own house in Menard. And yet, his mind was telling him he had never been here before.

As they approached the commissary, the smell of the food was incredibly familiar, sending a dagger of memory right through him. Not that it was good food—it was hardly that—it was just damn familiar.

He was certain now that he'd been subjected to hypnosis so that he wouldn't think about this place. It was a security measure. Too bad it hadn't helped Dr. Miller.

Frankly, he was excited about taking Mac to Bio. His friend had found a seam that was almost microscopic. As he was, the man had what was called exquisite vision. When they were kids, he'd been able to pick out the moons of Jupiter, not to mention see a tree rat crossing a wire at night and blow it to kingdom come at a distance of a couple of hundred yards. And leave the wire untouched.

"This is not food," Mac said. They were passing down the steam table in the commissary.

"I believe those are chicken wings," Evans said.

"From what planet?"

Flynn remembered what he'd eaten the last time he was here. In the hope that reenactment would release more memory, he got the same meal again, a quarter chicken, green beans, baked potato, and pineapple yogurt for dessert. He, Caruthers, Evans, and Mac sat together. The others had gone to a table of their own.

"I enjoyed my time here," he said. "When I was working with Dr. Miller." Mac gave him a sharp look, but the other two didn't react. It wasn't a good sign, but he continued anyway. "I thought maybe we could go down to the Biology section and have a look around."

Both Caruthers and Evans stopped eating.

"I mean, I was there. That's where my physical enhancement was done. I'd like to look the place over again."

Laughing, Evans said, "I think I need to consult Legal."

The cavalier reply made him so mad, it was all he could do not to reach across the table and splatter the guy's face against the far wall.

He put his anger firmly in a drawer and smiled. "Well," he said affably, "that's probably the best thing. On the other hand, I have a cop out there in Texas who could at any time get picked up and have his eyes cut out of his head, not to mention what will happen to his family. But you consult Legal. However, know this, all of you: If they die, I am liable to become very damn irrational, and that's not going to be comfortable for you."

He reached over and tapped Evans on the ear, moving so fast that the gesture couldn't be seen by normal eyes.

Evans shot out of his chair and sprawled on the floor, holding his head and crying out.

The buzz of conversation in the room died away.

As Evans sputtered and gagged and struggled to his feet, Flynn stood up. "Excuse me, ladies and gentlemen, is anybody here from the Biology unit?"

Nobody reacted. Here and there, people began leaving the room.

"I was there. Some of you probably worked with me."

The trickle of people leaving became a flood.

"You did good," he said. "I'm quite a piece of work, folks. Fastest gun in the West." He drew the Bull and reholstered it. "Anybody see that? No?"

The flood surged toward the doors.

"Okay, folks, don't have a heart attack—I'm harmless. At the moment."

The only table still populated was theirs. A couple of security guards, one of them with a stun gun, stood in the doorway. Flynn returned to his seat. "I'd advise you to tell those guys not to make any sudden moves," he said to Evans and Caruthers. "I don't care for sudden moves. Frankly, you know what I do when I see childish bullshit like guards with Tasers? I just think to myself, 'Bullshit. Empty, childish bullshit.'"

Flynn picked up his table knife and tossed it into the wall. There was a crash, the window above the point of impact cracked, and nothing could be seen of the knife except the hole where it had entered. He reached over and took Evans's knife, and began doing surgery on his chicken.

"You people have been at this what—sixty, sixty-five years? And look at you, four guys nursing a piece of equipment you can't even begin to understand. Where's the massive scientific effort? Where's the billion-dollar budget?"

"The parade's gone by. Twenty, thirty years ago at Wright-Pat, it was a different story. Some of the best minds in the world worked on this. The best. For years and years and years, Flynn. And we learned basically nothing. We lost. Now we're what's left, four trudging bureaucrats protecting the secret of the ages."

"I want to go to the Biology section. I want to meet the people who worked on me."

"As I said—"

"Let's roll. Right now." Flynn stood up.

"You're not cleared to go down there, Flynn," Caruthers said.

"Then get me cleared!"

"You can be. No question. But we have to go through channels, and you know that."

"Diana Glass cuts red tape like butter."

"So call her," Evans said. "Right now. The second she gets you cleared, off we go."

Flynn said, "Give me a phone. I lost mine."

"No cell coverage on the island. In any case, if classified matters are to be discussed, we need to go to my office and use the secure phone."

Flynn followed Evans down a hallway and up two flights to the sort of small office that defined the reality of the middle-level bureaucrat in the federal system. There was a picture of the president on the wall, one of Evans with a high-ranking but nameless air force officer, and an engineering diploma from Ohio State. On the desk were two photographs of which Flynn could see only the backs. There was an in-box with a great deal of paperwork in it and an equally busy out-box. For a man who had portrayed himself as basically a caretaker, he seemed to have a lot of work to do. But these days, when so much was done in digital media, the busy boxes could have been there just for show.

There were two telephones: one an old-style landline secure phone, the other a cheap wireless model. Flynn strode over to the secure phone and called Diana.

She said, "Complaint line."

"I'm laughing. Now I'm not. They're insisting that I need further clearance to go to Biology."

"I really don't know how to say this, but going down there could reduce your abilities. Put a level of awareness between you and your new skills that could affect your speed."

"What the hell are you saying?"

"It's dangerous for you to see your records—too much self-awareness could compromise your skills."

"I want to appeal to your superior officer."

"I have no superior officer."

"Sure you do."

"You can't appeal, and you can't know who he is or where he is or anything about him."

He hung up the phone.

Evans said, "You heard the same thing from her that we got in this command. Show you the disk, then show you the door."

Flynn spread his hands. "Okay, I lose. No contest."

Mac blinked, but said nothing.

They were due to be returned to the mainland at first light, in time to catch the dawn patrol commuter back to LaGuardia. From there, it was a nonstop to Dallas, then another commuter to Menard.

They were assigned two rooms in the small visiting quarters. Flynn had no further reason to spend his time talking to the locals, so he went to his billet and threw himself onto the bed. He assumed that there would be cameras and audio, so he did nothing to reveal his real intentions.

He closed his eyes and began mentally, and very carefully, reviewing the map of the island he'd made in his mind as they landed.

Mac followed him in. "What's the plan?"

"No plan, Mac. The long and short of it is, we busted out."

"So what happens next?"

He hated to lie to Mac, but right now, the two of them were certainly onstage. Caruthers was listening. His security team was listening. Diana was listening and probably whomever she worked for as well.

"We're due on the helipad at six sharp," he said. "From there, I think we need to go back to Menard."

"Menard? Why not Washington?"

"Because they've got their heads so far up their asses, they can see—"

"Oh, yeah, there is that."

"We need to do what we can to protect Eddie and his family. Just leaving Menard isn't enough to save them. If they even left."

"You think we're gonna die out there?"

He thought he was going to probably die, but not in Texas. If what he was about to do went wrong in any way, that was going to happen right here, tonight.

"We might as well get some sleep," he said.

Mac lingered. "Flynn, what was it like in that thing? I mean, that must have been amazing."

"What it was like is, we're never going to have anything remotely similar, not in our lifetimes or many lifetimes. As you move around inside, the entire interior of the thing changes, depending on what you want to do. It looks about twelve feet high at the center, am I right?"

"Yeah, I'd say so."

"When you first go in, you find yourself in the motor room. Counterrotating magnets, but we can't make them turn. We don't know exactly what they're made of or what kind of power needs to be applied. Then, say, you want to go to the control room. You just stand up, and it kind of appears around you. Nothing morphs or changes—you're just in another place. It's the most incredible experience I've ever had. The control room is not complicated. Two chairs before consoles with nothing but a couple of handprints embedded in them. Little chairs, but sit in one and it fits you, just like that."

"Put your hands in the handprints?"

"I did. Nothing happened. I felt like a monkey fooling around in a car. Not only did I have no idea how it worked, but I had no idea how even to *learn* to make it work."

"A monkey could be trained to drive a car. It'd be hard, but it's doable."

"Maybe, but he'd never learn to fix a car, or why it runs, nothing like that."

"Flynn, a fighter pilot can't begin to understand his aircraft. He knows the general principles. That's all. But I say again, he could be trained."

"They're telling me nobody knows how it works. They've had it for sixty years—more—and they haven't gotten to square one. What's worse, I can believe it. The thing is just amazing. And that feeling that we both had, that it was somehow alive—" He shook his head. There was nothing more to say.

"I gotta tell you, some asshole with a gun is not gonna pull down one of those things, no matter how much skill he has."

"Remember, we're not dealing with state of the art."

Flynn offered no sign to Mac of what he intended to do, but, as always, his old friend sensed something. He probed a bit, but thankfully in the wrong direction, asking him if there was any way to get the disk out of its containment.

"It's hundreds of feet underground. Access tunnel's filled in."

Mac seemed to look into himself. Flynn waited, watching him as he sank deeper and deeper into the truth. He said, "We've lost."

"Looks like it."

"We'll all move. We'll run."

Again, Flynn waited for him to realize what would actually happen if that scenario was played out.

"Goddamnit, Flynn!"

"I don't have a choice, Mac. It's me or it's you and Eddie, and his little family. That baby, Mac."

"You can't throw yourself at this thing, Flynn."

Flynn could not look at his friend. He said no more.

"I've never been a coward, Flynn. But I don't see what purpose is served by us going back to Menard, especially you. You already told Eddie to get the hell out. He *said* he would get out immediately. If he didn't, it's his problem. If he went to New York, tell him to stay there. Buy him an apartment there or in London or anywhere. You can afford it. Me, I'll live on the run. I'm good at that."

"Morris can be satisfied."

"Flynn, no."

"What the hell else can I do?"

"No!"

"I'm gonna go back to Menard, and I'm gonna take it from there. But you're right about New York. You stay there. Bury yourself in it. If Eddie's there, you'll have some company. When I come face-to-face with Morris, I'll bargain for your lives."

Mac stood up. "I've been mad at you a lotta times in my life. You're a person who's good at making people mad. I'd like to be mad at you now. But I'm gonna leave it. See if you start to make some sense in the morning. Because you're not making sense now."

"Mac—"

"No, don't talk. It is time to cut and run. Spend a little of that damn cash of yours to stay alive. Who knows, the longer you live, the more chance you have that Morris will slip up and give you the opening you don't have right now."

Flynn said nothing.

Mac left, slamming the door hard behind him. Flynn hated to see him go like that, but there was no choice. He stayed quiet, listening to the building. He'd already spotted all the visual surveillance. There was a good deal of it, typical of a facility that housed classified records and materials. Most of what was here had to do with biological warfare, though, not with the even more secret alien materials.

He turned out the light and then lay on his back in the dark again, waiting. He'd already planned his moves. He had a reasonable assurance that they would work. But care had to be taken. The least misstep, and this would all be over.

Before he made a move, he was going to need to figure out the cameras. While he was talking to Mac, he'd spotted both of them, fish-eye pinhole jobs—one in the back wall, one in the wall near the door. He could safely assume that the setup would be the same in all the rooms.

He was sure the surveillance team just saw a man who was waiting, hands behind his head, seemingly staring bleakly at the ceiling, wallowing in his defeat.

He noted that the edges of the two-square-foot ceiling tiles did not end above the closet door. Useful information. Because the roof was peaked and there were vents at each end, he knew that there was an attic above the tiles. To reach it, he would need to go through the hatch at the far end of the corridor outside.

The drop out of one of the vents was survivable, but only barely. Somebody using that escape route would need to land exactly right to avoid a sprain or worse.

Still, it was doable. He could get out of this place without alerting security. But how would he manage to take Mac along with him? Without Mac, there was no point in going. In fact, leaving Mac behind would mean defeat.

It was time to test security. He got up off the bed, paused to open the closet and put his jacket in it. Leaving the closet door open, he strolled out of the room. There was a guard station beside the only stairway, manned by no fewer than three armed guards. Their careful eyes followed him as he crossed the hall and knocked on Mac's door.

"Want to take a walk?"

"Outside? Are you kidding?"

"Just down to the vending machines. Get a Coke." He nodded, communicating necessity.

"Why not?"

As they walked down the hallway, one of the guards spoke into a walkie-talkie.

"Evening," Flynn said as they stepped around the desk.

"You're restricted to the structure," the guard lieutenant said.

"Not a problem. We're going to get some food."

There was another guard station at the foot of the stairs. Three more guards, all now on their feet, all with their holsters open, their hands on their weapons.

Had he wished, Flynn could have taken their weapons and knocked them all cold before they could take a breath. Whoever had set these guards knew it, too, because stations at both ends of the building were in sight of this one, meaning that anything he did to these men would be seen by six more pairs of eyes, and dealt with accordingly.

He knew exactly who had placed these guard stations in this way. The only person who knew enough about his skills to be able to thwart them.

"Hey, Diana," he said, "you'll be watching this little charade, so listen up. I'm gonna get a Coke and go to bed to cry my eyes out. Tomorrow morning I'm going to New York and I'm going to disappear. So this is good-bye, love."

Until they entered the small space of the basement vending machine room, he said nothing more. There was a Pepsi machine, a water machine, and a machine dispensing microwavable food. A microwave on the chipped white counter nearby.

He bought a burrito and put it in the microwave and turned it on. The machine wasn't so noisy as he had hoped, but it would have to do.

He spoke softly. "You willing to try it?" He waved his hands across his lips, indicating that Mac was to nod or shake his head.

Mac paused. His brows knitted. A question came into his face.

Flynn said, "Do a bedbug like when we were kids. Go out through the closet ceiling. We'll be dealing with a forty-foot drop to the ground. Is that okay?"

Mac's face, lips tight, eyes full of edge, said that he wasn't at all sure.

"Me, neither," Flynn said. The microwave turned off, and he added in a normal tone, "Like I said to Diana, I've decided to take your advice. Right now, I don't have an implant, so the longer I wait, the more danger I'm in. Tomorrow morning, I'm going to start running while I still have the chance."

Mac opened his arms and embraced him. "You oughta be in the movies," he whispered.

"See you on the other side."

Mac bought a Diet Pepsi, and they returned to the second floor.

The making of what they used to call a "bedbug" was a matter of getting in the bed and leaving it with the sheets arranged in such a way that a parent peeking into the room would—hopefully—think that it still contained a boy.

Would a subterfuge this simple actually work? Not for long, but hopefully for long enough.

To minimize the effectiveness of the cameras, he drew his blinds and turned out his lights. It would actually help a bit with the tiny nailhead units. You weren't talking all that many pixels. The best of them used computers equipped with sophisticated algorithms to supply the data that the lenses would be missing. With just a few pixels to work with, a good system could provide crystal-clear images in full light, but only adequate ones in the dark.

He sat on the side of the bed and took off his socks. They would form the "head" of the bedbug. Leaving his shoes on the floor, he got under the blanket and sheet. In fact, he got under both the top and bottom sheets. More bulk for the bedbug. He turned on his side with his back facing into the room and pushed the sheets until they formed a long wad sufficient to lift the blanket. Then he slipped the socks onto the pillow in front of his face and went deep into the blanket, until all but the top of his head was covered.

He slid backwards out of the bed and down to the floor. Remaining low, he slid on his stomach into the closet. Then he rose up, pressing himself against the back wall.

There came a knock at the door. "Mr. Carroll?"

"Yeah."

"Bed check."

"Who're you, the hall monitor?"

"Just doing my job, Mr. Carroll."

"Okay, let me get some sleep, then. I'm not going anywhere."

As he spoke, he reached up and slid one of the big ceiling tiles out of place, Then he raised himself by gripping a girder with his fingers. The air in the attic was choking, full of dust and insulation, and the pulsing of an unusually complex ventilation system that, judging from all the electronically controlled flues, was capable of being sealed in an instant. Shades of the biological-warfare days.

Above the layers of insulation and massive equipment, a thick cable harness ran from one end of the building to the other.

Moving quickly, he found a supporting beam and climbed along it to the rear of the structure, knowing that a man of his weight would cause sounds below in this otherwise lightly framed building.

He reached the metal vent, which was two feet by two feet in size, as he had observed from outside the building. Feeling its edges, he determined that it wasn't wired, and was screwed into the building's frame with standard construction screws, which he removed with his pocket-knife.

Behind him, there was the breath of a whisper.

"Guard came to my door," Flynn said.

"How deep is their security going to be?"

"On the way in, I identified a motion-sensor grid, but we can avoid it."

As he was working, he realized that he could see his shadow. Immediately, he dropped down, pulling Mac with him. He watched the beam of a flashlight play along the girders.

The light continued to explore the space for a time. Finally, there came the faint scrape of a hatch closing. Still, Flynn and Mac didn't move. Flynn waited a full minute, but nothing else happened.

He pulled out the vent and looked down at the drop.

Immediately below the vent was a window, the one at the end of the second-floor corridor. The sill was about an inch deep, just enough to enable a jumper to balance, assuming that he would be able to cling to the inch-deep upper ledge.

"Mac, what I'm going to do is lever myself out until I'm hanging from my forearms—then you're going to climb down my back. You got that?"

"What about you?"

"I can take the fall."

"You're sure?"

"It's just a guess. Now, move."

Mac was lithe and as strong as twisted wire. Flynn felt him slide quickly across his back, then overhand himself until he was dangling from Flynn's ankles. Then he let go, landing silently and efficiently.

Flynn lowered himself until his arms were stretched and his feet were about eight inches above the sill below. He dropped.

As his feet contacted the sill, he thrust his fingers hard against the upper window frame and pressed his body into the window itself. He was still in control of the descent, so he immediately dropped down, letting his feet slip off the sill and cutting the speed of his fall as much as he could by grabbing it as it passed eye level.

He hit the ground jarringly hard, rolled, then got to his feet and moved at once away from the building. A moment later, Mac followed him.

Darkness didn't matter to security in places like this, not anymore. Security would certainly be able to see them, so speed was essential.

As they moved off, lights began turning on all over the building, including outside lights—bright ones, many of them.

Staying low and close to the miserable little shrubs that stood around the building, Flynn ran. Mac followed.

They blended with the shadows and were gone.

CHAPTER TWENTY-FOUR

THEY HAD reached the shell road that led to the biology labs, and were trotting down it when Flynn heard the whine of electric vehicles. They darted off the road and into the scrub, but there was little cover. Anybody with infrared look-ahead or a starlight scope would spot them instantly, and Deer Island security would undoubtedly have both.

"Why are they doing this?"

"Something's wrong."

"What?"

"Flat on the ground, flat as you can be."

Lying very still, protected by a slight indentation in the ground, they heard a sound nearby, a low grunting and snuffling.

"Russian boar?" Mac whispered. They were all over Texas.

"Not up here. Probably a feral—"

There was a sudden burst of very weird, very complex chattering.

An instant later, the lights of three electric carts flooded the area.

"Shit," Mac whispered.

Their motors screaming, the carts shot straight at them—and flew over the indentation, missing Flynn and Mac by so little that they were washed in heat.

The moment they passed, Flynn leaped to his feet. In the glaring lights of the fast-moving carts, he glimpsed what may have been a running figure, pale and humped.

Mac said, "Did you see that?"

"Barely."

"Muscular rear legs, short forelegs, hairless, with a long, whipping tail."

Mac's eyes were truly amazing. "Anything else?" Flynn asked him.

"That's not enough?"

"What about the face?"

"Not human at all. One of them looked back. The eyes were powdery green. They were rounded. Maybe a new form of alien."

"That's all we need."

Now that it was clear they weren't the objects of the hunt, Flynn and Mac went back to the road and headed toward the floodlights that surrounded the Biology section. They were still half a mile away, and as they approached it, Flynn left the road again. They proceeded into a slightly higher area, where they had a broader view of the facility.

Flynn could see that the fence was covered both by cameras and motion sensors. He said, "We're going to walk up to the front door and just knock. But first take a good look—what do you see?"

"Tracks in the sand inside the compound. Boots, also dog prints."

"What kind of dog?"

"Long, thin print." He glanced at Flynn.

"Which is why covert penetration won't work. Come on."

The road was set deeper, and when they were on it, they could see only the roofs of the facility floating above the glare of the lights.

As they moved closer, Flynn said, "We have somebody behind us, about sixty feet. Closing."

Mac began to walk faster.

"No, stay cool." In one smooth movement, he drew his gun and whirled, landing in a crouch with his legs spread. Standing there frozen with fear, hands raised, and eyes practically bulging out of his head, was Evans.

"Mr. Evans, out for an evening stroll?" Flynn made the gun disappear.

"Gentlemen, may I approach?"

Flynn nodded.

"I'm here on behalf of your boss. She's urging you not to go in there, and we concur."

"She saw us from satellite?"

"Yes."

He looked up and waved. The starry night looked back.

"We need to do this," he said.

"We don't control that facility."

"Who does?"

"That's unclear."

"I was down there a few months ago."

"I know it."

"Who controlled it then?"

"We thought we did. We were working there. Dr. Miller worked on you."

"Come down with us," Flynn said. "Maybe you can help us get in."

Evans shook his head—a short, sharp, decisive movement. There was no way he was going a step closer to that gate.

Flynn began walking. Mac hesitated, then caught up with him. "How dangerous is this?"

"We need to try."

The gate was locked with a padlock on a hardened steel frame. The lock had no key and no combination.

Flynn called to Evans, who was still standing back in the road. "How does this work?"

"We can't open it."

Flynn said to Mac, "What we're looking at here is an alien facility. I wonder if it has embassy status."

"Okay, good. An alien facility that's locked and doesn't have a doorbell. So let's just move on."

"Mac, you have the vision of a buzzard. You need the vision of an eagle." He did a quick draw and replace. "Whoever's on the other side of that fence did this for me. I think it's at least worth asking if they could help you."

"Why don't you go in there and get *your* eyes fixed up?"

"Come on, you start way further up on the bar. My vision is normal."

Evans had left the area. The night wind rustled in the saw grass; a riot of stars looked down. On the distant horizon, a light rose and was gone—a car, perhaps, safe on a mainland road.

"Flynn, the only reason I'm still standing here is that I'm afraid to go back to the main building alone."

"Makes sense."

"If aliens killed Miller and took this place over, why in holy hell do you think they'll help us?"

"Because that's not what happened."

"Sure plays out that way in my book."

"Miller was working here with a human crew. I remember the place, and there were no aliens involved—not in what he was doing. The technology was alien, though, that's for sure. Miller was killed and probably so were a lot of other people who were working in there. By Morris. No question in my mind."

"So why are we here, if it's abandoned?"

"It isn't. The grays are in there."

"The ones on kids' lunchboxes?"

"You read up on the grays, you will find that they're quite real, they're very advanced, and they take a serious interest in Earth. I'm hoping they're mad as hell about what's happening, and they'll give us a lot more help than Aeon can. Basically, I'm hoping they have cops, too."

The wind rose again, scudding through the grass, moaning in the eaves of the old building.

"There's nothing out here but us and these floodlights, under which we are fools to be standing." He stopped, then held his hand up to shield his eyes from the glare of the floods. "Oh, shit." He pointed.

Just visible around the corner of the far end of the building was a figure. It came all the way around the corner. It had a black dog on a lead. This animal had a broad head, very unlike the dogs Mac had inherited from Morris. It was huge, and as black as night.

The two of them came closer, the man striding, the dog rippling with muscle and tension, its eyes never leaving them.

"Christ," Mac said under his breath. "See that?"

"What?"

"That guy's got seams, man. That's a—a—holy God, Flynn, it's the dog! The guy is just—look at him! The dog's running the show."

It wasn't a man. It wasn't biological at all. As it approached, Flynn could hear the hum and whine of motors. The dog, though, watched them with an intensity you see only in animal faces: the calm, cruel care of the predator.

The two of them came to the gate. They stopped. The artificial man stood motionless. The dog drew closer to the fence. It inhaled deeply of their scents, its nose pressed hard against the cyclone fencing. Flynn reached his hand out and felt the cool night air being sucked past his skin.

The dog backed up.

Flynn knew why the artificial man had been built—so that nothing would appear unusual from satellite.

The dog stared at the lock, which moved, clanking faintly as it did so.

Without the slightest click, it opened and then slipped off the hasp. It turned again and locked itself. The gate was now open.

"Why don't they just send somebody real out here?"

"The grays are extremely secretive."

"Flynn, *are* these the same grays you see painted on kids' lunchboxes and those crazy books? Because that's bull crap. I don't care *what* Caruthers says."

"I've never seen one in person, but yeah."

"I'm not buying in to this, and I'm not going in there, either."

"Fine." Flynn opened the gate and stepped into the compound. The surface was the same as the surrounding landscape. The lights seemed even brighter, now that they were focused on the area.

The compound consisted of three buildings. The more imposing one, which wasn't saying much, was the only one lit up from inside. The other buildings' windows were dark.

"I'm going in," Flynn said.

"Been nice knowing you, pal."

With the dog shadowing him by inches, Flynn crossed the twelve-foot strip of land. "Either you come or you don't."

The main door was glass that had been painted black. This operation was being run on the cheap—or just made to look that way.

As he approached, he heard an elaborate series of clicks the complex locking system opened itself.

"Mac, you coming?"

"I can't walk, man. I didn't know I could be this scared."

"You want to be carried?"

"Screw it." Mac came up beside him. "This feels like the gate of hell or something. It's radiating menace like heat."

"I know it, and I don't understand it, either." He put his hand on the stainless-steel grip in the center of the glass door. "Just let's push through it."

Beside him, the dog made a faint sound, a growl. Flynn wondered again what he and Mac had seen out there in the scrub. Was it yet another species of alien? Security had been chasing it, or perhaps herding it, obviously keeping it away from the other facilities on the island. But why was that necessary?

"Man, I can't handle this."

"Nobody can." He pulled the door open. He heard a hiss and a faint pop as the air pressure equalized. The place was not quite airlocked, but tight-sealed like the house Oltisis had inhabited in Chicago.

"Look," Mac said.

He was staring at the door of the nearest office. Beside it was a nameplate, MITCHELL, T. TRAFFIC COORDINATOR. Above the English-language strip were three more tags, all in different and entirely unrecognizable lettering. The door itself looked like something that belonged in a submarine—steel painted high-gloss gray, with hinges and a lip designed to withstand significant pressure from this direction.

"So there are three species besides us working in this facility. Plus, the hall can be pressure controlled."

"Is Aeon represented?"

"I don't think so." He gestured toward the door's multilingual nameplates. "None of that looks like their alphabet."

"Here comes trouble."

A man in a white medical coat was walking toward them, coming down the long hall. As he came closer and his face became clearer, for once even Flynn Carroll was surprised. This couldn't be another trick of Morris's, surely. But then what in hell was really going on here? As the man drew closer yet, and his identity became undeniable, Flynn just let his mind blank. His right arm was ready to move at lightning speed.

"Hi, Flynn. We were expecting you a little later. I'm afraid I've lost some money in the office pool. You've done very well to get here this fast."

Standing before him was a man he now recognized as an old friend and comrade in arms, Dr. Dan Miller.

"Dan, you look a hell of a lot better than you did in that bog."

Miller smiled softly. "We had to strip me out of my former life. Evie'll be okay, though. She has—"

"The sheriff, I know. Who died in your place, Doctor?"

"A long story."

"If Morris didn't do it, why would he think it's you?"

"He did it, and we hope he was deceived."

Flynn didn't inquire any further. He decided to assume that no crime had been committed and leave it at that. He was just incredibly glad to see Dan here.

"So this is Friend Eddie," Dr. Miller continued.

"I'm Mac Terrell."

"Oh, the black sheep. Looks like we got Flynn's thinking a little bit off. I expected the other cop."

"Mac's the one with the skill we need," Flynn said. "I brought the right person."

"And what skill would that be?"

"He's got incredible vision. I want you to make it miraculous."

"May I know why?"

"We have a disk to shoot down."

"That's impossible."

"It isn't."

"Exactly how do you plan to go about it?"

No reason to take a risk here. Strict information control was called for. "I don't think you'd be need-to-know on that."

He shook his head. "As you wish."

Mac said, "If there's all these alien species here, why won't any of them just shoot Morris's disk out of the sky?"

"Good question," Flynn said.

Dan Miller said, "We're going to have to go down into the red zone, guys. Mr. Terrell, you need to understand just how radically different this is going to be. We will not see aliens as you understand them, but we will see machines that are so advanced, they might as well be alive. Extremely advanced and far more intelligent than any human being. You will feel the power of their minds all around you. You will experience profound fear."

"I've noticed that already."

"A little of it. There's a generator outside that cues brains to feel danger and fear. It keeps animals and people well away from the facility. What goes on down below will be much more disturbing."

They reached the elevator's large black door, reminiscent of the brutal barriers that sealed a supermax.

"Okay, through that door we're going to be in a species-neutral atmosphere. There's less carbon dioxide in it than we have, a little more oxygen, and a cluster of rare gases. We can breathe it, but it smells a bit odd and it will affect your sense of taste. It's been designed so a maximum number of different species can use it."

At a wave of Miller's hand, the door opened to the complex interior, all of it strikingly familiar to Flynn, from the shimmering, powdery silver light to the blurred shapes and odd, twisted angles of the many different machines. In one direction, there was a pathway to what looked like infinity, in another, a black, twisted knot that was hard to look at without getting a headache. Stretching ahead was a catwalk over the main machine floor. There were three sets of rails at different levels—one in the right position for human hands. The catwalk hung ten feet above the floor of the facility. Below, there was a series of what appeared to be windows on the floor, each one a soft square of equal size. Some were gleaming black, others gray and filled with shadows. Two looked out on vivid scenes. One displayed a rose granite building, with long rows of black windows. The other revealed a path in a rich

jungle scene. There were huge trees covered with long green strands like hair. Leafy shrubs crowded the jungle floor. A well-worn path led off into the distance.

Abruptly, the window with the building went black.

"One portal to go," Miller commented.

"They're openings to other worlds."

"I'm looking at another planet?"

"You are," Dr. Miller said.

"How does that work?"

"As far as we understand physics, it can't."

"If I jumped down there right now?"

"You'd end up in that jungle. Probably fifty, a hundred light-years from here."

"Could I get back?"

"Who knows?"

Flynn noticed that a couple of the uniformed security people had appeared on the catwalk. People blocking his exit were not wanted. Also, there'd been a lot more traffic in the past. He remembered aliens down on the machine floor. "Where is everybody?"

"Flynn, the station's being retired. The grays are leaving Earth. Everybody's leaving."

"*What?*"

"You know this thing—what these fools released into the universe—"

Doors ahead opened silently onto a room that was at once startlingly familiar and exceedingly complex. Flynn said, "Mac, there are machines in there with hyperdimensional shapes. This means that human eyes and human minds can't make sense of them any more than a bird can figure out a living room. Don't look around in there, it'll disorient you."

"More than disorient you," Miller added. "You can become psychotic, and the effect can be permanent."

There were now four workers—three following them, and one linger-

ing at the end of the catwalk. So they weren't workers, they were guards, as Flynn suspected. He felt a familiar tension rise in his muscles.

"Come on, guys," he said, "the sooner we get this done, the safer everybody's going to be."

Mac asked, "Can Morris do anything to us down here?"

"Unknown," Dr. Miller snapped.

"What about those creatures on the surface?" Flynn asked. "We saw security preventing them from moving out of the restricted zone."

He shrugged. "Something somebody left behind. A failed experiment in human–alien hybridization. They have human genes, so we're not going to be killing them, as per E. O. 2241-R."

"Which means what?" Mac asked.

Flynn said, "A restricted executive order that states that anything carrying more than ten percent human DNA is human and subject to human law. It was promulgated during the second Bush administration."

"You never told me that—or any of this—before," Mac said.

"His memories of this place were blocked. Morris can get into the mind, remember, so we sent him out with his skills but not his memories."

"Okay, question time's over," Flynn said. "Let's do this."

"Past the catwalk, we move on the red lines only. Don't ever step off. Not ever. If you do, you'll become lost and we will not be able to find you."

"It looks normal."

"It's not. Come on."

They moved carefully along the catwalk, keeping their eyes on the path ahead, not looking at the machines that loomed around them.

"They're watching us," Mac whispered.

"Back off your guards," Flynn said.

"They're not guards. They're a dismantling team. The facility's going to be mothballed. Earth is being abandoned."

"You said that, but will you say why?" Mac asked. "What's been released into the universe?"

Dr. Miller stopped. He turned and faced Flynn and Mac. "Aeon is doomed. At least, the natural species is. They're going to be rendered extinct by their own creation."

"We know that," Flynn said. "There has to be more."

Miller nodded sadly. "The species they created—"

"The biorobots?" Mac asked.

"They're much more than robots. They're self-evolving and full of bad programming."

"In what way bad?"

"As Aeon woke up to the fact that they weren't alone in the universe, they got scared. They saw they were primitive. They saw that others were more intelligent. They felt threatened, and used their knowledge of genetic engineering to build what is essentially a self-programming warrior species."

"Which is what me and Flynn are fighting. Two people, only one of which is presently any good at it."

"It's an isolated band," Miller said.

"So why not just tell the more advanced aliens to get rid of them. Then we can all go home."

"Flynn, do you remember why we're doing it this way?"

"I'm a low-tech weapon. If the other aliens use their powers, there will be subspace echoes that stand a chance of being detected by the main body. So will their communications, all their activities. I assume that they're not leaving to abandon us, but to hide us."

He thought of the wire back at headquarters. It would undoubtedly be on the way out, which would be all to the good, as far as Flynn was concerned. He wondered about Geri. Could her mere presence here be a danger?

"No angels to protect us?" Mac asked.

"Not around here."

Flynn thought about that. No angels. The universe full of dangerous life. Somewhere out there, surely something better would one day be found. But clearly today was not that day.

"Let's get this done, Doc," Mac said. "I'm ready. Sort of."

CHAPTER TWENTY-FIVE

THE GREAT, black thing stopped Mac in his tracks.

"Take it easy," Flynn said.

"What in holy hell is that?"

If evil had a color, this fat cylinder—nine feet long and standing on four squat legs—was painted that color. Flynn remembered how frightening its absolute darkness had appeared to him the first time he saw it.

Mac stood staring at it, gripping the rail that followed the catwalk the three of them were on.

Flynn noticed that two of the guards who weren't guards were now close behind them. Too close.

"What's going on?" he asked Miller.

"Not sure." Then, to Mac, "This is a bioeditor. It's what can do what you need done."

"What's that down there, a black hole?"

Miller said, "The best way to explain that formation comes in a poem by W. H. Auden. Do you know his work?"

Mac said nothing. Flynn remembered the lines from Dr. Miller's explanation the last time he'd been here and quoted them: "'The crack in the tea-cup opens / a lane to the land of the dead.'"

"We think what you're looking at is an entrance to a parallel universe. Not another planet, but the undiscovered country, the land of souls."

Mac took a step back. He gestured toward the machine. "It looks like some kind of torture chamber from hell."

"No, actually, it's from California. It was built at the Trident Group in Palo Alto."

"Built by us?" Flynn asked.

"Built at the Trident Group, not by the Trident Group, unfortunately. By the grays. It's soul science, this thing. We're not there yet."

"You can smell the evil. You can see it." Mac turned away from the thing. "Soul science the hell, it's satanic."

Dr. Miller said, "There is no supernatural, only the natural world, some parts of which we understand and some we don't. It's natural to fear the unknown."

"It looks evil to me. Gotta say."

"Mac, it works."

Looking at it now, being in this room again, took Flynn back to how he had been before his time in the machine. What had changed in him went way deeper than biology. He had come out of it with new reflexes, but also with a better, more careful, quicker mind, and a deep new river of spirit within him.

"It's not evil, it's just . . . different. Here"— he took Mac's hand— "touch it."

Mac pulled back, but Flynn was faster. When Mac's hand touched the wall of the thing, the same thing happened as when Flynn had done it before. The whole side of it shuddered like the most delicate flesh, or the surface of a pond.

"It feels alive," Mac said. "Just like that disk, only more so."

"It's not a creature," Dr. Miller said, "but it is intelligent."

"What's it going to do to me?"

"When you enter it and concentrate in an organized way on the alterations you want, as long as they're possible, it's going to make them."

"Does it hurt?"

Flynn said, "It's going to be the strangest thing you've ever experienced. But it doesn't hurt."

"Go on."

"Your body seems to disappear. It's like you've become a kind of chaos, a sort of storm. You're roaring, rushing, all confused. But alive. Incredibly, totally alive. The feeling will scare you worse than anything you've ever known, but you won't want it to stop. Then your body will focus around you in the same form as the machine. A liquid blackness. You need to think about your eyes. Imagine seeing things two miles away. Seeing microscopically. Sparks will start hitting your eyes the same way they hit my hands when I began thinking about my draw speed. I went into the depths of myself, the why of me, my hopes and loves and fears. You mention angels—I felt like an angel, Mac, an angel in the light. Then all of a sudden, thud, and I was lying there in the thing, just me again in that cold, dark hole. I cried, Mac. I sure as hell did."

"If I want to stop, can I?"

"No," Dr. Miller said.

Mac walked up to it. "Why don't you do this to more people? Flynn needs an army."

"We worked on that. Hard. So did the grays. To make somebody truly exceptional, they have to start out at the top of their game. We can't put an ordinary person in there and have a man with incredible abilities come out. And now it's too late. Machines like this, soul editors, are real easy to detect. This thing has to be gotten out of here pronto. To tell you the truth, this whole facility has been kept in operation by the grays, in hope that you'd make it in before they had to pull the plug."

Flynn burst out, "Why in hell don't they just help us?"

"This isn't help?"

Mac stood even closer to the machine, looking at it, caressing its trembling flank. "Has anybody ever died in it?"

"There have been heart attacks. The first person to test it died of a stroke. That was in Palo Alto."

"Flynn, if this kills me, I want my ashes scattered in Big Bend, down along that ridge near Panther Junction—you know the place."

It was where Mac had almost won Abby, in a flaring sunset, on an evening so long ago it seemed like it belonged to another life. He'd kissed her, and Flynn saw Abby melt into him, and the joy in his eyes when she did. Later, around their campfire, she had searched Flynn with her own teary eyes. After moonset, she came to him in the inky night and whispered, "Hold me," and Mac, lying in his sleeping bag under the stars, had silently mourned.

"I know it. I'll do it." He wanted to say that it wouldn't happen that way, Mac wouldn't die, but what did he know? Not even Dr. Miller knew.

Dr. Miller said, "You go around it, Mac. Stay on the red trail. When you reach the entrance, it'll look like a tunnel with red glowing walls. You just lie forward into it, and the machine will do the rest."

"It's like the first time your ma ever held you," Flynn said, "like remembering your birth."

Mac shook his head, stood still for a moment, then strode around the machine and was gone.

It made no sound.

"Is it working?"

"Stand back."

There was a sound of something vibrating, followed by a wave of ice-cold air coming off the thing. Then it frosted over, the liquid blackness hardening and becoming covered with pale frost.

"What the hell?"

"We don't know, except that it's normal."

"Have you ever been in there?"

"I tried for an increase in intelligence."

"And."

"IQ 148 before, 152 afterwards."

"That's not nothing."

"We put a guy in, an IQ of 190. He came out completely insane. Killed himself right here on this platform where we're standing."

The guards were very close now. When one of them started to follow in Mac's steps, Flynn put up a hand. "No."

His eyes met the guard's. And he recognized him. It was the airman killed by the biorobot at Wright-Pat, or rather, it was the biorobot, impossibly, incredibly not only alive, but here.

Flynn drew his gun and blew the creature in half.

CHAPTER TWENTY-SIX

"WHAT THE hell, Flynn, have you gone crazy?"

"It's one of them."

"No, that's impossible."

Others were crowding forward, and Flynn could hear movement behind the machine as well. When he turned to look, it was still frozen solid, doing its mysterious work. It had better be quick, because this was not going to last. He had the Bull and the Special, but Mac and Dr. Miller were unarmed. A quick calculation told him they would be done in under ten minutes.

"Any other way out of here?"

"What's going on? You say these are Morris's people?"

"Four of them. Three now. Five or six more in the facility. We have about eight minutes, that's all."

Another one came forward, and Flynn dispatched it with another roaring shot. In the distance, there was a loud pinging sound, repeated again and again, each ping farther away than the one before.

One of the creatures launched itself at Dr. Miller. Flynn took it down also, and it fell shrieking to the floor below. It missed the vortex, though. Blood flooded out of the chest, but it immediately leaped back up the twenty feet to the catwalk and came straight at Flynn. At the same moment, another of them jumped over the machine, which began to make a high-pitched sound that reminded Flynn of an animal in pain.

"This is coming apart!" he yelled to Miller. He fired again, then a second time, this time at least rendering the two on this side of the machine unable to move, at least for a while.

There were only the four of them, but they had obviously evolved yet again, because they were coming back from lethal shots in seconds, not the hours it took the one he'd "killed" in Mountainville to recover.

He drew his knife and handed it to Martin. "They have to be cut apart."

"These are people!"

"Doctor, do as I say, or we'll all be dead—"

The fourth one dropped down onto Flynn from somewhere above. It was in the form of a strongly built, athletic man, and it threw him sideways and off the edge of the platform. He fell toward the vortex, which seemed almost to bend toward him, as if it were hungry for him.

As he dropped, he reached out and grabbed the leg of the creature that had unbalanced him, then twisted himself upward and threw his own leg over the platform.

For an instant, they were frozen, the two of them, their strength in balance.

Blood poured down through the platform as Miller cut up the one that had been lying there, cut it up and screamed out his revulsion as he did it.

Flynn's adversary shuddered. It redoubled its efforts.

But then Flynn was back on the platform, back on top.

Miller stood over the remains of the one he'd butchered, staring down at it with stunned eyes. Flynn grabbed the knife out of his hands and spun around, taking off the head of his attacker.

Then there was stillness. Flynn wasn't sure if there were some that had backed off, or if they were all incapacitated.

He ran around the machine. For a moment, he didn't understand what he was seeing. Then he did. The whole side of the thing had been laid open like a man's guts. Hanging out was a pulsating complexity of what looked like organic wiring, wet tendrils in a thousand different colors. One of the creatures lay slumped against it, its eyes glazed with what might be death. The other one was nowhere to be seen.

"Mac!"

No reply.

"Doc, how do I pull him out of this thing?"

Dr. Miller came around it. "My God."

"Where's Mac? What happened to him?"

Miller peered into the dripping tangle of wires.

Flynn knew they had little time. The creatures were all linked. Morris would know exactly what had happened here, and would be regrouping right now. Obviously, he was low on soldiers or he would have sent more.

"Mac, sing out."

"There's a body," Miller said. "Under there."

Flynn could just see it, a jeans-covered thigh under the machine. It was bulging horribly, as if the unseen part of Mac's body had been crushed.

Flynn's heart broke. At the same time, anger on a level he had not known possible swept him. This was more than rage, more than what he had thought of before as human emotion, a pillar of fire within him.

Bending down, he reached forward, thrusting his arms under the slumped remains of the machine. Using his leg and back muscles, then every muscle in his body, he lifted the thing. It was like cradling an injured man, just as intimate and sad.

"Hurry!"

"I'm trying."

"Can't hold it." He let it down.

Mac's leg was no longer visible. Flynn turned around. "He must have gone down into the vortex."

"The hell I did."

"Mac!"

He was standing beside Dr. Miller on the platform.

"It protected me. Held me like a baby. I could feel it dying all around me, but it would not let them get me."

Flynn took his friend by his shoulders. "You got a hell of a lot of guts."

"Listen," Miller said.

It was a rushing sound, like a great wind or the long thunder of breaking waves.

"What?" Mac asked.

"I don't know."

It was coming from back along the catwalk. Flynn could feel deep trembling.

Flynn went to the end of the platform, followed by the other two men. As they moved toward the door, the entire room seemed to fold in on them. Rolling out from behind them, there came a thick mass of dark blue smoke and a choking odor, sharp and hot, of some unknown fire. Flynn didn't turn; he didn't slow down.

Ahead of them, the door began closing automatically. Klaxons started, then emergency lights.

Flynn dived through the door and onto the catwalk above the portal to the jungle world. Mac and the doctor came behind, but the doctor's shoe got caught as the door slid closed.

He ripped it out, but then fell backwards and off the catwalk.

The portal appeared to be about twenty feet below them, but the doctor did not fall twenty feet. He kept falling and falling, his body twisting, his arms and legs windmilling. As they watched, he grew slowly smaller and smaller, until he was a dot moving across the green of the jungle.

There was a flash of light, and Dr. Miller was much more visible again, lying on the jungle path, one shoe missing, his legs twisted. As they watched transfixed, he shook himself. He stood up. Looked around. His hands went to his head. He understood what had happened to him.

He stood there screaming silently, looking up, his eyes wild with terror, as the portal grayed and went dark. The portal shuddered like the surface of a lake, and then Flynn realized that the whole room was liquefying around them.

They ran, dashing down the catwalk and out into the staging area, stumbling and falling as the pressure door closed behind them.

The elevator was across the room, its forbidding black steel door closed.

"Can we get out of here?"

"I don't know."

He went to the elevator and pressed the button. There was a moment's hesitation, but then it slid open. Before they could board the elevator, Flynn noticed that the Klaxons had stopped. Movement behind him caused him to turn, gun at the ready.

The pressure door was reopening.

"Jesus," Mac said as they got closer and looked together into the now completely empty space, a large bare room, its floor twenty feet below the doorframe. It was gleaming white, lit from above by rows of ordinary LED panels. There was a faint odor of something that had burned, but a long time ago. Old smoke.

The aliens had withdrawn.

"That poor guy," Mac said.

Flynn nodded. Dr. Daniel Miller had become the most profoundly lost man in the history of the species.

They got into the waiting elevator and returned to the surface.

The signs on the office doors were now all in English only. Here and there, a white space marked a place where a sign in some alien language had been removed.

Flynn touched a door handle. It was unlocked. He opened the door and stepped into the office of a Dr. William Richards. It was a typical office in a secret lab: There was a heavy-duty file safe, locked. On the desk was an in/out-box, which held some trivial memos about supply issues and a lighting problem. No references to aliens, nothing about what must have been taking place here just this morning.

"The parade's gone by," he told Mac. "Let's get out of here."

"What about that dog?"

"They'll be gone, both of them. And the aliens we saw out in the mounds. All gone. This place has been sterilized—and so has the rest of the planet, would be my guess." He thought of Aeon's more primitive portal, a massive gravity well out near Saturn. "Probably the whole solar system."

"And the disk?"

"Morris is still here, you can be sure."

"Here, in this place?"

"Obviously his crew got here somehow. But he got his nose bloodied tonight, so I'm thinking that he'll pull back, at least for a time. He'd better—we have exactly two bullets left in the Bull. The Special doesn't matter, since it's not accurate enough."

As they talked, they walked toward the main exit. Outside, the floodlights were off. The gate in the compound's fence stood open. The dog was nowhere to be seen.

Flynn tried his cell phone, but there was no coverage.

"I guess let's walk up," he said.

"Is it safe?"

He looked up at the sky. A late moon had risen, and still hung low in the east. To the south, the faint glow of the Northeastern megalopolis created an illusion of dawn.

"Three thirty," he said. "Hard to believe we were down there that long."

They started up the road. Flynn was alert for any movement, any sound, but all was quiet.

The disk rose up from behind a saw grass–covered dune and was on them in an instant.

Flynn threw himself to the ground and rolled off the road, but it was too late. It had been too late since the moment they left the facility.

Morris had really surprised the hell out of Flynn this time. "He got me, Mac. The attack down in the facility was there to put me off my guard."

He found himself looking up into the center of the disk's underside, a roiling circle of fire that would soon generate the light that would drag both of them into the hands of somebody who was going to hurt them very badly before killing them.

"Can you see that seam?"

"Man, it's dark."

There was a dull booming sound, and the light hit them. They rolled in opposite directions, and the light followed Flynn. As he felt himself rising, he grabbed the Special and thrust it at Mac. "Don't miss!"

The gun tumbled up into the light and was gone. Flynn felt his body leaving the ground. He yanked out the Bull and made sure it was in Mac's hand. "Two shots, but get outta this light!"

He rose further, seeking as he did so for his knife—not to defend himself, but to kill himself. His mind flashed regretfully to the cyanide capsules.

The end of the game, and the human side had lost.

What in hell could he expect?

The glowing maw of the thing was just above him now. He spread his arms and legs, and was just able to catch himself on the edges. Immediately, though, he began to slip inside.

A shot rang out. He heard the bullet whine off past his head—passing so close, he could feel its hot slipstream. The fingers on his left hand lost their grip. His arm thrust up into the thing. Hands, cold and strong, grabbed at his wrist, then clutched it.

His right leg went in. It also was grabbed.

"I'm goin'!" he screamed. He who was never scared was scared now—he was scared sick. It was going to end like this for him, in this monstrous machine, being cut to pieces, dying in his own vomit and in agony.

There came a tinkling like the laughter of children, cruel children.

A sharp sound followed, but in the distance. A shot? He was unsure.

There was a rush of air, then a flash of agony. Then there was darkness.

The darkness gathered him into itself. It was nice. It was good and kind and he belonged to it. Then he saw something that at first he didn't understand: a circle of fire overhead, slowly spinning.

There was a flash like a million suns, which left them both night blind. The flash was followed by a chest-slapping shock.

There was a silence.

"Are we still alive, Flynn?"

"Mac?"

"Are we?"

Flynn realized that he was on the ground, not in the disk. He said, "I'm thinking that we are." He tested himself, moving first one leg and then the other, then his arms. "I've got an issue with my right hip and arm. Must be my landing."

Mac sat up. "You fell a long way."

"I'm good at falling. I've practiced."

"The machine worked. I could shoot that fisherman over there right between the eyes."

Flynn looked around. "We're in the middle of the island."

"Look due south. See that little piece of water?"

"No."

They both got to their feet. "There's a boat that's got three guys on it. Two of 'em are asleep, the third one's got a line in the water."

They were both hurt bad, which became clear when they began trying to resume their hike up to the main building. They moved along arm in arm, leaning on one another.

"How in hell did I break my leg?"

"What's that wet stuff? That goo?"

"That's blood, Mac. You damn well shot yourself."

"I did not!"

"Yeah, you did. You winged your own leg with the first shot."

"Aw, shit."

Lights bore down in their faces, hard, bright rows of them.

"Is it another disk? 'Cause the gun's empty."

"It's the security patrol."

"Hey, we need help down here!"

A shadow moved out from behind the lights, an unrecognizable silhouette. The hands went up. A voice called out, "Flynn? Flynn Carroll?"

"Diana!"

She came closer, breaking into a run; then she was there before him. She threw her arms around him. He swayed against the weight of her, then inhaled the scent of her, and her sweetness made him dizzy with relief and desire.

"What the hell happened down there? I thought you were being examined by Dr. Miller."

"Morris got into the facility. Miller was— Oh, Christ, Diana, do you know what was down there?"

"Some advanced machines is what I heard."

"It's clean now. You could eat off the floor."

Diana and a number of the security personnel helped the two of them into the back of two of the carts, and they went together back up to the main building.

"Mac got the disk," Flynn said on the way.

"The wire is gone. Geri is gone. She left the way she came, from Area Fifty-One."

"I wonder if she made it."

Diana didn't reply, and Flynn didn't pursue it. There was no reason to speak more about Aeon. The planet had sealed its own fate, and would disappear into the history of the universe.

"Did you get Morris?"

"He wouldn't have been on the disk, but his assets are gone."

"Then that's the best we can hope for. A good result."

Diana wasn't happy, and Flynn knew it—and why would she be? Morris was their mission.

As he thought about that, he tried to put himself in Morris's position, to see matters from his enemy's viewpoint. He would know exactly why they were here, and how dangerous Mac would be to him if the bioedit was allowed to complete. Thus the logic of sending some of his last few entities into the facility where they would meet certain destruction. They might be destroyed, but so would the bioeditor, hopefully Mac, and ideally Flynn.

Finally, there was the surprise attack with the disk. So Morris wouldn't be in it. Far too dangerous.

So where would he be?

They arrived at the main building, and Mac was loaded off and carried toward the infirmary. Flynn's leg injury had flared up and he was hobbling, too, but at least he could walk.

He looked out across the water, a blackness touched here and there by the light of a fishing boat.

He stopped. He thought back. "Diana, where's the helicopter?"

"Now?"

"Right now."

"It took off after it dropped me. I guess the traffic director would know."

"Never mind—is there a boat? A fast one?"

"There are two boats that I know of."

He ran after Mac. In the infirmary, a sleepy-eyed nurse in a bathrobe was cleaning Mac's leg wound.

"Can you walk?"

"Can you?"

"Not really."

"Me neither."

"We have a chance to get Morris. It's our last chance, maybe for years, maybe forever."

"I can walk. In fact, I can run."

"Same here."

Mac got up off the table.

"Sir?" the nurse said.

Mac gave her a rictus grin, tight and hard. "I like pain, ma'am. In fact, I enjoy it so much, I'm going out for more. I'll likely come back later. In a bag."

Back in the corridor, they were met by a captain who looked like he'd pulled on his uniform over his pajamas.

"This is Captain Gilbertson, island chief of security," Diana said.

"I want both boats to converge on the south of the island. Make a wide loop, no lights. And I want that chopper called back. What I want it to do is start patrolling the Connecticut shore with its searchlight on."

"Excuse me, Miss Glass, is this the man you were telling me about?"

Flynn said, "There's a fishing boat out there with three individuals on it. It's going to be heading for the Connecticut shore, but slowly. It won't want to be drawing any attention. That boat is to be taken, and the individuals on it not just shot, but destroyed. Do you understand this? I want their bodies detonated, ripped to pieces."

The captain's face had turned to stone. Horror rimmed his eyes. "Shot? Destroyed? What are you saying, here? This sounds highly illegal."

"Diana, is there anybody on the island who's on our side of the line?"

"No, there is not."

"What about Evans and his crew?"

"They're not cleared for bio."

Flynn returned to the captain. "Captain, this is a national security matter, and you're not cleared to know even what you already do. You and your unit are ordered to stand down."

"On whose authority?"

"Do it, Captain, or you will be in a world of trouble. Trust me."

"He's right, Captain," Diana said. "Just get us the boats."

"A boat," Flynn said. "One boat. Your fastest."

Captain Gilbertson started a call to his superior officer. Flynn took his cell phone from him. "Prepare the boat at once, or you'll be charged with insubordination, dereliction of duty, and aiding a terrorist in the commission of acts that lead to loss of life. The last charge carries the death penalty, and it will be imposed, I can assure you. Now, get your ass in gear and get that boat prepped, and I want three high-powered rifles, scoped, on it, some flash bombs, and some hand grenades."

"We don't have grenades—"

Flynn grabbed Captain Gilbertson by the lapels and went close in. *"Don't lie to me."* He thrust him away so hard, the soldier flew across the corridor and hit the wall with a thud that shook the place. "Do it now!"

Ashen, his hands trembling, Gilbertson pulled himself together and rushed off.

"Let's move," Flynn said.

They headed for the island's small boathouse.

CHAPTER TWENTY-SEVEN

AS FLYNN guided the boat around the island, Mac lay on its long prow, watching the water. The boat was a Donzi, lean and low, powered by a 300hp MerCruiser engine. It was in excellent condition, kept ready for patrol and intercept duty.

Diana was beside Flynn, watching the boat's radar under a hood made of her coat. No light could be allowed to show, none at all.

As he ran the boat, Flynn kept a careful lookout to the sides and back. His chief worry was that Morris had anticipated this maneuver and was planning to ambush them. Given that he was almost certainly down to his last two entities, he would be desperate. As far as Flynn was concerned, Morris could appear anywhere, anytime—just not with the disk, and thank God for that.

Mac came down. "There's one fisherman out there with three guys in it, heading for the Connecticut shore." He pointed to a faint light. "Two miles out. Moving slow, like they were trolling."

Diana said, "I see him."

"We need that chopper," Flynn commented. He wanted it doing a grid search along the shore, making it appear that the focus of their interest was not on the water itself. Hopefully, this would cause Morris to turn around and head for Long Island. The farther they were from witnesses when what was about to happen went down, the better it would be.

"I've got a point-to-point measure on him," Diana said. "He's moving at about five knots."

"Mac, what's your maximum confident range?"

"Give me a thousand yards."

"At night? Are you sure?"

"I can count the number of threads in a shoelace."

Flynn did a quick mental calculation and increased speed to 7.8 knots.

"Keep watching. I'd like a positive ID before we can do this."

Mac, who had returned to the front of the boat, slid back down again. "You aren't gonna get positive. Positive is impossible, even for me."

"What will I get?"

"The best I can offer. But it's never going to be absolute, not at three thousand feet."

"Then if we make a mistake, that's what happens."

"I'm not a murderer, Flynn."

"With certain exceptions."

"Which don't include innocent civilians."

"We can't risk not taking the shot."

Saying it made him feel kind of sick.

Diana, he noticed, had not protested. She remained huddled under the coat, peering at the radar.

"Diana?"

She came up. "Yes?"

"Did you hear?"

"I heard. They could be innocent bystanders."

"Let's hope it's them," Flynn said.

"Let's hope." She went back under her coat. The faint glow of the radar reappeared around her feet. "They've increased speed. By an additional five knots."

Morris had detected this boat and was testing it. If it increased speed when he did, he would know its intentions. Flynn held steady.

"We'll be in range shortly," Diana said.

Flynn's hand hovered over the throttle. The boat would do thirty knots, easy. All he had to do was push it to the firewall, and they'd leap up on plane. If Morris's boat was just the little fisherman that it appeared, he wouldn't be able to get away.

"An extra six and a half knots. That makes eleven and a half knots."

Morris was slowly increasing speed. In other words, he was running. That meant two things: First, they had the right boat. Second, Morris was vulnerable.

"He'll be at the mouth of the harbor," Diana said.

"How many yards ahead of him?"

"Fifteen hundred and fifty."

"Too far. What port is it?"

"A little community called Easterly. Couple of marinas, a fishing fleet of maybe five boats. He's up to twelve knots."

Unless Flynn increased speed, he would never come into Mac's range at all, because Morris would reach port first.

He gripped the throttle. But then a realization came, which was that, if Morris had enough speed available to him, he was already close in enough to beat the Donzi.

Morris had won again, as always by thinking farther ahead. No matter what Flynn did, he wasn't going to catch the psychopath.

"Chopper's up," Mac said.

"I don't see it."

"You will. Two minutes."

"He's at thirteen knots. Four thousand one hundred yards ahead of us. Opening the gap now."

Flynn held steady.

The seconds practically crawled—five, ten, twenty.

Flynn watched the dark shore.

Two minutes came and went.

"We're losing him," Diana said.

A spear of light came down from the sky above Easterly, then ran along its shore. A moment later, another, farther down, appeared. Then a third one up the coast a few miles.

Three helicopters instead of one.

"Slowing. Ten knots. Five. Dead slow now."

Was he buying it? Or just being cautious?

The Long Island shore was dark.

Five searchlights now swept up and down the Connecticut coast, centering on Easterly.

Diana said, "He's increasing speed. Fourteen knots."

"What in hell?"

"No, wait he's going dead slow—no—oh, Jesus, it's a turn, a tight turn. He's heading this way! He's still turning. Now he's going for the opposite shore."

It had worked—maybe. Flynn held steady.

Diana said, "On his current heading, he'll be in range in two minutes."

Mac went back up to the front of the boat. Flynn held the boat absolutely steady, still on the same heading, now closing rapidly with Morris, who would cross their bows at 2,200 feet.

Without warning, without a flash or a sound, there came a tremendous shock wave, invisible until it hit the boat. Flynn was knocked back off the helm, sprawling into the seating behind him. Diana, whose head was below the level of the cockpit dash, lurched with the boat but kept her footing.

Flynn scrambled to his feet, grabbed the helm, and righted the lurching boat. *"Mac!"*

"I got it, I'm okay."

"Hold on, it *will* come again!" Then, "Di, you okay?"

"I'm good."

"I hope it's the same shock wave weapon Geri used, because it didn't work worth a shit."

Twenty seconds to go. Ten.

"It's speeding up, it's coming straight at us."

Mac fired. A second time. A third.

Flynn pushed the throttle to the dash, and the Donzi leaped to life.

Mac came down, sliding into the cockpit. Flynn said, "We gotta stay up on plane—the bow's full of burst seams."

Flynn swerved the boat so he could see ahead. The fishing vessel was dead in the water. In it, he could see slumped forms.

"Di, crack the grenades."

"We can't set off grenades in the middle of Long Island Sound."

"Maybe you can't," Flynn said.

When they came up beside the fishing boat, which was wallowing in the water, Flynn surrendered the controls to Mac and jumped aboard at once. "Give me some light!" he shouted up at Diana, who turned one of their floods on the scene in the craft.

A figure lay sprawled on its back. It looked entirely human. "Jesus," Flynn muttered. He turned over a second figure.

The face was not the same as that of the first, but its shape was. Flynn pulled out his flashlight and lifted one of the eyelids, and there staring up at him was the unmistakable steel gray of Louis Charleton Morris's eye. In his temple, there was a hole oozing blood. Geri's weapon was in the bottom of the boat, floating in the bloody water.

Morris's only mistake had been to trust it.

Flynn picked up the pulse weapon and put it in his pocket. Might be of some use to somebody. He'd turn it in to the tech team at HQ.

The third and last body had a human form as well, but the face of a biorobot. It stared, but not sightlessly.

"This one's rejuvenating fast," Flynn said.

Diana handed down the grenades, and Flynn thrust one in each mouth, breaking jaws to ram them in. Morris seemed to be resisting, so Flynn used his knife to also cut back the muscles at the hinges of the alien's jaws, then rammed the grenade farther down, into his throat.

Morris began spasmodically attempting to regurgitate it.

Mac cut into Morris's thorax and put in another grenade.

They got back into the Donzi and pulled out, planing away at high speed. When they were a mile out, Flynn detonated the grenades by radio.

Modern hand grenades were not small explosives, and the boat burst apart in a deafening explosion that slammed from the Connecticut shore to the Long Island shore and back. In the distance, car alarms along both coasts began sounding. A deeper siren, perhaps a volunteer fire department, joined them.

"There are going to be water patrols from ten sheriffs' departments out here within half an hour, not to mention the coast guard," Flynn said as they headed back to Deer Island at full throttle.

"Did we do it?"

"Mac, you're one of those guys who's going to get a medal you can't tell anybody about, because the answer is yes, we did it. We have sterilized our planet of a psychotic alien and his deranged posse of biorobots."

As the boat ran on, Flynn looked up at the half moon now hanging in a deep purple predawn sky, and at the stars beyond, fading now. He thought of the scourge that Aeon had unleashed, and what must be happening there now, and of Geri gone on her perilous journey, taking with her the last echo of Abby that he would ever see.

Diana leaned against him for a moment. Nothing was said, and then she was gone from his side, back to her seat.

He drove the boat onward, staying up on plane to reduce leakage, toward the dark bulk of Deer Island and the life of the future, whatever might come, whatever lay beyond.

mL   8-14